READYMONEY COVE

ALSO BY THE AUTHOR

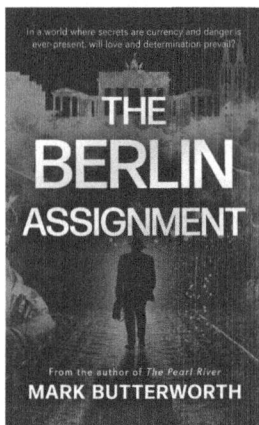

MARK BUTTERWORTH

THE PEARL RIVER

Adam Devon's principles and loyalty are put to the test, in a tale of love, war and intrigue...

In a world where secrets are currency and danger is ever-present, will love and determination prevail?

THE BERLIN ASSIGNMENT

From the author of *The Pearl River*
MARK BUTTERWORTH

PUBLISHED IN THE NAME OF MC BUTTERWORTH

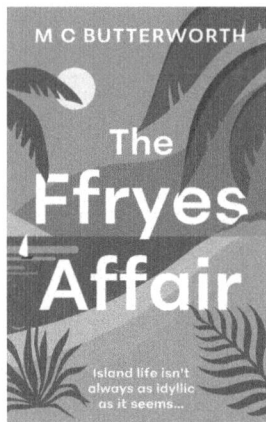

M C BUTTERWORTH

The Ffryes Affair

Island life isn't always as idyllic as it seems...

READYMONEY COVE

MARK BUTTERWORTH

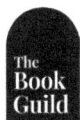

The
Book
Guild

First published in Great Britain in 2025 by
The Book Guild Ltd
Unit E2 Airfield Business Park,
Harrison Road, Market Harborough,
Leicestershire. LE16 7UL
Tel: 0116 2792299
www.bookguild.co.uk
Email: info@bookguild.co.uk
X: @bookguild

The manufacturer's authorised representative in the
EU for product safety is Authorised Rep Compliance Ltd,
71 Lower Baggot Street, Dublin D02 P593 Ireland (www.arccompliance.com)

This work is entirely fictitious and bears no resemblance to any persons living or dead.

Typeset in 10pt Adobe Garamond Pro

Printed and bound in Great Britain by 4edge Limited

ISBN 978 1835742 419

British Library Cataloguing in Publication Data.
A catalogue record for this book is available from the British Library.

To John Porter, remembering that first visit to Cornwall.

ONE

July 1959

Too much champagne had been drunk for anyone to care that the guest of honour had quietly slipped away and was climbing into his chauffeur-driven Jaguar in Horse Guards Road. It was almost 10p.m., but there was just the vestige of deep blue twilight over St James's Park. It was a windless, balmy summer evening, perfect for the night ahead. No instructions were spoken to Lionel. He knew his destination in Pimlico, and he also knew that his passenger was heading to a liaison with another senior party member; their relationship was an open secret.

Amanda Spencer had avoided the celebration. Her job was to manage the politician's career and ensure he progressed through the hierarchy. Since he'd become a Member of Parliament in the 1951 General Election his progress had been astounding: he'd gone from a backbencher to serving on the Defence Procurement Committee, and now he'd been appointed Undersecretary of State for Defence.

The next election was just around the corner. Although she had absolute confidence that the Conservatives would win and Henry Fitzjohn would be returned as MP for Sudbury and Woodbridge, it was the appointment of the next cohort of senior ministers in the new government that interested her. She had checked into her favourite suite at the Thames Vista Hotel and spent the early evening listing serious contenders that Fitzjohn might face. She also spent some time in front of the mirror. Now edging into her mid-fifties, she was a realist; extra work was required to keep her Amazonian figure and striking good looks in the kind of shape that men couldn't resist, or at least one man in particular couldn't resist. She answered a knock at the door.

"Ah, come in. How was the reception, Henry?"

"Splendid, my dear. The party faithful were in good form. Any excuse for a booze-up on the firm with that lot. For what, a minor bloody promotion?"

"Don't be unkind. And don't play down the promotion – you know it's a stepping stone to higher things."

Fitzjohn pulled a face to show his agreement and walked over to the drinks tray. "Good show, I see you've had the Talisker delivered." He poured himself more than a large one and added a single ice cube.

"Yes, but take it easy, we're going to be busy tonight at Imogen's. Sir Robert will be joining us – with Anthea, of course – and I want you to be on good form. He will be making the recommendations for promotion next month."

"Worry not. I hardly touched the plonk they had at the ministry. And I know how you like to present your precious commodity, my wonderful personality, in the most sober light," said Fitzjohn, in mock seriousness.

"Very funny, Henry. And keep your hands off Anthea on the dance floor tonight; Robert's very possessive of his wife."

"She will be safe in my hands, dear lover."

"Mmm, that's what concerns me. Now listen, here's what you need to know." Amanda opened her leather-bound notebook and talked through her ideas for the main messages they needed to impart to Sir Robert Darnell, the party chairman. He was known to dislike young, up-and-coming candidates for high office unless they came from a good family – titled, preferably, and certainly landed. The Fitzjohn family did not have all these attributes, and Fitzjohn was going to need all the backing he could get.

"Have you arranged for the car to pick us up?" Amanda asked.

"Certainly. At eleven thirty."

"Great, we'll be there before midnight. I will get a secluded booth to host his lordship. Now go and get showered. Your dinner suit is in the wardrobe."

Twenty minutes later, when Fitzjohn stepped out of the bedroom to the lounge he stopped in his tracks, open-mouthed. Amanda had changed into a slim-fitting midnight-blue silk dress, off the shoulder and with straps crossing her full cleavage.

"Goodness me, you look fabulous. Darnell won't be able to take his eyes off you in that dress. Come here." He took her by the waist and kissed her intensely. "Hey, we have some time yet…"

"Oh no we don't!" Amanda laughed as she pulled Fitzjohn away from the bedroom. "Later, maybe."

***

When they stepped through the glass and bronze entrance into Imogen's Club, the lights were so dim it took the pair a minute for their eyes to adjust. They walked through double satin-lined doors and past two enormous, muscled concierges, there to discourage the wrong type of guest. A receptionist sitting at a desk registered their names in the members' book. An obsequious waiter took Amanda's coat and escorted the pair to a small alcove furnished with a pair of padded red velvet banquettes opposite a small round table with a shaded lamp and an ice bucket on a stand. The place was busy: a five-piece band played and a crooner sang the latest ballads, doing a good job imitating Bobby Darin and Frank Sinatra. Many of the guests were already dancing, illuminated by the shards of light cast across the floor from the mirror ball. Just minutes after they arrived, Sir Robert Darnell was shown to their table, walking ahead of his wife, a self-important statesman at all times.

By 2a.m. Fitzjohn, Amanda and their guests had consumed several bottles of Imogen's champagne, but Amanda stayed focused. She wasn't going to let the evening pass without pressing Darnell on the matter of future Cabinet ministers. After dancing a lively cha-cha with the party chairman, she guided him to their booth and sat close to him. She had been careful with her perfume, wearing just enough to catch his attention, but not enough to seem gauche. Henry had been right about her dress.

"Look, Robert, I know Henry is one of our younger stars, but you have seen him operating. Loved by party members, great with the press, works hard in the constituency and at Westminster. Solid business interests in Granta Airlines and an impeccable military career – Spitfire pilot and all that."

"Impeccable?"

"Well, certainly good enough. Let's not split hairs."

"What exactly are you looking for, Amanda?" said Darnell.

"After the election, the new government will need new thinkers with new ideas. Building Britain Great is the mantra that Henry promotes, and he means it. Old Mac is a great figurehead, sure, but even he admits that the Cabinet needs shaking up. Henry's – well, our – interest lies in furthering his career in support of our military strength and defence industries, and not just the aviation sector." Amanda leant forward and said quietly, "It's time for Henry to be appointed Minister of Defence."

Darnell sat back and glanced furtively towards the dance floor. Fitzjohn had persuaded Anthea to stay for a second dance, a nice slow waltz, allowing him to hold her close. Darnell frowned and looked back at Amanda. "I wouldn't disagree with you on the future of the party, but don't get carried away with the notion that being young and enthusiastic is the route to senior appointments. And Henry has only recently been appointed Undersecretary. Perhaps he needs another ten years or so to mature?"

"Now come on, Robert, he's not actually as young as he looks. He's mid-thirties. How old were you when you became Home Secretary?"

"I had passed forty!" Darnell said with a forced indignation that did not impress Amanda. Darnell placed his hand on Amanda's knee and ran his fingertips across her inner thigh. He smiled. "Alright, fair enough, leave it with me. I'll have a chat with Macmillan and see what we can do. Come over to my flat next week and I'll let you know how I get on. Would Thursday evening suit you?"

"Certainly, shall we say nine o'clock? Will Anthea be at home?" asked Amanda.

"Actually, she normally spends a couple of nights with her dear mother in Marlborough during the week, so I'm afraid we will not have the pleasure of her company."

Amanda returned Darnell's warm smile.

"One other thing. He's clean, isn't he, Henry? No skeletons in any cupboards that might cause an embarrassment at some later date?"

"He's a regular Boy Scout."

"That's what I like to hear. Now, how's my old friend Sir Douglas? Still shooting every pheasant in East Anglia?"

"Father is in good shape, thank you, Robert. Yes, still roaming the Fens."

"Excellent. Pass on my regards, will you?"

"Of course."

Darnell looked at his watch and raised his eyebrows. "I think I had better rescue Anthea and be on our way. Busy day tomorrow. Goodnight, my dear." They stood and brushed cheeks just as the music ended and Fitzjohn and Anthea arrived back from the dance floor. As Sir Robert and Lady Darnell departed, Fitzjohn took a half-full champagne bottle from the ice bucket. "Shame to waste this. Let's finish it off and you can tell me how you got on."

Amanda related the short discussion and added her assurance that the chances of a senior appointment were good, but Fitzjohn must start acting the statesman, less of the man about town.

"Understood, old girl. Now, fancy a dance?"

They made it three dances, to Amanda's delight. She felt that tonight would be remembered as a very significant night as she pressed herself against Fitzjohn. The club was quieter now, with guests mainly sitting and finishing off their drinks. Fitzjohn could see to the far side of the dance floor and had noticed a group of men and some very attractive females. Sounds of laughter from the men floated across, giggles from the girls.

"Who's that group over there, Amanda?" said Fitzjohn.

"That's Stephen Walmsley and his lackeys – entertaining last year's debutantes, by the look of things."

"Seem to be having quite a party. If you know him, why don't we go over and you can introduce me?"

Amanda gripped Fitzjohn's wrist and pulled him towards her. Her face was set in a severe, tight-lipped stare. "Listen to me, Henry, don't even think about it. You keep away from Walmsley. Promise me!"

"Steady, lover, no problem." Fitzjohn was shocked by Amanda's intensity. "Who is he?"

"He's an architect, works mainly for the seriously rich on their country seats and Fitzrovia pieds-à-terre. But he's also a mover and shaker for the younger set – they idolise him, for some reason. He throws lavish parties, gives out invites to his chalet in Verbier, and of course, he'll pick up the tab for tonight." Amanda couldn't hold back a sneer. "He's never seen without a flock of girls around him, pressing them on his wealthy men friends for his own benefit, if you see what I mean. Nasty piece of work, in my opinion. Come on, drink up. It's time for us to go."

TWO

Adam Devon eased back the throttles overhead the Isles of Scilly and commenced a slow descent to the RAF airfield at St Mawgan. He would hand back control of the aircraft to his student pilot, James Braithwaite, to prepare and execute the landing, but for the moment Devon was enjoying flying: it was a beautiful day with just a few high-level cirrus clouds, and the air was crystal clear. Devon used the Wolf Rock lighthouse as a marker for the approach to Land's End and asked Braithwaite to fly the route using visual references, rather than navigating by instruments. He liked to see his students retain the elemental skills in flying, not just rely on technology.

Braithwaite set up the Shackleton on a gliding track along the north coast of Cornwall and at 2,000 feet gently reapplied power to the four engines to ease the rate of descent, then steered a wide curve over the River Camel estuary and lined up with the runway.

Devon glanced across to Braithwaite. He wished the man wouldn't look so nervous, particularly every time they approached to land; it showed an apparent lack of confidence. He was a good pilot with plenty of hours flown on the Shackletons and other heavy transport aircraft, but Devon insisted on absolute precision in flying, and even as a civilian instructor he had the authority to reprimand, or praise, all aspects of a pilot's performance.

Braithwaite needn't have worried. The landing was smooth and within minutes the aircraft was parked outside the debriefing room. The two navigators, flight engineer and five-man technical team deplaned into the warm sunshine and walked across to the olive-green wartime buildings. The two pilots followed them in.

It was a quiet trip with no hostiles encountered, either surface ships or submarines. Was it a holiday in Russia? Devon thought. As he set to the task of writing up the aircraft and his own logbooks, an orderly approached him and said the station commander would like to see him in his office as soon as his admin was completed. It was a request, not an order. Devon was no longer a serving RAF officer, but as a civilian he knew he should treat it with the respect that the CO was entitled to. As it didn't sound urgent and he wanted to give Braithwaite feedback on the flight, he said he would be along in half an hour. The orderly frowned, but said nothing.

The CO was a good sort, in Devon's opinion: Bomber Command during the war, then a testing assignment commanding a squadron of Halifax freighters in the Berlin Airlift. After five years in maritime reconnaissance, his series of promotions ultimately meant an office job and no more flying.

Devon glanced at the name plate on the CO's door – Wing Commander Louis Valentine – then knocked and entered. He stepped into an anteroom where the orderly sat behind a desk and pointedly looked at his watch. Devon knew he had taken forty minutes to do his paperwork.

"One moment, please," the orderly said in as friendly a tone as he was ever going to use, got up and went into the wing commander's office. Devon could hear their quiet discussion but couldn't pick up what they were talking about. He sensed a tension in the air, and became more curious about what the CO wanted to discuss.

"Please go through."

As Devon entered, the orderly closed the door behind him and returned to his desk.

"Ah, come in, Adam. How was the flight this morning?"

"Quiet, sir, nothing untoward sighted." Devon knew he need not use 'sir' within the privacy of the CO's office as he was a civilian, but felt it was simpler to keep to service protocols.

"And the aircraft?"

"Solid as a rock, no problems at all. The technicians were all happy with their kit. Braithwaite did a good job – he will soon be ready for signing off, I think."

"That's good to hear. Now, there's something I need to discuss with you." The CO sat up straight and looked serious. Devon could see his staff file on the desk. "You signed up for a two-year tour with Coastal Command and you have, what? Three months left of your contract?"

"That's right, sir."

"And how do you feel about your role here?"

Devon was taken aback; he hadn't expected to be interviewed about his job. "I believe I have fulfilled my requirements."

"Indeed. The feedback from the officer commanding the surveillance staff has given you a glowing report: he's very impressed with the precision of your flying and how you instil the same in pilots. So important when hunting subs."

"Thank you, sir. My time with de Havilland as a test pilot taught me that."

"Good show. Our role here is becoming even more key to the security of the British Isles and the rest of Western Europe, and at last the Ministry of Defence is diverting more money to fund a rapid increase in aircraft and personnel. The growing threat from the Russians' long-range submarines has to be countered, and recent reports show that the launch of new boats is increasing all the time. Now, this means that we're going to require more pilots, and instructors to train them, particularly those with experimental flying experience such as you were undertaking at de Havilland. So, I have been authorised to offer you a new, open-ended civilian flying contract. You'd have the same role of training for ship and submarine identification and monitoring, but you'd also head up the whole of the training arm at St Mawgan. Ideally I would like to see you join up again, but you have made it clear that you wish to remain a civilian pilot. Your salary will be enhanced by around 25 per cent to take account of the wider role, and you will qualify for a housing allowance, should you wish to move your family down to Cornwall. The contract would be subject to termination by either side on three months' notice. Well, Adam, would this be of interest to you?"

"This has come as quite a surprise, sir. I have been planning my next career move at the end of my contract. Although there are some great flying opportunities out there, I really enjoy working with Coastal Command. I have to say, this new salary is very generous. But as you know, I have been commuting back to London most weekends to be with my wife and son, and I'm not sure how she would view relocating down here. She has her own career to consider, and living apart is not something we would want to do on a long-term basis."

"Understood, old chap. It's never easy for services wives. When are you next going back up-country?" said Valentine.

"This weekend, sir. In fact with the urgent work last week keeping me here, it's been a fortnight since I've been home. I shall be driving up on Friday morning."

"And will you discuss the offer with your wife then?"

"Certainly, sir. I should be able to give you my response next week."

THREE

Hannah was pleased and relieved that the managing director of the bank had agreed that after maternity leave she could return to work on a part-time basis. She had cut down to three and a half days a week, taking Monday off and allowing her to leave the office at lunchtime on Fridays. She collected Michael from nursery and was always home when Adam arrived from Cornwall. That had started nearly two years ago, and she was looking forward to Adam completing his contract so they could live as a family again. The arrangement had worked well enough, but she missed Adam when he was away and inwardly felt he was neglecting his fatherly role with their son, who would soon be three. But she never complained to Adam; his job was so important to him.

Her reduced hours meant a salary cut when finances were already tight, and another increase in mortgage interest rates was predicted. So, she relished the weekends when they were together as a family and she looked forward to the coming Sunday, when her parents would be visiting from Cambridge for lunch. The weather forecast was good, and she planned a walk in the morning across Wimbledon Common for the three of them. An hour or two of normal life for them, she hoped, when their married lives had been anything but ordinary.

Arriving home just before lunch, she bent down to pick up the post strewn across the terracotta tiles in the hall. Bills, of course, a newsletter from their local MP, a postcard from her brother on holiday in Scotland. And the bulky envelope that usually arrived on a Friday morning.

On the days she was not at the bank, she worked at home on another job. It was unexciting research, and she had promised herself many times that she would resign. But something inside her wouldn't let her give up the work. It was vitally important to her: it connected her to her past, her family, whom she feared she might otherwise start to forget. But that could wait until Monday when once again she would be alone in her office at the top of the house. She ran upstairs with the envelope and filed it away unopened in her desk drawer.

***

The traffic on the A303 slowed to an annoying crawl. Devon wished they would build a bypass around Stonehenge so that motorists who wanted to gape at the stones wouldn't just slow down, holding up the traffic. But as he passed the monument he gathered speed and made good progress for the next hour. Since it was late on Friday afternoon, the stream of commuters coming out of London was well under way; his journey ran smoothly against the flow and as he approached Walton-on-Thames he glanced at the clock on the dashboard. Nearly half past five. He would be home in twenty minutes: pretty good going, less than six hours from the airfield to Wimbledon. He had invested in a decent car when he accepted the contract in Cornwall, and the Rover 90 was a delight to drive. The CO's job offer occupied his thoughts throughout the journey, and he knew he was going to disappoint Hannah by suggesting they all move to Cornwall. But the contract was well paid, and there were not many flying jobs around that he would want to do, and that paid so well. And of course, it gave him the sense of purpose he had valued so much when he flew for the RAF.

As he parked outside the house he saw Hannah at the window holding young Michael, with his arm waving. Seeing Hannah's smile sent a thrill of love through Devon. She was so beautiful. He reached the door just as it opened, and Michael jumped into his father's arms. He seemed to have grown in the two weeks since Devon had seen him, and held in his hand a stick of blue chalk. After kissing Hannah quickly, Devon obeyed his son's cries to go into the living room to admire the picture he had drawn on his blackboard. Although it wasn't immediately obvious, apparently it was Daddy's aeroplane flying over the sea.

After ten minutes of amusing Michael, Devon walked through to the kitchen, took Hannah in his arms and gave her a lingering kiss. "So good to see you. How has your week been?"

"Pretty good. Busy at the bank, of course. Michael has had great fun with his train set."

"Excellent. It was lovely of your parents to buy it for him."

"Yes, and by the way, they're coming for lunch tomorrow."

Devon hesitated, then said, "Good, good. Will be nice to see them."

Hannah had turned to the cooker and taken a dish out of the oven. She didn't notice Devon's momentary look of concern. He had hoped for a clear weekend so they could discuss his job – he expected a long debate over the merits of moving to Cornwall.

"That smells good – what are we having?" he said.

"Chicken and leek casserole. There are some potatoes in the oven, and an apple pie."

"You've been busy!"

"All easy things to make, and you need a proper meal after the drive up from Cornwall."

"Will Michael have the same as us?" Devon said uncertainly.

"Sure – all his food is the same as ours now. Cut small, of course." As they ate their meal, Hannah reflected on her earlier thought that Adam was losing touch with his growing son.

"Ah, that was excellent – so much better than the mess at St Mawgan," said Devon.

"Glad you think so! Would you like to bath Michael and get him ready for bed? I'll clean up the kitchen."

"Good plan, I'll take him up now. Are his pyjamas in the chest of drawers?"

"Yes, usual place."

After Michael had been settled into bed, Hannah switched on the record player and put on the long-playing record of the soundtrack of *South Pacific*. She found a bottle of port in the sideboard and poured two glasses. Devon felt warm and relaxed as they lay back together on the settee, his arms around her shoulders and back.

"The film was excellent, wasn't it?" said Devon. "That was our last visit to the cinema I think."

"Yes, you're right. And the music is wonderful, but the story is so sad."

"Well, it tries to be honest about relationships. They don't always end in happy-ever-after." Devon sensed that Hannah was in a sombre mood, and knew this was not a good time to talk about his work. He changed the record to a Nat King Cole LP, which did the trick and livened up the mood. "Why don't we go over to the common with Michael in the morning? The walk and fresh air will do us all good."

Hannah clapped her hands. "I was going to suggest that very thing!"

After they had finished their second glass of port, Devon went around the house, checked the doors were locked and turned off the lights. Hannah had already gone up to the bedroom.

FOUR

Richard Dunn arrived late for his meeting with Henry Fitzjohn at Cambridge airport. He was the chief pilot, flying the air charter services; he wasn't cut out for arranging the relocation of a business, but he felt he just had to get on with it. He had driven back from Gatwick that afternoon at speed in order to make the meeting.

Dunn unrolled an architect's drawing and smoothed it out on the desk. "These are the plans for our new offices, the check-in desk and the reception lounge. The aircraft parking areas are here and here." He had a red pen in his hand and drew a series of crosses on the plan. "We have standings for up to six aircraft, allowing an increase from our current three."

"Excellent!" said Fitzjohn. "And are we all set for the move next month?"

"Yes, no problem. I met the airport manager this morning and he showed me around. The whole place is brand-new and beautifully kitted out. We will be ready to start operations as soon as we get the aircraft down there on Wednesday 12th August. Roger Harris and Jos

Richardson will fly the Consuls and I will fly the DC3. A van will go by road with all our office equipment, filing cabinets and papers. Will you be joining us?" said Dunn.

"No, I have to be in the House the whole of that week. Although it's the summer recess I have committee work to attend to, but I'll come down to Gatwick on the Saturday morning. I'm hoping the first of the Viscounts will be delivered by the beginning of September and the second a week or two later, and we can really get going with the new routes. With the interest in the ordinary man having his annual holiday on the Costa del Sol or Majorca, there's going to be a huge surge in demand for charters." Fitzjohn clapped his hands. "With the Viscounts carrying more than fifty passengers, the money will be rolling in!"

"Let's hope so. You're putting a lot of money into this venture, Henry," said Dunn.

"Well, certainly the banks and investors are."

"Indeed. Now, how are you getting on with recruiting pilots? Those with experience on the types of aircraft we have."

"Good point, Dickie, glad you're thinking ahead. I've been very busy in Westminster, you know, haven't had time to talk to potential pilots. So please go around your old RAF pals and see who wants to join the airline of the future. And with BEA ditching the Viscounts from their fleet, there will be plenty of good pilots looking for a job. Can I leave it to you, old chap?"

Dunn inhaled deeply; Fitzjohn knew he was overworking him and his increased absence due to parliamentary duties meant he had to leave some key decisions to Dunn. But the core part of the newly expanded business would be a team of excellent pilots who could be trusted to fly safely and look after the customers. Dunn would do as asked and find some good people, but Fitzjohn felt that the final choice of pilots should be his responsibility.

"OK, Henry," Dunn said slowly. "I'll get some pilots lined up, carry out the initial interviews and check them over, make sure they're a good fit for our business. Then you can meet the best of them and decide who you want to employ. We also agreed we need to recruit a head of cabin crew, remember? I've got some good people in mind. He or she can then bring in the stewards and stewardesses."

"Very well, Dickie, sounds like a good plan. Go ahead with it. I'll be in my office in Westminster from tomorrow, should you need me."

***

Fitzjohn had completed his weekly surgery with constituents in Sudbury and driven over to Cambridge to meet Amanda at the University Arms Hotel. She wanted to go through the campaign plans. Very tiresome, in Fitzjohn's opinion; no date had yet been set for the general election, so what was all the fuss? His was a perfectly safe seat – he couldn't see Labour making too much impact in the farming community of Suffolk.

Amanda had booked a table in the restaurant for a late lunch and arranged for it to be a four-seater, with plenty of room for her to spread out her papers. Most diners had departed, leaving them able to talk in private.

"I think Macmillan will call the election by the middle of September," she said, with a degree of certainty such that Fitzjohn wasn't minded to argue; he knew Amanda had all the right contacts in the party. "That would give us about three weeks of campaigning. This is what we're going to concentrate on."

Flipping open her notebook, Amanda ran down the list of village halls, golf clubs, Royal British Legion meetings, schools and factories that she would book for him to present the Tory manifesto – and, of course, to showcase Fitzjohn's engaging personality and win the trust of the constituency.

"I will arrange a car and a driver to take us to all the venues. Let me have your diary and I'll make sure each event is noted down."

"Do we really have to go through all of this again, Amanda? It's hardly going to influence the outcome, is it. And I've got lots on at Granta, with the move to Gatwick and new aircraft arriving. We want to get the new services off to a good start, don't we? You are our main outside investor, after all."

"Yes, of course, but think about our immediate priorities, Henry, and don't forget you're not just winning over the local voters in this campaign, you will be under the spotlight with central office. Particularly Sir Robert. He will want to see you as a leading light in the election nationally – a poster boy, you could say – if he is going to consider you for promotion. I will work on him to make sure he listens to the message and backs you with Macmillan."

Fitzjohn sat back, pursed his lips and stared silently at Amanda for a few moments. "Look, old girl, you've given me a huge amount of support since the election in '51 and now you're ramping up your workload for me. But I've never asked why you want to do all this – what do you get from my progress in the party and government?"

"Easy. I'm a committed Conservative and I don't want the country to be ruled by Labour, Liberal, communists, fascists or any other crazy group. And that's why I joined the local party and took on the campaign manager role."

"Oh, come on! It's not just your political leanings, there's more to it than that. We have our … let's call it a special relationship, and I might at times feel you genuinely care about me. Is that it?"

"Certainly I care about you!" Amanda laughed and tossed her head back. Small tears of happiness formed in her eyes. "In fact, I care *for* you, Henry. I'm sure you appreciate that." She looked stern. "But I can always separate business from pleasure, and the work we are doing to get you into the Cabinet after the election is very much business."

"Agreed, but if that all works out, the only reward you'll get is the satisfaction of a job well done."

"No, Henry, there is potentially a much greater reward."

"Which is…?"

"Alright, if I have to spell it out for you: Number 10. From the position of Minister of Defence, a senior Cabinet role, the next step is to stand for leader of the party and, of course, prime minister. I want to get you to Downing Street. And you'll be taking me with you, as your wife or your senior adviser, I don't care. As a teenager, maybe even as a child, I always dreamed of becoming prime minister, of walking through that black door. Yes, you may well laugh – there's a cat in hell's chance of a woman being elected leader and PM, so the only way for me to get to Number 10 is through you. That's the plan."

"Well, now I see why you have shown such interest in me. And I thought you were simply doing the work out of fondness for me."

"That's the business side. There is, of course, the pleasure side to think of."

"Glad to hear it. By the way, have you booked a room here for this evening?"

Under the table Amanda put her hand on Fitzjohn's thigh and said quietly, "Actually, I have, but we have to go through the details of the campaign first. There's a lot to agree."

"Alright, if you insist. Let's have a quick look at the itinerary."

FIVE

The first harbingers of autumn were showing on the yellow and gold leaves of the oak, sycamore and London plane trees that covered nearly half of Wimbledon Common. Feeling the freedom to run unbridled, Michael surprised Devon with his speed, chasing his small football across the grass heathland.

"Come on, Mum, keep up!" Devon called as he kicked the ball ahead of Michael, making him run even more.

Hannah was thrilled to see her husband and son playing together. It was such a rare sight, and she wished they could be together more often. Although she wanted to spend more time on the common, Hannah called to Devon that it was time to go home so she could prepare lunch.

Devon took Hannah's hand in his right hand and lifted Michael with his left arm to carry him home; he was too exhausted to walk any further. Devon knew time was getting on, and he had to raise the matter of his job with Hannah.

"While we're walking back, there's something I need to mention to you, darling," he said. "The CO called me in during the week to talk about my contract."

"Right, what did he say?"

"Well, he offered me a new contract – one with an open period. With the increase of Russian activity, the ministry wants to expand Coastal Command. They're happy for me to continue as a civilian employee training pilots on long-range surveillance work, and he's offered me a promotion to lead all training at the air station. The good news is that I would get a salary increase and we would have a housing allowance – we'd be able to live rent-free. I said I would give the CO my response this week."

"But would that mean we'd sell up here and move down to Cornwall?"

"Yes. Living in two places at once has been fine for a couple of years, but we can't go on like this, can we?"

"No, that's true, and not just for my sake. You hardly see Michael."

"That's how I feel, too."

"But, Adam, what other flying jobs are there? The plan was at the end of your contract you would find something more local, back to de Havilland or one of the other aircraft manufacturers."

"Yes, that is still an option, in theory. But there just aren't the right sort of jobs around, and none of them pay what I earn at the moment. There is a huge increase in holiday passenger flying but I'm not sure I want to be a bus driver, flying backwards and forwards to the Continent. Very dull."

"But it's regular work, and you'd be home most nights."

"The airlines are looking for pilots, sure, and it pays quite well. But such boring work. You wouldn't wish that on me, would you?"

Hannah couldn't find the right words to answer. She turned around and took Michael from Adam. No, she would never want Adam to do work he didn't enjoy, but she felt he was being selfish, not giving any thought to her and Michael, not seeing married life as a partnership where her needs were considered too. He certainly wanted to keep flying; there was no question of him taking one of the many office jobs BOAC were advertising. But international travel was expanding all the time, and lots of his ex-RAF pals had taken up airline flying. And if they moved to Cornwall she would have to give up her position at the bank, which she enjoyed. But she would continue her specialist work – which Adam knew about, but they never discussed.

"I want you to be happy at work, of course. But I'd have to look for a job in Cornwall too."

"Hannah, there would be no need for you to work. You could enjoy life, have more time to yourself and with Michael."

"That's true, but he will be going to school next year, and then what? I'd join the local WI and make tea and cake every day? That's not really for me."

"Yes, I know that, but you do have your other work to keep you busy. That's all done by post, isn't it?"

"Mostly, yes, but some meetings are required in London. I'd have to travel up once or twice a month."

"Well, there we are, it would all work brilliantly! And perhaps we should keep the house here in Wimbledon – we can let it out and use the income to help pay the mortgage. Then with the Command paying our rent on a house in Cornwall, it adds up to a very nice deal."

When they arrived home, Hannah asked if they could discuss it further in the evening, after her parents had gone home. She wanted time to think about what would be best for them as a family, not just Adam and herself as individuals. It was a crucial time for them, as they were being asked to think about what they wanted from life, where they wanted to go – not just geographically, but in terms of their careers. They had already agreed that they would like more children at some time in the future, and then Hannah knew she would have to take a career break, or perhaps give up work entirely. Being a stay-at-home housewife did not appeal to her one bit. Other women with children carried on working in many areas: doctors and nurses, secretaries, even factory workers and bus conductresses. But she knew that it was not about what other people did; it was what would work for her and Adam.

***

Hannah was thrilled to see her father playing in the back garden with Michael after lunch. Even though he was only three, Grandad was trying to teach him cricket, how to hold the bat, the correct grip for a leg spinner, and how to catch two-handed. Adam acted as fielder and comforter as Michael fell over rather than hit the ball, and poured the lemonade at their 'tea' interval.

After Hannah and her mother had washed up, Hannah asked her to come through to the front room. Their possible move to Cornwall had played on her mind since the morning, and she didn't want to wait until the evening to chat about it with Adam. She decided to seek her mother's opinion. Perhaps part of her was hoping that the decision would be made for her, if her mother objected strongly to her daughter and grandson moving to the far side of the country.

But after talking through Adam's job options, Hannah began to convince herself that it was actually a great opportunity for them all: Cornwall was a lovely place to live and the job would be financially very rewarding. When her mother's face lit up at the news, Hannah was so relieved that she was keen on the idea and suddenly became excited about the thought of living in Cornwall, away from the bustle of London. It would be wonderful for Michael, with plenty of fresh air and regular visits to the beach.

When the boys came in, Hannah couldn't contain her enthusiasm. "Oh, Adam, I've been talking to Mum about your job and the prospect of moving to Cornwall. She thinks it's a great idea and would be very nice for all of us."

Hannah's father had come in the French windows with Michael and just caught the last few of Hannah's words. "What would be a great idea?" he said.

"Adam has had a job offer from Coastal Command: an open contract, lots more money and a bigger role. It would mean us all moving to Cornwall. What do you think, Dad?"

He turned to Devon. "Weren't you planning to return to test piloting or something like that after your current contract expires?"

"That was one of the options I wanted to consider, but jobs like that are few and far between. The one with Coastal Command pays very well, it's work I like, and if we move to Cornwall I will be home most evenings."

"Isn't it dangerous work?"

"No, not really. The Shackleton's a great aircraft, very reliable. And although the Russians are expanding their submarine fleet, in peacetime no one is going to shoot at us!" Devon laughed gently, as did Hannah's father.

"What if we have a change of government at the next general election? Isn't there a risk there could be a change in defence policy and you'd be laid off?"

Devon nodded. "Yes, there is always that possibility, but if there is a reduction in defence spending I would be confident that our monitoring of the Russian threat will be one of the service branches that would be protected by either party that gets in."

"Well then, it seems like an excellent opportunity for you all. And we can book our holidays in Cornwall and come down on the train. Would your parents travel down there as well, Adam?"

"Oh yes – I mean, I haven't discussed it with them but I'm sure they will be supportive and, like you, come for holidays."

"Visits to the beach and ice creams – won't that be marvellous, Michael?" Hannah's dad swept the boy into the air and caught him, giggling and happy.

"Oh, thank you, Dad." Hannah kissed him on the cheek and embraced her mother.

SIX

One of the perks of being a senior politician that Henry Fitzjohn enjoyed to the full was the regular flow of invitations to social events, all expenses paid. He had taken Amanda to the July Festival in Newmarket, with their tickets provided by a small but ambitious construction company that was hoping for planning permission for a new town development in Suffolk (which they were granted, after Fitzjohn's intervention), and they enjoyed good seats at Wimbledon each year, courtesy of a large accountancy firm in his constituency.

Fitzjohn decided to stay overnight in London to enable him to make an early start to the Oval cricket ground for one of his favourite events – the first day of a Test match against India. The early September weather was set fair. He talked his way into the members' pavilion and had a good breakfast before wandering around the ground ahead of the start of the match, enjoying the atmosphere and the smiles and nods from people who recognised him. It's nice to be famous, he thought.

Just before the first over he found the private box that his host, Edward Collins, the Chief General Manager of National Provinces

Bank, had reserved for the day. Very soon after his arrival, the guests were invited to take their seats for the match. Fitzjohn was glad he had remembered to bring his aviation sunglasses and a cream panama with a hat band in the dark blue, maroon and light blue of the RAF.

Collins took the opportunity to air his views on the direction government corporate tax policy should be heading. Fitzjohn nodded and agreed enthusiastically, but without taking his eyes off the cricket. Boring, monotonous businessmen didn't seem to appreciate the wonder of Truman's bowling, tearing through the Indian batting order. As the teams walked off the field for lunch, the bank's guests returned to their host's box for a few drinks before their own meal. Fitzjohn looked around at the usual collection of industrialists, Lloyd's underwriters, some newspaper men, and a woman he vaguely recognised from the Treasury. They all seemed to be enthralled by a man who was holding court, overdressed for a cricket match in a light tan suit, white shirt and a gaudy pink tie. Fitzjohn suddenly recalled he had seen him before, at Imogen's club: it was Stephen Walmsley.

***

After lunch several of the guests took coffee out to their seats, but Fitzjohn was one of those who stayed behind to enjoy a glass of port. Forgetting Amanda's pleading, he went over to Walmsley. "Great bowling from Truman, wasn't it? My name's Fitzjohn, Henry Fitzjohn." They shook hands.

"Stephen Walmsley. Yes, I recognise you. Conservative MP, I believe, and owner of one of Britain's leading air charter operators," Walmsley said with a knowing look.

"Guilty as charged on the parliamentary front. Still some way to go with the airline, but I'm happy with our progress so far. We've just moved to Gatwick and acquired a couple of Viscounts."

"Really? Not just an air taxi service, then? A proper airline, by the sound of things."

"That's the plan. Key to success, of course, is having a good man to run the show when I'm not there. And I have a very good man. What brings you here today, Stephen? Not just the cricket, surely?"

"No, I can't say I'm the world's biggest fan. But in my business socialising is important – most of my firm's engagements come from people we know."

"And that's your architecture practice, am I right?" said Fitzjohn.

"Yes, indeed. You're well informed. My team also procure the construction side of things. Usually refurbishment of London houses and apartments, and some work in the country. And we have been known to act as development surveyors when a client wishes to acquire or build something new."

"Sounds very lucrative."

Walmsley waved a hand in the air and said quietly in a between-you-and-me tone, "Well, we only work with those who can afford the quality we provide. Not just residents but those who know a good investment. You're probably aware of the huge interest from foreign investors in London property at the moment."

"Quite. And I'm sure you have all the right contacts."

"I believe I do," said Walmsley, pursing his lips and staring at Fitzjohn.

An attentive host, Edward Collins was circulating, ushering the guests outside as the cricket was restarting. Fitzjohn found his hat and was about to walk to the door when Walmsley touched his arm. "Henry, if you're not otherwise engaged, why don't you come along to my flat in Marylebone on Saturday evening? We're having a little party – some very good friends of mine, a few drinks, perhaps some dancing."

"Thank you, Stephen. It happens that I am available this weekend."

"Splendid, old boy." Walmsley handed Fitzjohn his card. "From around ten."

***

In fact Fitzjohn had a very busy Saturday: he drove down early in the morning to meet Richard Dunn at the new offices in Gatwick airport. The first of the Viscounts had been delivered, looking resplendent in its new livery of silver and red, with Granta Airlines' logo. The two new pilots had passed their conversion tests and were now certified to fly the Viscount. In the afternoon he signed a lucrative contract with True Sun Holidays, the fastest growing package holiday operator in the UK, with Terry Graham himself coming to the signing. In a couple of months the first passenger charters would be taking off, flying to Malaga in Spain and Palma in Majorca for some autumn sun, followed the next summer by frequent flights to France, Greece and Italy.

Fitzjohn recognised how important Dunn was to the operation, and had decided to make him managing director. As well as a good salary increase, he gave him a profit-sharing bonus framework, which could see Dunn earning up to an additional 50 per cent of his salary. Naturally, Dunn was delighted, and Fitzjohn became even more confident that the new airline would be a success. Next time he met with the banks it would all be good news, and he'd hopefully steer them towards further loans as the business developed. He also felt the need to repay Amanda's loan as soon as possible; he was inherently uncomfortable that he was in her debt.

Amanda was away for the weekend with an old schoolfriend in Bristol. Fitzjohn was bursting to tell her about the progress with the airline and how well the bookings were doing, but that would have to wait until the coming week. For now, he had to get back to his flat in Kensington and get ready for Walmsley's party. On the way he picked up a new Dormeuil steel-grey suit from his tailor's in Savile Row, along with a light-blue shirt and a dark-blue tie. Fitzjohn was of medium height and substantial build – not muscular but well rounded. He kept fit by swimming and doing regular gym work. He had a round, suntanned face, brown eyes and lank tawny hair combed over to behind his right ear. His moustache was a leftover from his RAF days, but he kept it neat and trimmed, as he felt it added a touch of sophistication to his looks. He found himself looking in the mirror several times before his car arrived to drive him to Marylebone.

Fitzjohn was immediately impressed with the flat. It occupied the top floor of an Edwardian block and had a huge living space, a well-fitted kitchen, three bedrooms, a balcony and a lofted workroom with an architect's drawing board. A bar had been set up, serviced by a waiter in a crisp white jacket. Waitresses in tight black dresses circulated with canapés. Music was from a stereogram, all lively stuff, and some guests were already dancing.

Walmsley introduced Fitzjohn to a tall man of about his own age who described himself as a diamond merchant. Fitzjohn thought he looked every inch a dealer, with his manicured nails, flowery silk square in his top pocket, and neatly waved fair hair. But beside him was a very attractive lady whom he introduced as his wife, Lucia. Fitzjohn looked at her again. Yes, definitely some Italian in there somewhere. She moved away, to Fitzjohn's disappointment, but only to place her champagne glass on the bar. Then she came back and without a word took Fitzjohn's hand to dance. He was very happy to oblige, and found she was an expert dancer: could have been a ballerina in the past, he thought. She was also a sensuous dancer, and kept her face very close to him. Fitzjohn decided he wouldn't mind if he saw her again, and slipped a card from his inside jacket pocket into her hand.

As the evening wore on, he found that the men seemed to be comfortably outnumbered by the lady guests and recalled Amanda's comments about last year's debutantes. That explained why so many of them looked barely twenty years old and were immaculately dressed and well spoken. Now he could see why Amanda wanted him to keep away from this set; there were any number of beautiful women to tempt him.

Around half past one people began to depart. Fitzjohn didn't want to be seen as overstaying his welcome. He found Walmsley in the kitchen, deep in conversation with perhaps the most beautiful of the girls. Fitzjohn expressed his thanks for a delightful evening and went to leave. But Walmsley said, "Henry, before you go, may I introduce my good friend Vanessa Paget?"

Fitzjohn took her hand. "Lovely to meet you. Have you enjoyed the evening?"

"Oh yes, Stephen always ensures I have a good time."

"Jolly good. What do you do for a living, Vanessa?"

"I'm an actress. Shakespeare and West End theatre, mainly," she said, tossing her long dark-brown hair across her shoulder. "I'm resting at the moment."

"Wonderful. Well, I hope we meet again sometime."

Walmsley touched Fitzjohn's arm. "I'm sure you will, Henry, sure you will."

SEVEN

Hannah and Adam Devon were thrilled with the house the agent had recommended in the pretty village of Cardinham, not far from Bodmin. Just a couple of miles off the A30, the main road through Cornwall, it was an easy half-hour drive for Devon to the RAF St Mawgan airfield.

Since it was close to the mainline station at Bodmin Parkway and its regular service to Paddington, Hannah would be able to travel to her meetings in London swiftly and in comfort. The house was just a short walk from the church, village hall and a small post office and shop. It had a large south-facing garden and four bedrooms – plenty of room for family and other visitors. The village had a junior school and tennis club, and Hannah felt they would soon make friends for themselves and Michael. The rent was in budget and the house was so much nicer than the two they had looked at in the morning, which were smaller and further away from the station. They made the decision on the spot: they would take it and move down to Cornwall in about a month, just in time for late summer in the West Country.

Hannah arranged for their house in Wimbledon to be put in the hands of a letting agent, who assured her there would be high demand for the property, as more commuters to the City were settling around District Line tube stations. And he was right: the very next day the house was let to a young couple who both worked in shipping offices in Leadenhall Street. The rental income would start straight away, putting Hannah and Devon in the best financial position they had ever been in.

Devon would commute to work in the Rover. They bought Hannah the two-year-old Land Rover that she wanted, which would allow her to negotiate the undulating countryside and narrow roads. They had a phone connected at the house, and they placed orders with the milkman and baker. In the post office window were a couple of advertisements for nanny services, which Hannah decided to investigate, for times when she needed help with Michael. Although the house was beautifully furnished, Hannah bought new linen for the beds and a new food mixer, which was sent down to Cardinham by Selfridges. She was so pleased that they had made the decision to live in Cornwall.

But the one thing she felt sad over was her resignation from the London and Hong Kong Bank, where she had worked for over ten years. She had a quickly arranged leaving party at the Lamb in Leadenhall Market and was given a lovely card, signed by almost everyone in the bank. But the most special note was the good wishes she received from John-Paul Cohen, the senior manager who had given Hannah her first opportunity in the bank. He had also been influential in signing off her secondment to the Hong Kong branch back in 1948, where she had met Devon.

Hannah had notified her contact at Mossad, the Israeli intelligence service she had worked for since being recruited for a mission in Hong Kong to hire British Spitfire pilots to join the Israeli air force, about her move to Cornwall. That assignment failed, and she was sent back to the UK and rejoined the bank in London. After a while, she got involved in an assignment to Berlin to rescue Devon, her then fiancé, which was only possible thanks to Mossad's support. Consequently, she became an intelligence agent with the service. Although she was required to attend regular briefings in London, her job was now desk-based. She had been assigned the task of monitoring and analysing radical groups and political parties that existed in the UK: right-wing nationalists, communists, fascists and any others that could be a threat to Jewish people or that might plot against the Israeli state. She did the work because of her Jewish heritage; most of her family had been lost in the Holocaust. The pay was also helpful and gave her a sense of purpose.

Hannah had a network of agents around the country who tracked the activities of these groups and organisations. Some joined and infiltrated groups, while others simply attended meetings and recorded the formal proceedings, staying behind to gather the informal views and plans of the group members. All these agents sent their reports to Hannah, and her job was to triage the intelligence and compile a report on the key risks for Mossad in London.

As well as her London briefings on developments in the politics of the Middle East, relations with the United States and the work of other Israeli spy networks, Hannah was required to take periodic refresher courses on small arms and self-defence at a centre on the Essex coast, an hour from London. Just before they left Wimbledon she spent a day there handling and firing Beretta and Browning pistols and the Uzi machine gun. Although she was no longer operational in the field, it was important that she maintained the ability to return to active service at short notice, should the need arise. She had agreed with Adam that she would not talk to him about the work she was doing, unless she had to return to the service to take part in an operation in the UK or abroad, where guns might be involved. What Devon didn't know about, he couldn't accidentally mention to anyone who shouldn't know.

Hannah soon became friendly with Mrs Tregothan, the postmistress in Cardinham, who ensured that her incoming packages and outgoing reports were dealt with efficiently. For Mrs Tregothan, it made a change from the usual postcards and pension payments, and she clearly believed Hannah's cover story: that she worked as a journalist on government affairs.

***

The reconnaissance operations at St Mawgan had been assigned a new, wider sector by the ministry: an area covering the Atlantic western approaches from the south coast of Ireland, down to Brest in Brittany. Instructions from the ministry in London were becoming more frequent and focused: Russian submarines must be constantly under observation and their routes tracked. That was the aim. In practice, the submarine commanders were developing greater skills at evasion and the tactics of surfacing and diving at times when they could avoid their hunters. As new aircraft and trainee pilots started to arrive, Devon often had to work long days on extended-range missions. The ability to take some time off and see his family, now living just half an hour from the airfield, was a huge benefit, and he was glad and relieved that Hannah had agreed to the move.

The village shop in Cardinham stocked the daily newspapers, which arrived on the overnight train from Paddington. One clear, calm Saturday morning in September, Hannah walked to the shop with Michael and bought *The Times* and the *Daily Express*. Hannah enjoyed reading about world affairs in *The Times* and knew that Adam would take time out to read the sports pages of both newspapers. They studied the editorials. Journalists were speculating about the likelihood of a general election being called, and Hannah asked Adam what would happen to his role with the RAF if there was a change of government.

Would defence spending cuts mean he would be out of a job, as her father had suggested? But Devon was confident that maritime defence capabilities would be supported by whoever was in power; the role was not defined by Westminster but by the Russian government's aggressive stance. He was sure his job would be safe, no matter which political party was in power.

EIGHT

Henry Fitzjohn had spent the evening at Park Castle near Saffron Walden, the family's country estate in north Essex, with his two older brothers and Sir Charles Fitzjohn, his elderly father, mostly debating the subject of death duties and how to avoid them, and the future rents of the farms on the estate. The old man went to bed just before midnight and discussions between the brothers, usually a tense affair, were amiable and productive and went on into the early hours, helped along by generous measures of a good malt whisky.

Fitzjohn had no desire to get involved with the practicalities of running the estate – he never had – but he was keen to know that his long-term interests would be protected. After all, he was a beneficiary in his father's will, and when the time came he had a working plan to sell his share to his brothers and walk away with the money to invest in his airline, and perhaps a nice mews house in Chelsea. All a long way in the future, thought Fitzjohn, as the old squire was as fit as a fiddle, despite his years.

Fitzjohn was woken by a knock on his bedroom door at what felt like an ungodly hour, but when he glanced at the clock on the bureau he saw it was almost 9a.m. He called out a grouchy "come in" and felt his headache pulsing as he struggled to sit up. Arnold, who had once been the butler to the household but was now the general factotum, crept in wearily with a tray, a pot of coffee and a glass of water, designed to defer the flak he knew he would receive from Master Henry.

"What do you want, Arnold? It's too sodding early for that!"

"Yes, sir, I'm sure you are correct in the usual course of affairs, but today I have an important message for you." He crashed the tray down on the bedside cabinet and allowed himself the smallest of smiles as Fitzjohn winced at the throbbing in his head.

"Terribly sorry, sir."

"Leave it there and clear off – let me get back to sleep."

"Certainly, sir. Shall I also leave the important message from Downing Street until later?"

Fitzjohn spun round and sat up. "Downing Street? What message?"

"I'm sure it's nothing urgent, sir."

"Just tell me, damn you!"

"Of course, Master Henry…"

"And don't call me that, I'm not a child!" The effort of shouting taxed Fitzjohn's reserves of energy, and he slumped back into the pillows. "Oh, for crying out loud, just give me the message."

"Mr Macmillan's private secretary telephoned this morning, sir, and asked if you would be so kind as to attend a Cabinet meeting today at 1p.m. In Number 10, of course."

"*What?* Really? Why didn't you wake me earlier, you fool? Run me a bath straightaway and have Cook send up a tray of breakfast. I'll get the 10.30 train."

***

Despite the shortage of taxis at Liverpool Street Station, Fitzjohn arrived early for the meeting, saluted the duty policeman and walked through the black door into Number 10. An assistant secretary took him through to the Cabinet meeting room, where four or five ministers were gathered. They welcomed Fitzjohn politely and he joined in their small talk, each of them studiously avoiding speculating on the purpose of the meeting. Fitzjohn felt he was being indulged; the group were mostly Old Etonians, members of a club he could never aspire to, and his presence at the meeting was only as a stand-in for Duncan Saunders, the incumbent Minister of Defence, who was abroad. Nevertheless, Fitzjohn was determined to make a good impression at his first Cabinet meeting.

At 1p.m. on the dot Harold Macmillan came in with his three private secretaries, said nothing and sat straight down. After a wave of his hand, everyone else took their seats.

"Gentlemen, thank you for attending at such short notice. You may well have anticipated the purpose of the meeting, but don't let that take away the importance of what I am about to say. And note, please, absolute confidentiality is required until we make the public announcement. I am pleased to say that we shall declare at 11a.m. tomorrow that we are dissolving parliament and calling a general election. The date of the election is to be 8 October." Macmillan sat back. Silence prevailed until he said, "Comments, please."

Peter Titheridge, the Home Secretary, was the first to respond, but then he was Mac's closest ally. "Bravo, Prime Minister, very timely. We have won over the country with the measures we have taken on living standards, employment and taxes. I've no doubt the country will back you."

Fitzjohn heard the Chancellor groan under his breath at Titheridge's sycophancy. Not everyone thought it the right time for a general election, but it seemed that no one was willing to voice opposition to Macmillan.

"Why now, Harold?" Fitzjohn jolted in shock as he heard himself ask the question. He just blurted it out without thinking and, he realised too late, it sounded like a challenge. There was silence as everyone turned to him, and for a moment he found he couldn't breathe. He knew it breached protocol for an Undersecretary, only at the meeting for good form, to ask a question. And to address the prime minister by his Christian name in a Cabinet meeting? Some might have said that amounted to insubordination. Sometimes acceptable for the Home Secretary, but few others would dare. It was too late to shrink back now. Fitzjohn clasped his hands on the table and looked squarely at the prime minister.

Macmillan raised his eyebrows and leant forward to get a clearer view of Fitzjohn. "Now that's a very germane question, Henry, and thank you for being so succinct."

Fitzjohn relaxed, and a warm blush rose up his cheeks. The PM took the question on face value and, by using Fitzjohn's first name, gave him a credibility that some around the table had not managed to achieve in years of working with Macmillan.

"The British people will be looking forward to the next decade, less than four months away, leaving behind the austerity that characterised the 1950s, and they will want the Conservatives to take them forward. International trade, defence, industry, the health service, schools, employment levels – all in good shape. The polls are turning in our favour, so we shall make use of our momentum. I want everyone in this room to display the confidence and belief in our country that will carry the voters with us. When you return to your constituencies I want you to rally all party members to the cause. If we can show our belief in our plans for the future then all of our MPs will do the same. The campaign begins today, gentlemen."

Fitzjohn nodded meaningfully through the PM's speech, almost, but not quite, expressing a condescending approval rather than just understanding. It was a familiarity that came naturally to him and he extended his support for the PM by glancing around the table, eyebrows raised, at the other members of the Cabinet, almost daring anyone to disagree.

Macmillan coughed, and everyone turned to face him. "Gentlemen, any more questions? No? Right, you will be given a copy of the final draft of the manifesto as you leave, and this will be launched with our announcement tomorrow. I wish you good fortune in the campaign. Now, I have an audience with the Queen at Buckingham Palace at three o'clock. Good afternoon, gentlemen."

The Cabinet members departed without a word, either inspired by the prospect of a new term in office or in fear of losing their jobs. As Fitzjohn headed for the door, Sir Oliver Colton, the PM's senior private secretary, stopped him. "Don't go too far, Henry. Mac wants to see you this afternoon, at 5p.m., if that is convenient with you?"

"Yes, of course, Sir Oliver," said Fitzjohn in his most affable voice. He decided he would spend the night in London, and went direct to his flat to kill some time before the meeting. He called Amanda to tell her about the election. Although she acted surprised, Fitzjohn couldn't help feeling she already knew.

NINE

Fitzjohn did not wish to be seen as being in awe of the instruction to meet the PM, so he made sure he was not early for the appointment, arriving at Number 10 at just one minute to five. He was shown to Mac's office, and was surprised to see it empty. It was nearly half past the hour when Sir Oliver Colton came in, sat down, and advised Fitzjohn that the PM would be another fifteen minutes. Fitzjohn felt Colton had structured Macmillan's diary to give him some time alone with him.

"Henry," Colton said, pausing to make sure he had Fitzjohn's full attention. "Henry, you are of course aware of the various threats to the United Kingdom, our Empire and allies around the world that our enemies pose. You will also be aware that the cost of running our armed forces is such that reductions in the budget are inevitable and our capabilities will be reduced – all for vote-winning tax cuts for the working man. The PM is under serious pressure from the party to ensure that, as we go into the sixties, we secure Conservative governments for a generation. My question to you is, should you find yourself in a position of authority in a future government, what stance would you take in regard to these matters? And would you support or oppose the cuts?"

Fitzjohn knew he was being put on the spot. Why should he answer such a question, put by a civil servant? Was Colton speaking on behalf of Macmillan or garnering his own intelligence on senior members of the party?

"A difficult question, Sir Oliver. Have you canvassed Duncan Saunders for his opinion on this? He is, after all, the Minister of Defence."

"It's your opinion I am enquiring after." Colton stared fixedly at Fitzjohn.

Fitzjohn dodged the question. "This position of authority you mention, what exactly do you have in mind?"

"Oh, come now, Henry. It is well known that you are one of the PM's blue-eyed boys." Colton changed his tactics, offered an obsequious smile. "And I'm sure you have a very clear picture of what he has in mind for you after the election. Assuming the Conservatives win, of course."

"Of course, Sir Oliver. But wouldn't it be more appropriate for me to discuss the matter directly with Mac? His intention, as I understand it, is to reinvest in the armed forces to address the growing threat, and he would want a team of like-minded supporters around him."

"Indeed. And Saunders has been one of those people. Unfortunately, in my opinion, he is now out of favour with Macmillan, thanks to his views on the Suez crisis." Colton looked at his watch. "The PM will be here in a moment – he wants to talk to you in private. But before I go, please remember this. The country cannot afford the defence expenditure that the PM is proposing. He is being pressured into building larger armed services by the chiefs of staff – no surprise there. If you should find yourself in one of the lofty government positions I alluded to, I am sure I can trust you to oppose the PM's defence expansion plans."

"It's certainly something that has to be considered," Fitzjohn mumbled, then fell silent as the door opened and Macmillan entered with a sprightly stride that surprised Fitzjohn: he might be known as Old Mac, but he had the vitality of a much younger man. Colton said nothing more and left the room.

***

After his session with the prime minister, Fitzjohn telephoned Amanda and asked to see her for dinner that evening. Not only was she available, but she said she had thought Fitzjohn might call her, and she would meet him in the bar of the Thames Vista Hotel at seven o'clock. When Fitzjohn arrived she was already there, well into a large gin and tonic.

"What exactly did Mac say?" Amanda asked.

"Pretty straightforward. Would I or would I not support the defence expansion strategy that he would bring to parliament in the first session after the election?"

"And you said…"

"Certainly I am in favour, as I told him. But I also said I gathered that not everyone feels the same. Without blinking, he asked me if Colton had had a chat. So I related the discussion I had just had with Sir Oliver. Macmillan just smiled and nodded. I don't know why he doesn't just sack his private secretary and be done with it."

"Not that simple, Henry. These senior civil servants carry significant weight in Westminster. Mac uses Colton's position of influence to his own advantage and works around their differing views on policy. If he fired all those who disagreed with his views on all the matters that cross his desk, Westminster would be half empty."

"Right, well, the bottom line, old girl, is that Harold and I are on the same page. Isn't that the important thing, from your perspective?"

"If you mean will it help you to be appointed Minister of Defence after the election, then certainly, but it's not guaranteed. Mac will have to build a Cabinet that is seen by the voters, party members and the press as a winning team – he will have plenty of choice in who he appoints."

"So what does that mean for me?"

"Smile at the right people in Westminster, make sure you win your own seat and just keep your nose clean, Henry, there's a good boy. Not so hard, even for you."

TEN

September 1959

Adam Devon was given his patrol sector by the station intelligence officer, including his take-off time and the crew for the mission. The area south of Ireland was designated a high-risk zone, as intruder submarines often patrolled seas where a high level of maritime traffic could be expected. The crew were vastly experienced technicians, experts in using the submarine detection equipment on board the aircraft. No one needed to be briefed on the growing importance of the reconnaissance patrols, given the tension between the West and the Soviet Union, and if war should break out, the possibility of attacks on British and allied naval and commercial shipping.

It was a typical early autumn day in the Atlantic, with a low pressure system bringing large formations of cloud and rain. Visual identification of Soviet ships and submarines was impossible, but the radar and sonar equipment on board the Shackleton identified vessels that, in a war situation, the aircraft would seek to destroy. The purpose of this mission was to allow two student pilots to alternate, flying prearranged segments of the patrol area as the technicians scanned the sea for ships and surfaced submarines. Two frigates from the Royal Navy were on station to the south of Bantry Bay in the role of seaborne interceptors working with the aircraft.

Devon found both pilots to be very capable, and he was confident they would soon finish their training and move over to an operational squadron, either in Cornwall or at the northern base at Kinloss, Scotland. But Devon needed to ensure he was impartial in his assessment of one of the pilots, a man he had flown with in Singapore and Hong Kong in the late 1940s, Flight Lieutenant John Corrigan. Devon remembered him as a good friend who had left the squadron in 1948 to join BOAC but had signed up again with the RAF in the last year, citing the attraction of operational flying.

Around an hour after take-off they were nearing their furthest waymarker. It was time to commence a pattern of criss-crossing the sector, leaving no part of the ocean unexamined. Corrigan took the controls. Precise headings were to be flown; no drifting off course was acceptable, because that's how enemy vessels could be missed. Devon was pleased – Corrigan's excellent flying was a testament to his many years of experience on all types of aircraft.

***

Two hundred miles west of Land's End, a Soviet submarine broke the surface of the sea. Men emerged from the conning tower, glad of the fresh air and the wind on their faces. Captain 1st Rank Fyodor Yegorov followed within minutes and ordered a rota of crew members over the next hour to come up and take the air: a concession that every man knew was not an operational requirement, but a reward for the work they had done on the boat's maiden voyage. All crewmen were experienced submariners and understood the honour the Soviet Union had given them in manning the *Leninski*, Russia's first nuclear-powered submarine.

The assignment was simple: test the UK's submarine detection capabilities. When submerged, conventional submarines' engines ran on electric power from batteries. These needed to be recharged regularly, using diesel engines that could only be operated when the boat was on the surface. And this made it easier for submarine interceptors in the air to spot them. But the *Leninski* used nuclear power to charge its batteries, so it could stay underwater, and undetected, for months at a time, if necessary. The Russian North Atlantic fleet commanders wanted to test the tactics and capabilities of the British interceptors, both on the sea and in the air. After another half an hour, the captain ordered all crew members to return to operational stations and prepare to dive. The next move would be to head east and stand fifty miles off the Isles of Scilly. There they would stay submerged and carry out their simulated attacks on enemy shipping; if the British anti-submarine warfare operations showed their hand, then all the better. The *Leninski* spotted by sonar a cargo ship en route from Harwich to North America. Using quiet running, it stealthily tracked the ship, keeping within torpedo range. After forty minutes the radio operator called to the senior lieutenant on duty – he had picked up a transmission from a British destroyer patrolling the seas above them. They were being hunted.

***

Devon heard through his headset the radio operator's excited voice: "Hostile submarine, five miles east." He immediately instructed Pilot Ian Chant, who had taken over flying the aircraft, to take up a heading of 090 degrees and patrol the area where the submarine was detected. The two navy ships were already in the hunt and headed towards the

Isles of Scilly at maximum speed. After several tracks back and forth by the Shackleton, no trace of the submarine had been detected. Devon ordered Chant to move back out to the west, guessing that a Soviet captain would seek the safety of the open Atlantic Ocean then head north around Ireland and ultimately to his Soviet home port.

Chant kept his head down, concentrating on flying the Shackleton over the designated area, monitoring the compass, airspeed indicator and altimeter. He wasn't expected to look out for enemy ships or submarines; that was the job of the technicians. Knowing that Devon would be expecting accurate distance and headings, he flew the sector precisely. After just ten minutes there was another update: "Target one mile west." Chant looked across the cockpit at Devon, who simply nodded. Chant banked the aircraft to the left.

Within two minutes they were overhead the expected location of the submarine, but the technicians remained silent. Had the sub captain diverted back towards the east in a double bluff to avoid the hunter, or sped away out of their patrol area? The technicians in the back of the aircraft were glued to their headsets and screens.

Devon gave the order to return to the Isles of Scilly, but the search was fruitless. After another half an hour of patrolling he decided they had been outfoxed and were not going to find the Soviet submarine. It was time to head back to St Mawgan.

ELEVEN

Fitzjohn's daily post in his office in Westminster was largely dealt with by his secretary, Sian Shelby and her junior, Mea Pengelly. Fitzjohn had made it clear to her that he had no interest in reading the complaints and idiotic demands from constituents – or anyone else in the country. From the substantial postbag he rarely had more than a couple of private letters, and the usual requests to appear as an after-dinner speaker; some he even accepted. Good for PR, Amanda said.

Only a week had passed since the election was called. Fitzjohn had enthusiastically undertaken all the engagements in his diary, rallying constituency support, shaking hands with local people, and giving interviews to the press. He surprised himself by how much he enjoyed the campaigning: the truth was, he revelled in being in the limelight and was enjoying being popular. He was delighted that it also meant several nights at the Thames Vista Hotel, with Amanda giving him all the encouragement he needed to perform.

One day Sian came in with his morning coffee and a letter that was clearly personal – it had an impressive crest on the back of the envelope.

She was fanning her face with it. "Mea just passed this to me – you might like to read this one, Henry, it's almost from royalty."

"If it isn't actual royalty, then why should I be interested?" he replied with a throaty laugh.

"I think it's from Lord Valley – William Valley you may know him as, if I read the crest correctly. He's one of our biggest supporters. Shall I open it?"

Fitzjohn stifled a yawn. "Alright, go ahead. No doubt he wants to press me to abolish death duties."

Sian slid an invitation card from the envelope, raised her eyebrows and gave a soft whistle. "Well, how about that? It is indeed from the man himself."

"And? Come on, old girl, to what do I have the pleasure of a despatch from such an important man?"

"He has invited you to be his guest at a fundraising party at his pile in the country, Valley Lodge. It's down in Sussex. It's this Saturday, and you're invited to stay over until Sunday, with a shoot in the morning."

"I'm not paying for the privilege – what a cheek!"

"Calm down, you won't have to pay anything – you're invited as a guest of His Lordship. A famous face to get the punters to part with their cash."

"Ah, well. But should I really be doing this during the election campaign? Doesn't he know I have no time for jollification?"

"It's all part of the game – getting the rich to donate their money while all the hoo-hah of the election is under way. Actually there's something else here." Sian took a slip of paper out of the envelope. "You are asked to donate something for the after-dinner auction." She picked up Fitzjohn's desk diary. "You have Saturday and Sunday blocked out for meetings at the airline in Gatwick. Valley Lodge is not far away – you could do both."

"Good point. Very well, please send my most grateful thanks. And tell them I will donate a pair of Granta Airlines return tickets to Palma. Take them from the advertising budget."

***

Fitzjohn was more than satisfied with Richard Dunn's planning for the first operational flight for the Viscount, which would head to Valencia the following Tuesday. New pilots had been recruited and the second Viscount delivery was only a couple of weeks away. He had brought his weekend bag with him and changed into his dinner suit at Granta's offices.

Valley Lodge, like all country houses, was designed to impress and to demonstrate wealth. This house did that job well. With a broad frontage only three storeys high, mullioned windows with leaded glass, the building was probably 200 years old but was clearly kept in pristine condition. The grand hall was furnished in art deco style, with an impressive collection of modern art, statues and pictures. It seeped wealth, and Fitzjohn immediately felt comfortable. He was shown to his room by the housekeeper, who pointed out the drinks tray, including a rare malt whisky. Fitzjohn didn't hesitate to help himself to a measure.

Canapés were served in the ballroom, an opulent salon with a view of the parkland at the rear of the house, where Lord Valley was welcoming guests. Fitzjohn estimated there would be about fifty people at the party, given the size of the house, and he knew that most were paying a substantial sum for the privilege. Good for them, he thought. Labour's union funding couldn't match this level of support. Lord Valley welcomed Fitzjohn as one would an old friend, even though they had never met.

Fitzjohn noticed the label on the champagne bottles as the staff generously refilled glasses: a 1948 Mercier. Impressive. He was enjoying the role he naturally adopted as he was introduced to other guests: the charming, amusing, good-looking MP, the darling of the party and a man of the future. He circulated and shared the universal sentiment that the Conservatives were bound to win the election by a landslide.

He was buttonholed by a petite woman in a black trouser suit, wearing a silver brooch in the shape of a leaping fox. She was explaining her role in the newly formed anti-foxhunting association. Fitzjohn had no strong views one way or the other but felt the lady would be on to a loser if she thought the country set would happily give up their horsey pursuits. As she was no doubt a valued donor to the party, he listened attentively, but as he was wondering how he could politely move on, he became aware of someone standing close to him on his right side. He glanced across to see it was Stephen Walmsley. Taking the opportunity to step away from the fox lady, Fitzjohn turned on his best bonhomie. "Stephen, how nice to see you again, old chap!"

"And you, Henry. I was delighted to hear that William had added you to the guest list. I have to say that it was my nudging that prompted His Lordship to send the invitation."

Fitzjohn was taken aback. This Walmsley must carry some status if he could influence Lord Valley's guest list. "Well, good show. Is William one of your clients?"

"He certainly is, both here at Valley Lodge and up in Knightsbridge, where he has a lovely townhouse. I'm also hoping to be given the brief for the design of a new beachside house in Guernsey that William is planning."

"Guernsey?"

"Yes. There are excellent tax advantages on the island, of course..."

"I see, very astute. But so long as he continues to direct some of his pre-tax income to the Conservative Party I don't think anyone will complain, do you?" said Fitzjohn with an almost imperceptible wink.

"No, indeed." Walmsley looked past Fitzjohn's shoulder. "Ah, here are a couple more of my guests – let me introduce you."

Two very attractive girls were at the door, each sipping from a champagne coupe. One blonde, the other brunette, in their early twenties, Fitzjohn guessed. As they approached the smiling Walmsley, Fitzjohn remembered he had met the brunette at Walmsley's party, Vanessa something.

"Henry, may I introduce Penny Vaughan-Hart? Penny is an actress – West End theatre."

The blonde lady stepped forward, smiled and fluttered her eyelashes.

Fitzjohn shook hands. "Pleased to meet you, Penny. Are you a friend of Lord Valley?"

"Oh no, I'm here at Stephen's invitation. How about you?"

"Guest of our host." Fitzjohn turned to look at the brunette. "And if I'm right…"

Before he could say anything further, Walmsley interjected, "You will remember Vanessa Paget, Henry."

"Indeed I do." Fitzjohn shook her hand and noticed her firm, lingering grip. Her brown hair had a neat fringe and was curled outwards at her shoulders. She had a wide mouth and full lips. When she smiled, her left cheek creased into a dimple. She wore just a touch of pale-blue eyeshadow above her brown eyes.

"We met at Stephen's flat, as I recall. A pleasure to see you again, Vanessa."

"And you, Henry. This is such a lovely house, isn't it? One of my favourite places."

"You've been here before?" Fitzjohn was intrigued.

"Yes, I was here for a garden party earlier in the year. I was with an old schoolfriend."

"Well, I'm sure we'll have a great weekend. Do enjoy yourself." Fitzjohn had seen one of the Conservative central office administrators across the room and went over to say hello. She told him she was there to make sure all the fee-paying guests were well fed and watered and in good spirits for the evening's fundraising auction. Soon dinner was announced and the guests walked through to the dining room, where six large round tables were laid out, beautifully dressed with flower displays, Royal Doulton china with the Valley crest, and Royal Brierley crystal. Fitzjohn was first to his table and soon found his seat. He quickly looked at the other name cards and was delighted to see that the guest placed immediately to his right was Vanessa Paget.

TWELVE

From the array of cutlery before him, Fitzjohn estimated there would be seven courses, and as many accompanying wines. He thought that Lord Valley was laying it on thick but the dinner was sure to gain the approval of all guests, particularly those who had bought tickets to attend. A great deal of money would be heading to the Conservative Party coffers after the weekend's entertainment.

Fitzjohn's assistant secretary, Mea, had briefed him on Lord Valley's business interests: international banking, shipping and commodity imports, rubber, metals, coffee, timber – all goods that required stable international trading conditions to prosper. Mea also mentioned the arms manufacturing division of his empire, but she had found little information on this. Valley had a clear interest in a UK government that supported his businesses.

Vanessa Paget was a good conversationalist: amusing and erudite, at times she had the whole table in thrall as she told stories about famous actors and actresses she had worked with during her time at the Royal Shakespeare Company. Fitzjohn noticed she was careful not to mention the parts she had played in these productions but acted her persona as the glamorous starlet to perfection. Her white satin dress was close-fitting but modest in cut. Fitzjohn noticed her expensive jewellery: a choker with three rows of diamonds, a solid gold bracelet and pearl earrings.

During a quiet spell, he asked her, "Where do you live?"

"I have a lovely flat overlooking Regent's Park. York Terrace, if you know it?"

Fitzjohn certainly did – a very exclusive place to live. She must come from a wealthy family, he thought. "Yes, I know it well – a charming part of London. Have you been there long?"

"Nearly a year. My family live in Cornwall, but I really have to be in London for my work. I'm so lucky to have a good friend who supports up-and-coming young actresses. You must come over to my flat one evening for a drink."

From that, Fitzjohn understood that she was living rent-free and welcomed male visitors. He had a sudden realisation that she might well be earning an income from talents outside acting and was well rewarded for her services. No wonder Amanda had been so disparaging about Stephen Walmsley. Fitzjohn instinctively looked across to Walmsley's table and was not surprised to see Penny Vaughan-Hart sitting next to him. He felt he had been set up: Walmsley thought he was doing him a service by introducing him to a very attractive and apparently willing girl, but why would he bother? Fitzjohn felt he had very little to offer Walmsley: he didn't have the sort of property that needed a high-class architect.

But whatever was going on, Fitzjohn was determined to enjoy the weekend to the full. After dinner the guests moved back to the ballroom, which was now set up with discreet lighting, a five-piece band and female vocalist. More champagne was already poured into tall flutes, and several couples had taken to the dance floor. The representative from central office came over to Fitzjohn, all smiles, very pleased at the sum raised in the auction – even Fitzjohn's airline tickets had sold for fifty pounds. She didn't hesitate to ask him if he would like to dance. This took Fitzjohn a touch by surprise, feeling as she was on duty she wouldn't take time out to dance, but he instantly accepted.

He danced with another four or five ladies before he noticed Vanessa sitting on her own. He asked her to dance and soon found she was a good dancer and responded effortlessly to his lead. She maintained eye contact throughout the dance. As the music ended she pressed her cheek to his. "Let's have a drink."

Fitzjohn went to the bar and got himself a malt whisky with ice and a gin and bitter lemon for her. It was getting on for 1a.m., and Fitzjohn felt in need of some fresh air. He suggested they walk back through the hall to the orangery, where the doors were open to the garden. England had been enjoying an Indian summer, and the night was balmy and still. As he stepped out to the terrace, he felt Vanessa's fingers touch his hand, just momentarily.

They stopped at the edge of the lawn and gazed at the night sky. Her white dress had a silvery sheen in the moonlight and her eyes were wide and imploring. She took a sip of the gin, turned away from him and walked under a rose pergola. Away from the lights of the house it was almost dark. Vanessa was barely visible, but he saw her stop and put her glass down on a stone pedestal.

Fitzjohn silently followed suit, to free his hands. She turned her back to him and stepped further away in the darkness, but Fitzjohn had had enough of her teasing. He placed his hand on her left shoulder and span her round. Vanessa raised her arms and linked them round his neck. He embraced her and kissed her. The scent of the roses blended with the perfume from her skin as he swept his hands down her back. He almost gasped as her hand moved down his chest and her fingertips played a pattern across his stomach. Fitzjohn responded with exploring hands of his own and they kissed again eagerly.

Fitzjohn gazed at her. "Look, old girl, we can't have much fun out here. But perhaps we might meet later? Give it an hour or so; it would be a poor show for me to disappear just yet. I'm in the Sussex suite, first floor."

"I know. My room is next to yours, and there's a communicating door."

THIRTEEN

Devon filed his report on the exercise, focusing on the flying skills of the two trainee pilots and recommending that they each needed to complete two further missions successfully to be signed off as operational maritime reconnaissance pilots. But the potential identification of an unknown submarine meant he was required to complete a separate written report and be interviewed by the station commanding officer, Wing Commander Louis Valentine, and the duty intelligence officer. They would make enquiries to check if it could have been a British submarine – or indeed French or American. Devon was accompanied to the meeting by the senior technical officer on the aircraft, who was convinced it was a Soviet submarine and that it was still in the area, motionless and silent. Although he accepted this was just a gut feeling; he had no proof. Devon expressed the view that if the sub was still there, then the Russians would not be too impressed with the RAF and Royal Navy's submarine hunting techniques.

But the development of submarine tracking technology was not Devon's specialism and he was dismissed by the CO. He was now off duty for the rest of the weekend. After stowing his kit in a secure locker and changing into casual clothes he set off for home, elated that he would be with Hannah and Michael within an hour. But on the journey into mid-Cornwall his happiness dissipated as he felt a wave of fear for his family: the risk of war now could be as high as it was in the late 1930s, when the threat from Germany was ineffectively dealt with by appeasement. The Soviet leaders might be emboldened in their aim to spread communism across Europe if the Western alliance showed the kind of weakness that had prevailed in 1938. He had a chilling sense that the technical officer was right: there was indeed a Russian submarine prowling the waters around the UK, preparing for the day when it would be called to attack.

Devon turned off the A30 and passed through the village of Millpool, a quintessentially English village: the cottages had flowers tumbling from window boxes, hens pecked along the grass roadside, the local shop was just closing, and villagers were walking their dogs.

As he continued into Cardinham, he was sorry that there was no pub within walking distance of the house. He could do with a drink after the tense day he had had. But he knew Hannah would have dinner ready as soon as he walked in the door and quickly felt his good mood return at the thought of a couple of days with her and Michael.

"Hello, darling!" Hannah wrapped her arms around Devon's shoulders. "How has your day been?"

"Oh, not bad, thanks. And you?" Devon did not wish to worry Hannah with his thoughts about submarines and war.

"We've had a great day. Diane Trenwith from the toddler group at the church suggested we go to Fowey for the day with her and her daughter, Alice. So that's what we did. I drove the Land Rover and Diane brought a picnic, which we had on the beach."

Devon looked puzzled. "What was the town you mentioned?"

"Fowey – F.O.W.E.Y. Rhymes with joy, they always say. Funny name but a lovely town. We had coffee at the Fowey Harbour Hotel before walking along to the beach – a place called Readymoney Cove. And we had ice cream from the little shop there. We should all go there one day – you'd love it."

Devon picked up Michael. "Great stuff. Did you make sandcastles, Michael?"

"Umm," he said, slowly rubbing his fists into his eyes.

Hannah tickled his chin. "Yes, you did, and you helped Alice too. He's very tired, Adam, it's been a long day."

"What are we eating tonight?" Devon asked, but he could easily guess the answer: it was Friday, so they would have fish from the mobile fishmonger whose van came every week, direct from Mevagissey.

"A dressed crab to start, then Dover sole."

"Sounds great."

After dinner, Hannah suggested that Adam take Michael upstairs with a book while she cleared up. They were only three pages into *Four Naughty Kittens* when Michael dropped off to sleep. Devon straightened his blankets, lifted the boy's hand and kissed his fingers, and went downstairs.

"He's sound-o," said Devon.

"Good. He should be, we've had such a busy day."

They sat down in the living room with coffee. Devon poured two small glasses of dark rum.

"I had a letter from Yoel today," Hannah said slowly. She used her superior officer's first name to give a casual feel to the discussion; she knew Devon was not comfortable with her working for the Israeli secret service. "I'm to go to London in two weeks' time for a briefing and then a couple of days' refresher training in Essex. I'll be away for six days, including travel. But I'll phone Mum and ask her to come down to look after Michael."

"Right."

Hannah waited for Devon to say more, even to object, but he simply nodded and sipped his rum.

"You're OK with that?"

"Sure. I know the work you do is important, and what with everything going on in the world at the moment…"

"What do you mean?" said Hannah.

"Well, since Suez the Russians have been getting more and more aggressive. There is a risk, you know, that they will invade West Germany and the Balkans, and there we go, World War Three."

"But would they really risk it, given the strength of British, West German and French forces? And the Americans, of course."

"Who knows? If Khrushchev threatens nuclear weapons again, he might just be stupid enough to use them. And we would retaliate."

"That's a very gloomy picture, my dear," said Hannah, seeking to lift the mood.

"Yes, sorry, I guess I'm in the wrong frame of mind. We tracked a submarine off Scilly today, and the intelligence wallahs are convinced it's Russian. I've no doubt it will be back."

"Right. But for now let's enjoy the weekend."

"Good idea!" said Devon, clapping his hands. "I have some gardening to do tomorrow, but perhaps on Sunday we could go to that beach you mentioned? The weather forecast is good."

"Readymoney Cove." Hannah smiled.

FOURTEEN

With only a week left until polling day, Henry Fitzjohn had arranged to meet Amanda Spencer at the University Arms Hotel in Cambridge to plan his campaign for the run-in. He arrived the night before their meeting and was irritated that she had not joined him; she said she preferred to drive up in the early morning. As he finished his full English breakfast, Fitzjohn wondered for a moment what could keep her in London: what could be more alluring than a pleasurable night with him? But he put that out of his mind when he read the editorial in *The Times*. Contradicting all forecasts in the opinion polls for a comfortable Conservative victory, the newspaper cited a strong Labour campaign, cleverly using television appearances by their leaders to gain public support.

But Fitzjohn was confident: first in himself as the incumbent MP: his constituency was as safe a seat as you could expect, and second, he believed that the rise in standards that the Conservatives had brought to the working man meant more people saw themselves as middle class and worthy of voting Conservative. The poor handling of the Suez crisis, resulting in the resignation of Prime Minister Eden, even though it had only been three years earlier, was long forgotten, and Mac was proving surprisingly popular.

He spotted Amanda coming through the lobby. As always, he couldn't help admiring her elegance and Romanesque beauty – and he never added 'for her age'. She sat down and requested coffee. Getting straight down to business, she opened her attaché case and took out her notebook.

"I've drafted the itinerary for the week, Henry, and here's your copy. We will of course finish off the week on polling day at Sudbury town hall for the counting. The aim will be to put in appearances at the main employers in the constituency. I've got agreement from several already for you to go in and see how they work, shake hands with as many workers as possible. Over the weekend we will be knocking on doors, canvassing with the local party reps. Each evening next week we have either a WI or Rotary, and one school PTA meeting."

"Excellent, Amanda, you have been working hard. The opinion polls are looking good too."

"Well, that's true, but don't get complacent; we don't want any slip-ups. I've got the campaign volunteers fired up, reminding everyone they have never been so well off and it's all down to the Conservatives. Don't let them forget that."

"What about meeting the press?"

"It's too late for the newspapers to be much use to us, but the BBC are interested in you. Keen to know the views of one of the youngest MPs who is tipped for greater things and holds a strong seat. I'm trying to arrange a radio interview but we must be careful: remember, they will try to get you to say something controversial. You should avoid talking about defence issues, always an unsettling subject. All emphasis should be on the happy prospect of full employment and low taxes."

"But will that be true?" said Fitzjohn with a sideways glance.

"Near enough. They only have to believe it, of course, when it comes to voting."

"Understood. So, here we go for a fun week! Can't wait to get going and enjoy a resounding victory on election night." Fitzjohn sat back and stared at Amanda.

She blinked and raised her eyebrows slightly. "What?"

"What urgent business did you have that prevented you coming up to Cambridge last night? Gone off me, have you?"

"Henry, I can't be answerable to you every day of my life."

Fitzjohn saw something he had never seen before in Amanda: defensiveness. And a blush. "No, and I'm glad. Wouldn't do for us to be fully open and honest with each other, would it?"

"Oh, don't be ridiculous. What on earth would I have to hide from you?"

"A girl like you has many distractions in life." Fitzjohn wasn't unhappy that he had riled Amanda.

"A girl like me? What are you saying?"

"Oh, nothing. I know you have a very busy personal life, that's all, my love."

Fitzjohn's inference seemed to strike home. "If you must know, I had dinner with Robert Darnell, keeping up the pressure on him to ensure you are offered a Cabinet role after the election."

"I see. And did you have a successful and satisfying night?"

"Evening, you mean," Amanda said firmly; she was fighting back. "Very. I'm confident he and I can persuade Macmillan to appoint you to the defence job. But there will be conditions."

"Very well, and what are they?"

"That's up to Mac to brief you, but you can be sure he will be looking for tangible support for his defence strategy. As you know, he's keen for the UK and our NATO allies to invest in our armed forces in the face of the Soviet threat. Good for the defence manufacturers and employment, of course."

"But that's not the only reason he advocates increases in defence spending, surely?" said Fitzjohn.

"No, indeed not. Everyone fears the Russians will start simultaneous attacks on West Germany, the Baltic states and Yugoslavia in the next year or so. The defence chiefs of staff are unwilling to initiate anything that starts a war."

"I think Mac is too weak to direct them. My opinion is that we should make a pre-emptive strike into East Germany and some of the other states and push the Russians right back to their border and free the Poles, Czechs and the rest of them from communism."

"Hell of a risk – aren't the Reds likely to use their nuclear weapons?" said Amanda.

"It would be the end of them if they did, as we would hit back. Macmillan can leave it to me if I'm given the Minister of Defence job: the damn Russians need sorting out, and the sooner the better."

Amanda looked pensive. "But all of this is for the future – let's get going on our rounds today. You're making a speech at the Suffolk farmers union this afternoon and another at the Hadleigh Women's Institute this evening."

"Very exciting."

FIFTEEN

October 1959

Henry Fitzjohn's eyes ached and he had a pounding headache as he struggled to sit up in bed. The victory celebrations had gone on past 3a.m. and only came to an end when the champagne ran out. He couldn't remember walking to the hotel, but he knew it wasn't far from Sudbury town hall. Strewn across the floor, his clothes were mixed with Amanda's and the sheets were tangled around her legs and back as she quietly slept. She was on excellent form last night, thought Fitzjohn, tirelessly leading the party supporters in their revelry. And what he did remember was that she was no less energetic when they arrived at their hotel room.

He switched on the radio just in time to hear the eleven o'clock news bulletin. A resounding victory for the Conservatives; votes were still being counted in remote constituencies but the BBC was predicting a final majority in the Commons of over one hundred seats. Fitzjohn's own constituents voted overwhelmingly for him, and he inwardly rejoiced in seeing the Labour vote decline again.

Amanda stirred and rolled over towards him.

"Good morning, my dear, how are you feeling?" said Fitzjohn.

"Under the circumstances, not bad. Well done on a great result." She shuffled closer to him and ran her hand across his chest. Fitzjohn returned the favour.

"The BBC news just reported a landslide victory. Another five years in office! Old Mac will be absolutely beside himself." Fitzjohn laughed.

But Amanda did not feel quite so optimistic. She got up, wrapped herself in her silk dressing gown, went into the bathroom and turned on the taps on the huge Victorian bath. As steam filled the room, she returned to the door and said, "We'll take the day off, but tomorrow we must get down to central office – there's no time to waste. Sir Robert will be there and so will every other hopeful seeking a Cabinet post."

"Can there be no respite?" Fitzjohn stifled a yawn. "The job's done – time for a holiday. Darnell is unable to resist your charms; he'll put in a good word for me with Mac. A forgone conclusion, isn't it?"

"Far from it, Henry. Out of sight is out of mind. So tomorrow you will be all pleasantness and determination when we meet him. But, in the meantime, I think you need to take a bath…"

Fitzjohn's headache disappeared as he closed the bathroom door behind them.

***

The next morning, Fitzjohn was up before breakfast and put in a solid half hour of lengths in the hotel pool, followed by ten minutes in the sauna. He made a quick call to Richard Dunn, who was just opening up the Granta Airlines office at Gatwick. He said that he had found some good pilots, ready for Fitzjohn to make the final decision. They agreed that Dunn would ring central office and leave a message on who was available and when. Fitzjohn then found Amanda in the dining room having a fruit salad and black coffee. She had copies of all the newspapers in front of her and pointed out, on page four of *The Times*, a good picture of Fitzjohn waving and smiling as the result of the Sudbury and Woodbridge constituency voting was announced.

"Darn good coverage. Fancy me being picked out as the face of the Tories!"

"An old university friend of mine is the photo editor at *The Times*. I made sure she found room. How was your swim?"

"Very enjoyable, thanks. I'm ready for my bacon and eggs now. What time do you want to leave?"

"As soon as you have finished. We should get to Smith Square late morning."

"Good show. And what's the plan when we get there?"

"I have telephoned Sir Robert's secretary, who confirmed he will be spending the day there."

"Even on a Saturday?" asked Fitzjohn.

"This is not just any Saturday, Henry! He will be glad-handing all the central office people and dealing with the press, trying to get the best coverage from the Sundays. So it will be difficult to get his ear but we must try. I want him to promise me … promise us, I should say, that he will be pressing Mac to appoint you to the Cabinet."

After an easy drive into London, Fitzjohn parked his Jaguar in Great Peter Street and they walked the short distance to the Conservative central office in Smith Square. Amanda was right: the place was alive with joyous party workers and MPs who wanted an audience with the chairman.

Amanda called over her shoulder as she marched through the lobby. "Let's start with some coffee and get a table in the bar. I'm sure Sir Robert will be there."

Fitzjohn dutifully hurried to catch her up. Amanda was right again. Standing at the window, talking to two journalists feverishly writing in their shorthand notebooks, Sir Robert Darnell waved to Amanda, said a few more words to the reporters and sent them away.

"Robert, congratulations, a fine victory!" Amanda kissed Sir Robert on both cheeks.

"Thank you, Amanda, a great result indeed. Ah, and I see the Member for Sudbury and Woodbridge is with you."

"Yes – as I'm sure you are aware, Henry increased his majority."

"Yes, bravo, Henry." Darnell extended his hand. "An excellent outcome. And I'm pleased to tell you that you should expect a call from Colton, Mac's private secretary. You know him, I believe."

"I do indeed."

"He will set up a meeting with the prime minister."

"Good show."

"Just make sure, Henry, that you've done your homework on Mac's defence thinking. But don't make up anything you can't back up. Ensure you are very clear on your own views on strategy: if Macmillan thinks you're a yes man, he won't have anything more to do with you."

"Tha.'s understood. Thank you, Sir Robert."

After Darnell had gone through to the main committee room, Fitzjohn turned to Amanda. "If no more is required of me here, I'd like to head down to Gatwick. There's a pile of work to get through and Dunn wants me to meet a couple of pilots. Do I have your permission to earn my living, my love?"

"Not a great time to make yourself scarce."

"I'll be back up here by Monday morning – how's that?"

"Alright, that's fine. I'll see you then."

Fitzjohn wasted no time in making his way through the busy office and out into the square. He tossed his car keys into the air a couple of times, reflecting happily on the events of the past three days. A clear victory in the election and good prospects for further advancement. Now he could forget all about politics and concentrate on the airline

– much more fun. As he got to his car he remembered that he hadn't checked in with the office secretary for any messages from Richard Dunn about pilot interviews. "Hell," he said to himself, turned on his heel, hurried back to Smith Square, dashed up the stairs and through to the administration office. Sure enough, there was a handwritten note for him with three names and times on it.

As he skipped down the stairs, he passed a narrow passage that led to some storage cupboards. Something made him glance into the gloomy alcove, and what he saw gave him a kick in the stomach. Sir Robert Darnell and Amanda were entwined in a deep and sensual kiss.

Fitzjohn didn't linger. He muttered, "That bitch, that bloody bitch." He could see it all so clearly now. Yes, Darnell would put his name in front of Macmillan – but at the price of Amanda sleeping with him. And Fitzjohn thought he could trust her.

SIXTEEN

Captain Fyodor Yegorov's orders were clear: identify and monitor naval operations emanating from Plymouth's Royal Navy base. In wartime it would be the most dangerous mission as anti-submarine defences would undoubtedly result in them being attacked. In the tenuous peace that existed, the risk was of a diplomatic row or even the boat being seized as an intruder in British waters and the crew arrested.

Yegorov planned the route with the navigation officer. They would sail the *Leninski* from her base in Murmansk through Arctic waters then, near Iceland, would dive and turn directly south, passing the Outer Hebrides to the west. An audacious dash through the Irish Sea would allow the submarine to continue close to north Cornwall before turning past Land's End and into the English Channel.

As a nuclear submarine it could stay submerged for the entire voyage, reducing the risk of being seen by navy or airborne defences. But unknown to Yegorov, during a short period on the surface they had been spotted by a Shackleton operating from the RAF station at Kinloss that patrolled the north-east Atlantic. Alerted to the sub's movements, navy ships kept a watch with their sonar equipment, and were aware of the submarine moving down to the outlying area of the Bristol Channel. But from there, contact was lost.

***

More surface ships were assigned to hunt the submarine, and the job of airborne tracking was passed to RAF St Mawgan. As dawn broke, five Shackletons were scrambled. Three were assigned areas that covered the waters north of Cornwall, including Adam Devon's aircraft, and two were to monitor the whole of the south-west of the British Isles. Devon briefed his crew to be ready for anything up to a twelve-hour patrol. The sonar technicians revelled in the challenge: the cat-and-mouse sparring with the submarine officers, where the winner is the one with the most patience and ingenuity. And sometimes a touch of good fortune, but that was something the RAF wouldn't rely on.

After a morning of tracking along the north Cornwall coast and across to southern Ireland, there was no sign of the submarine. It didn't mean it wasn't there, of course; it could be stationary, biding its time, or it might have headed west and be comfortably out of range in the depths of the Atlantic.

But Devon had a hunch. The sub could have accelerated to maximum speed during the night and passed through their area south towards the Channel Islands. The whole operation was under the command of Squadron Leader Guy Carson in one of the aircraft on the south side. His call sign was Lion One.

Devon radioed: "Lion One, this is Lion Three, come in, over."

"Lion Three, go ahead."

"Permission requested to join your group, sir. No joy here."

"Current position, Lion Three?" said Carson.

"Ten miles north of Bude."

"Roger, proceed direct to Falmouth Bay and patrol as far as Plymouth, over."

"Direct to Falmouth. Lion Three, out."

Within a few minutes they were over Bodmin Moor. Devon peered through the cockpit glass looking for Cardinham, but low cloud over the moor obscured his view. As they approached Cornwall's china clay mining district with its distinctive white pyramids of spoil from the extraction works, Devon handed over control to student pilot Robin McCoy, another accomplished RAF pilot in the last stages of his conversion to flying the Shackleton. As they arrived overhead Falmouth, McCoy eased the aircraft round in a slow left-hand turn and took up a heading east towards Plymouth.

It wasn't until nearly 5p.m., more than nine hours after they took off, that Wing Commander Valentine called all aircraft to return to St Mawgan. The debriefing was solemn; none of the pilots and technicians enjoyed a mission that didn't result in spotting an intruder.

Devon felt this most acutely. "I'm convinced there was a sub out there, Louis," he said in the debrief after landing.

"Yes, me too. It looks like the Soviets are getting the better of us. The intelligence bods believe it's the *Leninski* on proving missions. If they're right, our navy ships out of Plymouth would be sitting ducks."

***

It wasn't until two days later that Captain Yegorov ordered 'ahead slow', taking the submarine out to the Atlantic for the long journey around Ireland and back to Murmansk. He was confident that his commanders would be delighted with the mission.

SEVENTEEN

When the telephone rang in his flat in Kensington, Henry Fitzjohn hoped it would be the broker acting for the seller of a Vickers Viscount he had bid for. He had offered more than a fair price, keen to secure an example in excellent condition, ready to be added to the Granta Airlines fleet without delay.

But it wasn't the broker. Henry's disappointment was tempered as soon as he recognised her voice. After their night at Valley Lodge he gave Vanessa Paget his phone number and invited her to call whenever she wished. Knowing another assignation would be reckless – foolish, even – nonetheless he had hoped he would hear from her.

"Hello, Henry, how are you?"

"Vanessa! Great to hear from you. I'm fine, thanks – hope you are likewise."

"Oh yes, quite in the pink."

"And are you calling from London or Cornwall?"

"In London. I'm at a loose end this evening and I wondered if you would like to take me out to dinner."

Fitzjohn didn't hesitate. "Splendid idea. York Terrace, isn't it? I can pick you up at eight, if that suits you?"

"Yes, perfectly. My flat is the top floor of number 28A. Ring the bell, I'll come down."

"Excellent. I shall book a restaurant. See you at eight."

"Goodbye, Henry."

Fitzjohn slumped down on the settee and let out a roaring laugh. "Bloody hell!" he said to himself.

***

Fitzjohn decided to take a taxi rather than call his chauffeur. He trusted Lionel to be discreet, but sometimes it pays to keep your cards close to your chest. After showering and dressing he poured himself a small malt whisky and contemplated the night ahead. Was it the thrill of anticipation he was sensing, or just a touch of nerves? Not something he usually felt in his relationships with women; this one had got under his skin... and he liked the feeling.

He arrived right on time and found her name on the doorbell panel. Vanessa must have been ready, as she was downstairs in less than two minutes.

"My dear, you look wonderful," Fitzjohn said, and he meant it.

"Thank you, Henry." Vanessa's mink coat was unbuttoned and revealed her pink silk dress, low cut and ending six inches above her knee. Her triple row of pearls glistened in the street lights as Fitzjohn held open the taxi door. Her dark brown hair was again curled outwards across her shoulders, and he caught the sweet smell of her perfume as she entered the taxi.

"I've reserved a table at Stella's in St John's Wood. Not far." Fitzjohn had never been there before and was relying on its excellent reputation. It was off the beaten track; he didn't particularly want to bump into anyone he knew.

"Lovely." Vanessa smiled, rested her hand on his and intertwined their fingers.

Fitzjohn ordered champagne and suggested choices from the menu. Vanessa readily agreed. Wines followed with each course, and brandy with their coffee. By midnight they were ready to move on. "Perhaps we can call into the Blue Angel, have some drinks, some dancing. Would you like to do that?"

"Oh yes please, wonderful idea."

In the dim, smoke-filled club, Fitzjohn and Vanessa moved steadily around the dance floor. He was holding her firmly, his arm round her back and their hands together on her right side, in front of her shoulder. The music was low and slow; Fitzjohn felt her sensuous closeness and her warm breath on his face. She rarely lost eye contact, seeming to look right into him and understand his emotions. He was swimming in a trance of desire for her when she suddenly said, "Henry, I'm getting tired – could you take me home now?"

His pang of disappointment soon vanished when he realised what she was saying. Fitzjohn paid the bill and they collected Vanessa's coat from the cloakroom. The doorman clicked his fingers and a taxi appeared in a moment. Driving along the quiet streets of the West End, they soon arrived at York Terrace. When the taxi stopped Vanessa said, "Come up for coffee or a nightcap."

When Vanessa opened the door to her flat, Fitzjohn gasped – partly in response to the effort of climbing the stairs to the third floor, but also because the flat was stunning. The living room was fitted out with cream leather chairs and a pale-blue carpet. Abstract artwork on the walls brought shocks of colour, and a television stood in the corner on a walnut stand. Vanessa pointed to a small bar with an array of drinks and glasses. Very chic, thought Fitzjohn.

"Pour a couple of whiskies, would you? There should be some ice in the bucket." Coffee wasn't offered. Vanessa disappeared for a few minutes before returning, freshened up. She turned off the main lights; Fitzjohn could see the only light was now coming from the bedroom. Vanessa turned on some music.

Fitzjohn took her arm and they danced again. But this time Vanessa placed her hands on Fitzjohn's shoulders, guiding him around the floor. As the music ended she took his hand and led him to the bedroom. Fitzjohn unzipped her dress. She wiggled her shoulders, and her dress slid to the floor. She pulled his tie away from his collar and he quickly slipped it over his neck. With deft fingers she undid the buttons on his shirt. She sat on the bed and slowly removed her stockings and the rest of her underwear then lay back, her breathing deep and regular, her lips apart.

Fitzjohn joined her on the bed. They kissed fervently as he ran his hands around her breasts and slowly across her stomach… and beyond. He didn't want the night to be the same as the one at Valley Lodge: a quick tumble and thank you very much. He wanted to put her pleasure ahead of his own and make sure she enjoyed every touch and caress. She slid her hand under the pillows and found a contraceptive. With practised hands she slid it on him. "You have to be dressed for the occasion, Henry." She giggled.

Soon, but not urgently, she pulled him to her. But he took his time, explored her body further until she gasped for him. Her sighs and moans rose in tempo as they reached satisfaction together. Afterwards they curled up in a tangle of legs and arms, and soon they both fell asleep.

***

The noise of traffic in the street below woke Fitzjohn. He glanced at his watch: nearly 10.30. Vanessa was lying face down and he could see her back rise and fall in her deep sleep. He crept to the bathroom, picking up his clothes as he went. Then in the kitchen he found a coffee percolator, filled it with water and ground coffee and switched it on. Walking back into the living room, he had a chance to have a better look around. A couple of pictures sat on a corner table, including one of Vanessa with a man. It looked like they were on an expensive yacht in a harbour in the Mediterranean – Cannes it seemed, with the Carlton in the background. No doubt he was one of her admirers, but Fitzjohn felt no angst; he had no claim over her. A jolly good night out and some fun afterwards was what he was after, and she could certainly fulfil that order.

The bubbling of the percolator stopped. He poured two cups and added milk to his own, then took both into the bedroom. She was still asleep, so he placed the coffees on the dressing table next to a jewellery box. He couldn't resist opening it. He was stunned by what he saw: a collection of diamond bracelets, long gold chains, a second string of pearls and three watches. Someone was treating her well.

Vanessa stirred. Turning over, she pulled the sheet up to her neck, in a show of new-found modesty.

"Good morning, my dear. How are you today? Here's some coffee," said Fitzjohn, sitting on the edge of the bed.

"Thanks, morning. I'm fine, just a little tired. Thank you for a lovely evening, Henry, I so enjoyed myself. I'm sorry I dropped off to sleep – must have been all that champagne."

"That's absolutely fine. I think I was pretty whacked myself."

"No, you were just wonderful in bed. Enough to tire any girl out."

Fitzjohn laughed. "Good of you to say so, and I didn't have a bad time myself."

Vanessa took his hand. "I can safely say I've never had it so good."

Fitzjohn smiled, and wondered where he had heard that before.

EIGHTEEN

The expected fine weather for their day at the seaside did not disappoint. It had been one of the mildest October weeks on record, with sunny days and clear, mild nights. When they arrived at Fowey, Devon parked at the Fowey Harbour Hotel and they carried all the kit they required for the day along Esplanade and down the hill to Readymoney Cove. Devon took the folding seats, Hannah looked after the food hamper and blankets and Michael marched along purposefully with his bucket, spade and rock-pooling net. A couple of times Devon stopped and picked Michael up so he could see the boats down in the estuary: yachts and motor boats coming and going out to the English Channel.

The cove was essentially square when the tide was out, with a sand and shingle beach. Larger rocks emerged from the sea on each side of the entrance to the cove. The view was straight across towards Polruan and the open sea to the right. On each side the black and grey cliffs climbed to a hundred feet, with houses on the Fowey side and a ruined castle on the coastal headland opposite.

Hannah suggested they walk to the left of the beach, where the sun would be shining late into the afternoon. The sheer rock face on that side of the cove would also give shelter from the light wind that was coming off the sea.

"This is great, a nice little suntrap," said Devon, pulling off Michael's sandals and socks and then his own, and rolling his trousers up to his knees. "Bring your bucket – let's go down to the sea and fill it up." They ran to the water's edge and waded in. Devon was pleasantly surprised: the water was certainly cold but not icy. He thought he might have a swim later.

Michael started digging a hole and piling up the sand to start a sandcastle. Devon helped with another spade, and they soon had a round pile of sand with a moat around it. Michael poured in some water, which immediately soaked into the sand. He called to his dad to come with him to the sea for more water, and they repeated this three times before Michael tired of the game. Devon suggested they take the net and go and hunt for crabs in the rock pools.

Hannah spread out the blankets and opened the hamper. She had made chicken and tomato rolls for her and Adam and a fish paste sandwich for Michael. She had bought small pork pies from the Cardinham village shop. Her own homemade Victoria sponge was sliced up, ready to eat. When Adam and Michael came back for lunch, she poured tea from a large vacuum flask and opened a bottle of orange juice.

"Just what the doctor ordered," said Devon as he ate one of the pork pies and cut a second in half. "Here you go, Michael – you can have one of these too."

"You're a hungry boy, aren't you?" Hannah tickled Michael under the chin and ran her fingers through his blond hair.

"These are nice snacks, Mummy!"

Hannah sipped her tea in between bites of her roll. "Adam, have you seen that old fort up on the headland there?"

Devon turned round and squinted into the sun. "Yes, I saw it on the walk down. Doesn't look much. I wonder if it's possible to get up there. We can go and have a look later."

"That would be fun, but we ought to keep an eye on the tide – it's just started coming in."

They finished their food and Michael climbed onto Hannah's lap, ready for an afternoon nap. She leant back in her chair and closed her eyes, warmed by the sun. Devon packed away the plates and cups then took a walk back to the top of the beach and peered in the little shop there. Not surprisingly, it stocked buckets and spades and an assortment of beach toys. It also had an ice-cream cabinet that he would visit later with Hannah and Michael.

He saw Hannah standing up and pulling a jumper down over Michael's head. The afternoon was wearing on and the temperature would soon be falling. He wanted to have a quick swim so dashed back to join them and grabbed a towel. After changing he ran down to the water's edge and, without stopping, dived into the waves. The shock of cold only lasted seconds as he swam out, curving round the left-hand side of the cove. He rested for a moment and looked up at the impressive triple-fronted house perched on the only flat area of the headland. White blinds were closed across the arched windows, and the grey walls glistened in the sun. Devon swam across the cove towards Fowey and realised the tide coming in was carrying him onto the shore. There was no problem with that; he had enjoyed his swim and it was time to return.

"How was it?" said Hannah, standing in the shallows with Michael.

"Excellent. Are you having fun, Michael?"

"Unfortunately I mentioned there was a castle up on the hill; now he's desperate to go up there."

"Great, give me a couple of minutes to dry off and get changed."

Michael ran ahead of them, back to the blankets, turned round and called out, "Hurry up, Daddy!"

Devon did indeed hurry. Within a few minutes he was fully dressed and they walked across the cove to a set of steps and a footpath going up to the castle. But they found it hard going, overgrown with brambles and gorse. They trudged on and within ten minutes the path levelled out. A broken sign sat askew in a hedge, its painted words were cracked and faded. The sign read 'St Catherine's Castle, c. 1540', although Devon could already see it was not much more than a small fort.

"Look, Michael, we're here now," said Hannah, having resorted to carrying him up the last hundred yards. "Come and look in the castle."

From the inside of the round tower, arched windows gave views across to Polruan and to the right out to sea. One level down, the land was flat with a grassed-over gun emplacement left from the castle's last operational use: naval guns ready to resist any invasion in the Second World War. After exploring every corner of the castle, Michael was again tiring.

"Adam, shall we go back down now?"

"Sure. I'll lead the way."

As they arrived back at their blankets, the sun dipped behind the headland and they were in shadow. "We've had a great day, but it's getting a bit chilly now. Let's pack up and walk back to the car," said Hannah.

"Why don't I nip back and get the car? I can park for a few minutes at the top of the beach – it will save us carrying all this kit, and probably Michael as well."

"Good idea. See you in about fifteen minutes."

As Devon started up the hill out of the cove he saw large wooden gates to the big house he had noticed from the sea, and read the name carved into a stone pillar: 'Point Saturn'. Over the boundary wall he could see the house better. He was no expert in architecture but believed it was in the Palladian style: beautifully built oyster-white brick and Portland stonework, with lovely well-maintained gardens. The gates suddenly opened inwards and a man in a porter's uniform locked each gate open. Devon stood back from the road to allow a grey and black Rolls Royce to ease its way out of the gates into the narrow lane. The car was chauffeur-driven but Devon noticed a man and a young woman in the rear seats. The man waved out of the window and called, "Thank you, Rufus – back in a couple of hours." Almost silently the car glided away up the hill. Devon stepped back into the road.

"Thank 'ee, sir!" called the porter. Clearly a Cornishman.

"No problem." Devon walked over to the gates. "Nice car."

"Aye, a Silver Wraith. 'E likes his cars, does the guvnor."

"And who is His Lordship?"

"Arr, 'e ain't no lord, but he has the money to live the life."

"And he is…"

"Sir Bartley Paget. Tin mine owner and local property baron. That was his daughter Vanessa 'e was with. They're taking her to Bodmin Station, on her way back to that London, where she do live."

"Right. Well, have a good day."

NINETEEN

Hannah arrived at the house off the Edgeware Road where she had been told to report in time for the evening briefing. A different location to the usual office. There were twelve agents. She knew three of the others, whom she had met at previous training events: Yardena, Zvia and Robert. There were plenty of new faces. She had felt a degree of unease when she heard that the course would last five days – there were usually only one or two days of discussions and some target practice with a pistol for her annual firearms sign-off.

The grand Victorian townhouse was previously used by the Israeli embassy as overspill accommodation for visiting dignitaries. Hannah admired the furnishings in the lounge and dining room, although her bedroom was no more than functional and she had to share a bathroom with Yardena. When she found the briefing room she was surprised to see its stark interior: pale-green walls, hard lino on the floor, and glaring ceiling lighting. There were twelve desks and chairs, a blackboard stood in a corner, and a projector rested on a desk in the middle of the room. There were no windows.

When Yoel Arbel entered the room, everyone stopped chatting and instinctively sat up straight. For the newer recruits to meet the head of Mossad's UK operations was both an honour and a reminder that the training week had a serious purpose.

Arbel's assistant placed some papers on the lectern, then left the room.

"Good evening, everyone. It's a pleasure to meet you all. Some of you I know well and others I will get acquainted with this week. I will remind you now – although it's only for good order that I mention it, as you are all experienced agents – that we observe the utmost secrecy in what we do here. Is that understood?"

All present said a clear, "Yes, sir."

"Right, let's get down to business. There is growing concern about the increasing tension with the Arab states, and the risk that they may act in unison to attack Israel, creating an overwhelming force on several fronts. We would not be able to defend ourselves if that occurred without warning. So our job is two-fold: first, all agents must recharge their readiness for active service and hone their skills in the use of weapons. Second, more importantly, our intelligence services must step up and get even more insight into what our enemies and their allies are doing. Any questions so far?"

"Yes, sir, if I may." It was a woman of a similar age to Hannah, with a slight East European accent, who had been introduced as Agata. "Why do we need to train in weapons use if we are based here in the UK, undertaking intelligence work? And could just twelve of us really make a difference if there was a war?"

"Rest assured that there are many others being trained around the UK and across the world. There is always the possibility that we may be called at short notice to go to Israel and fight to defend the country, and every soldier makes a difference. Hence all agents must be competent in a range of weapons. We will be spending some time at the ranges in Essex this week. Anything else?"

Hannah froze. She had never thought that she might be required to leave Adam and Michael and go to a war zone. But what could she do? This was not the right time to object. She said nothing as Arbel continued.

"Right, we will spend the next two days reviewing the intelligence reports that you have been supplying, and new information that has come in this week, paying special regard to planned Russian activities to interfere with arms supplies from Great Britain to Israel."

Arbel spent some time briefing the team on the amount of Russian influence there was on UK industry, detailing the known personnel operating from their embassy in London. This was all familiar to Hannah, as she had been through reports from her contacts on subversive activity within unions and political parties. But she struggled to concentrate as her mind wandered back to her younger days and the reasons she was still an agent with Mossad.

It didn't take much to trigger her anguish at the loss of her parents and members of her wider family in the Holocaust. She and her brother had escaped the horrors: sent to England in 1939 when she was twelve, as part of the Kindertransport movement, where thousands of Jewish children were sent to safety from the Nazi persecution of Jews. Following her post-war recruitment into the Israeli secret service she was sent to Hong Kong to source Spitfire pilots for the Israeli air force. The only happy outcome from this mission was that she met Devon. Twenty years had passed since she lost her family, but her desire to protect the State of Israel was still strong.

When Devon got into trouble in East Germany in 1952, during an assignment to extract a Russian defector from Berlin, it was Yoel Arbel who had helped Hannah rescue him, and she owed a debt of gratitude to him and the service. But now she also had an obligation to Michael, to stay safe and to be a good mother. She shuddered at the thought of leaving him and going to fight a war in Israel.

Arbel was looking at her. "Is that clear, everyone? Hannah?"

"Yes, yes, that's all understood, sir." She had taken in enough of Arbel's presentation to see the urgency in the intelligence work they were doing. She knew she had to put out of her mind thoughts about any other tasks she might be assigned.

Before dawn, two days later, the team stood outside, shivering in the cold easterly wind coming off the North Sea. Across the flat marshland they could see the Fingringhoe ranges and lights from half a dozen 3-ton trucks carrying soldiers to their shooting positions. Arbel directed them to their own range, safely hidden from prying eyes. They spent the days learning how to handle a variety of weapons: pistols, sub-machine guns, heavier, two-man machine guns.

At the end of the week, on the Bodmin-bound train from Paddington, Hannah thought about how the exercises had gone. She was glad her training was done and out of the way; she had a better understanding of the risks threatening peace in the world, and she had a clear agenda for the intelligence work she and her team were to carry out. She was on her way back to her idyllic home in Cornwall, with her lovely husband and beautiful son. She felt very lucky.

TWENTY

January 1960

Henry Fitzjohn decided that all his meetings with the chiefs of staff would be held in the newly completed Main Building in Whitehall. The modern, bright offices said much about how he would be fulfilling his responsibilities as Minister of Defence in the exciting new age of the 1960s. After extensive discussions with Prime Minister Harold Macmillan, they discussed a strategy of taking the initiative to the Soviets, although Fitzjohn felt that he had to press the PM hard to fully come around to his way of thinking. Britain would lead its European allies, as well as the United States – and of course the Commonwealth and Empire – to do more than simply stand back in the face of the communist threat. This was not just about increasing the defence budget; Fitzjohn convinced the prime minister that the only way of stopping the Russians was for the Western allies to take action to liberate the countries controlled by the communists, reunite Germany and push the Russians back to their own border. A bold, history-making move on the scale of the D-Day landings. One that would remove the communist threat entirely. Macmillan agreed.

Fitzjohn revelled in his role. He had been given licence to commit to the armed forces in a way that would place the UK in the forefront of world affairs. British global influence might be declining as more countries gained independence, but Fitzjohn saw a future where world security would be guaranteed through the strength of the Western alliance.

His deep-seated dislike for communism and the Russians was further fuelled by the way they crushed the uprising in Hungary in 1956. The invasion was so sudden, the West could do nothing to assist the Hungarians; since the end of the war, the West was unlikely to help any other country in the Eastern bloc resist the might of the Soviet army. Fitzjohn saw the allied leaders as being weak; the Russians could act freely, knowing there would be no response to their actions. The great fear Fitzjohn held, and all others present, was that they might seek to take control of the rest of Europe – and ultimately the UK.

As Fitzjohn sat at the head of the long, oval table in Whitehall, with fifteen senior officers around the table – men from the army, navy and air force – he said a few words of welcome then stood to give his presentation. He was impressed by the breadth of experience in the room. Each man's uniform glistened with medal ribbons, air force pilots' wings, army parachutists' wings, and pips and crowns shone on their epaulettes. They may be senior staff officers but Fitzjohn was the Minister of Defence, their boss, and he wouldn't let them forget this.

Impressive though the gathering was, Fitzjohn felt no nerves; his self-confidence shone through and he knew that the strategy he was about to present made sense and should appeal to them. Fitzjohn indicated to his private secretary, Sian Shelby, to distribute copies of slides that were to be used in the meeting. She then sat down with her shorthand notebook.

"Gentlemen, good morning. Thank you for attending this, our first defence strategy meeting under the new government. I will be outlining the way forward that we have planned. I have obtained support from the prime minister and Cabinet to adopt this. Then I will take questions. I believe the philosophy of the government matches your own, individually, as a group, and that of the people of the United Kingdom: it's time to stop the not insignificant threat from 'the Reds under the bed'." Fitzjohn allowed himself a small smile and added, "And ultimately secure a lasting peace for us all. Miss Shelby, the slides, please."

Sian placed a slide on the projector. It listed the strength of the Soviet forces: aircraft, tanks, ships and submarines, and men. And an estimate of Russia's nuclear arsenal. After Fitzjohn had pointed out the huge resources at the Soviets' disposal, another slide showing the British, French and West German forces, which were notably smaller than the Soviets', was projected onto the screen. A slide showing the US armed forces was shown separately, and Fitzjohn commented that American involvement in the strategy being discussed was vital, but past experience had shown that it could not be relied upon. Several more slides with more gloomy words and numbers followed, until Fitzjohn asked Sian to remove the projector.

"So, gentlemen, we know the threat is real and ever present. Our response must, of course, be to match their capabilities and continue with our efforts to develop more effective weapons and manpower. But that alone is not enough. The government's strategy therefore is to instigate a pre-emptive military campaign to force back the Russians and free the Eastern European countries from under the hammer and sickle. We will of course remove the threat of the Red Army attacking West Germany, the Low Counties, Balkans and ultimately, the UK. This will be a mighty campaign and very expensive, but the PM has given me his full support and that of the Cabinet. All the defence cuts you had to tolerate in the 1950s are behind us. What I want from you are your plans to re-equip, modernise and expand all areas of our armed forces to enable us to deal with the communist threat in the manner I have just outlined. Comments, please."

But the assembled chiefs of staff remained silent, to Fitzjohn's shock and consternation. He had expected rejoicing and congratulations for driving forward the forces' expansion plans – the very strategy that they had been seeking for years. Now they would have to put their military might to good use, and justify their pleas for larger, better funded armed forces. But were they doubtful of the government's commitment? They had all previously agreed that expansion of the services was the only way forward: were they now getting cold feet?

After several seconds of silence Admiral Sir Adrian Temple, the Chief of the Defence Staff and the most senior officer present, said quietly, "This is all very well as an idea, Minister, but where will the money come from? Will the government really add a penny, maybe two or three, to income tax to pay for all this? Not to mention a return to austerity that war brings. Does the nation see the need for the operations you have outlined? I don't doubt that we in this room would relish the plans, if we could be confident they will be seen through. Certainly we all agree that the best form of defence is an effective deterrent, but if we are being asked to go away and build the necessary capability, and deliver said capability, we need absolute assurance that the plan would be sustained over a number of years."

Fitzjohn looked around at the other officers. There was a murmured chorus of agreement and lots of nodding heads. Fitzjohn's instinct told him that more work would be required to bring them round. First he would report back to Macmillan.

***

At 7.15 that evening Fitzjohn sat in the bar at the Thames Vista Hotel, waiting for Amanda to arrive. He felt she was becoming more remote. Perhaps the novelty of promoting him was wearing off, even though he was tipped for the top job. Or, more likely, she was enjoying the benefits of friendship with Sir Robert Darnell. He couldn't care less; he had an invitation to another party at Stephen Walmsley's flat for the following Saturday night, and the lovely Vanessa would be there.

Fitzjohn didn't have to wait long. Amanda arrived in a flurry of excitement, took the stool next to him and kissed his cheek.

"My dear, lovely to see you," Fitzjohn said. "What have you been up to today?"

"Well, you will be pleased to hear that I have secured a new investor in your airline."

"Excellent, who is the fortunate one?"

"It's my good friend Christine Campsie – you know, in Bristol. Well, her husband actually – he's doing very well in his export business and has been looking to diversify. He will be matching my investment."

"Really? Good work, Amanda. We might be able to fund another aircraft with that. I'll get on to Richard Dunn and have him do some research into what's available. Great stuff!" Any doubts about Amanda's commitment to him disappeared from Fitzjohn's mind. A new aircraft would allow him to develop routes to Greece, Cyprus and Malta – something he had been thinking of for some time.

"And what about you? How did the defence committee go?" said Amanda.

"Ah, not so good. The chiefs are so slow to react, I really wonder if they have the stomach for a fight. And they don't trust the government to carry the expansion plans through. I need to see Mac again and get him to assure them that the rearmament will not fizzle out. They're right about one thing: if we want to sustain or grow the armed forces at a high level for years to come, that will hit the British taxpayer."

"Quite a challenge, Henry. Are you sure you are fully committed to the strategy yourself? Do you have enough support?"

"I certainly am. I have a plan that will see the end of communism in Eastern Europe for good, that I described to the chiefs. And by the way, be very careful about this – don't discuss military strategy with anyone."

TWENTY-ONE

After spending the whole afternoon and early evening at an audition for a new London musical, Vanessa Paget walked out of the theatre and flagged down a taxi to take her back to her flat. She was running late.

Stephen Walmsley was already there and had let himself in with his spare key. He sat with a G&T in the living room.

"I'm so sorry, Stephen. The silly head of casting couldn't make up her mind and had four of us sing another song and read bits of the script."

"Were you offered a part?"

"Only in the chorus! That casting director doesn't recognise talent when she sees it. The girl given the part of Nancy could hardly sing; she just has big boobs."

Walmsley laughed. Vanessa was well endowed herself. "Still, even a part in the chorus is worth having – gives you exposure to other directors," he said. "This musical is going to be big and will be a stepping stone to your wonderful career. Just be patient."

"You're a love, Stephen. And I should say that I'm to be Nancy's understudy."

"Excellent! There you are, you see, already on your way up. Now, can I pour you a drink?"

"Yes, please. I'll have the same as you. Bring it through to the bathroom for me when it's ready, there's a dear."

Walmsley took the drink and placed it on the side of the bath just as Vanessa stepped into the foam-covered water.

"Thank you, Stephen. Look, I hope you don't mind tonight if we don't – you know."

Walmsley often had the pleasure of an hour in the bedroom with Vanessa before they went out. "No, no, that's alright. Time is short and we'll be meeting some important clients so we can't be late."

"I won't be long." Vanessa sank deeper into the warm water and closed her eyes.

***

At Walmsley's usual tables at Imogen's Club, two champagne ice buckets and an array of finger food were ready for their guests' arrival. Two of his friends were sitting at the bar with a Tom Collins each and a bowl of olives. A few others had taken to the dance floor, even though it was not yet 11p.m. They all joined Walmsley and Vanessa when they arrived.

"Don't forget, it's Yuri Andreyevich that I'd like you to get to know," Walmsley whispered to Vanessa. "You'll like him, he's great fun. And very generous when it comes to entertaining. He may invite you to the Savoy for afternoon tea or to the Talk of the Town to see Frank Sinatra. These Russians like to think they have the best taste, so go along with whatever he suggests. And don't ask him what he does for a living; that's a taboo subject. But do tell him about your work – he will be delighted to have the company of a West End star. Have you got all that?"

"I get the picture, thank you," said Vanessa, irked by his manner. She would only go out with a man if she liked him, she told herself; she wasn't the sort of girl to give favours and pleasures just because Walmsley asked her to.

Less than half an hour later, three men arrived and joined Walmsley's party. Polite introductions were made. The men were all wearing double-breasted suits, post-war style, two in garish pinstripes and the other a plain dark grey. Each of the men had short, badly cut hair and two were very overweight. The slim man in the plain suit was Yuri, Vanessa was pleased to hear. He was clearly the senior of the three; the other two were deferential to him and laughed enthusiastically at his every comment. Nearly six feet tall, round-faced with brown eyes and a long, straight nose, Yuri shook hands with Vanessa and gave a polite bow. She was impressed, and felt the evening might be more promising than she had imagined.

The Russians ordered a bottle of good-quality vodka and a tray of small glasses. Andreyevich poured a round and made a show of toasting everyone before drinking the shot in one. The glasses were refilled and the ritual toast repeated before they drank again, throwing the vodka to the back of the mouth and drinking with a gasp.

Vanessa was happy to go back to champagne as the spirits she had drunk had made her light-headed. As Andreyevich took her to the dance floor she balanced herself with one hand on his shoulder. Her fingers brushed his neck. He smiled and held her close for a slow waltz, followed by two more dances before they took a seat in a secluded alcove.

"You speak very good English, Yuri," said Vanessa.

"Thank you. I spent some time in the US as part of my job. That was nearly a year ago and I have been here since."

Vanessa couldn't resist the temptation. "Oh really? How exciting. And what job do you do?"

"I work at the Russian embassy – cultural attaché, promoting Russian arts. Not so exciting, you understand, but a pleasant job. What do you do for a living?"

"I'm an actress and singer. I've been in Shakespeare plays and West End musicals but I've been resting recently. But the good news is I've just landed a part in a big new West End musical."

"Excellent, congratulations."

"Thank you."

"What is the name of the show?"

"*Oliver*. It's about Oliver Twist – do you know the story? The book was written by Charles Dickens."

"No, I'm afraid my understanding of English literature is poor, even though England is now my home."

"Well, consider yourself at home with me!" Vanessa laughed, and Andreyevich laughed politely along with her. "Anyway, you should come and see the show when it comes on. I will get you a ticket."

Andreyevich invited Vanessa to dance again. She enjoyed his firm lead and stylish moves – he wasn't at all the boorish Russian she imagined he might be when Walmsley told her he wanted her to meet him. Before Vanessa left the nightclub, Andreyevich invited her to dinner at the Dorchester that Saturday evening. She hesitated, then declined. As much as she admired him, she had already made a date with Henry Fitzjohn, and she felt he was much more fun.

What she didn't know was that Walmsley had given Andreyevich her phone number. A week later he called and invited her out for dinner again. This time she accepted.

TWENTY-TWO

Hannah's alarm woke her at 5.30a.m., and she rose to see a dark, dank winter morning. She went downstairs and made Devon a cooked breakfast: eggs, bacon, potato croquettes, fried bread, tomatoes and black pudding, then tea and toast with marmalade. She had the same, but without the black pudding, which she regarded as a strange, pungent northern food not suitable for anyone with good taste.

"Hey, you needn't have made all this," Devon said as he sat down and tucked into the bright orange yolk of one of their farming neighbour's fresh eggs.

"You need something more than RAF sandwiches on these long flights. Where will you be heading today?"

"Not sure. The squadron leader will be holding a briefing at eight o'clock. But my guess is south of the Scillies, down to the Channel Islands. They think that's where the Soviet submarines are most likely to be found. It'll be a big operation – every aircraft in the squadron will be involved, plus the navy, of course."

"Right. If you can, let me know if you will be home tonight."

"Will do, but the odds are that I'll be staying over. We won't be back until late in the evening, then there's the debrief. Probably another early start in the morning."

After Adam left, Hannah tidied the kitchen and went to Michael's bedroom. He was just stirring, so she made his breakfast before getting him bathed and ready for his toddler play group. She met her friend at the entrance to the church hall after she had dropped Michael off.

"Morning, Diane, how are you today?" said Hannah.

"Morning, my lovely. I'm well, thank you. What have you got planned for today?"

"Oh, just the usual paperwork."

Diane looked thoughtful. "What is it you do, exactly?"

Hannah had a stock answer to questions like this. "I'm a journalist working on government affairs, public opinion and that sort of thing."

"You must have been really busy during the election."

"I was indeed. Always busy." Hannah laughed gently and went to leave.

"Why don't you have a break and come to my house for coffee? Say eleven o'clock. We can pick up the children at half past twelve. In fact, why not stay for lunch? Michael and Alice play so well together."

"Um, well, I have a lot on." Hannah thought again. "No, the work can wait. I'd love to come over, thank you."

And she was very glad she did. Having to pore over reports and distil the key issues tested Hannah's patience, and a change of scenery and female company would be very welcome. Diane was Cornish born and bred with a wealth of knowledge about Cardinham, Bodmin and the Fowey area, and she was fun to be with. And she was right about the children: they played happily with a football in the garden while Diane warmed up Cornish pasties in the oven.

"What does your husband do, Diane?"

"Terry works at the china clay mines down St Austell way. Drives an excavator. It's good money and regular work."

"Is he from Cornwall too?"

"No he's from up country. Bristol. Your Adam, he's in the RAF, isn't he?"

"Not anymore. He's a civilian and trains RAF pilots at St Mawgan to fly the Shackletons."

"Right, them big four-engine jobs we see come over. I never know what they're up to. Not going to bomb us, are they?"

Diane and Hannah laughed. "No, they go out to sea, looking for Russian ships and submarines."

"And they bomb them, do they?"

"Ah, no. Fortunately we're not at war with the Russians. Adam's squadron just likes to keep an eye on what they're up to."

"Bloody Russians, always causing worry and stress. Sometimes I think we should just clear them out of East Germany and them other countries and shove 'em back to Russia."

The two women looked at each other as, with perfect timing, three Shackletons flew over Cardinham at 2,000 feet heading south. Their growling engines stopped any further conversation for several minutes. The children came in from the garden.

"Alright, my 'ansome." Diane ruffled Michael's hair.

In the early afternoon, Hannah said, "It has been lovely to see you, Diane, but I really should be off home now and get some work done."

***

Devon had handed over control of the aircraft on the taxiway to give student pilot Eric Appleby practice at taking off with a fully loaded, fully fuelled aircraft. The mission could last up to fifteen hours, so they needed three pilots and two flight engineers to share the workload.

Devon would be watching for any lapse of concentration from the pilots, any drop in the standards required for consistent, accurate flying.

He glanced out of the window and saw the green-brown mass of Bodmin Moor ahead of them and thought of Hannah and Michael somewhere below. He had a sudden rush of determination to protect them: he would work even harder to seek out Russian submarines, so their commanders would know that, in the event of hostilities, they would be found and destroyed.

Over the south coast, the Shackletons broke their formation to fan out over the English Channel and commence their tracking and soundings routines. They picked up numerous contacts with vessels coming and going, and identified them as cargo ships, ferries and one large liner, the *Queen Mary*, en route from Southampton to New York.

Devon's orders were to patrol the western approaches up to a hundred miles south of Fastnet Rock, the most southerly point of Ireland. The sea was steel grey, and a gale-force north-easterly wind whipped up high waves and foam. It was going to be an uncomfortable trip.

An hour into the mission, no submarine sightings had been made. Devon gave instructions for a change of pilot to Flight Sergeant Mike Bacon, another of his old colleagues from his days in the RAF in Hong Kong. Bacon had started his career as a ground-based aircraftman but had passed pilot training and spent some time in transport squadrons. Moving to maritime reconnaissance was a big step up for him. Devon felt he was a natural, relaxed pilot and was likely to pass the conversion course first time.

Flying directly west, with the wind behind them, the Shackleton's ground speed indicator exceeded 250 miles per hour. Turning back 180 degrees on the reciprocal track, its speed over the sea reduced to 150 miles per hour. Several of these exercises were carried out with excellent precision by Bacon, despite the buffeting wind. The technical team in the back of the aircraft seemed mesmerised by their radar screens and sat motionless, listening out for radio transmissions.

Nearly two hours after leaving St Mawgan, Devon suddenly felt the aircraft shudder and saw the airspeed drop. He frowned. This was more than turbulence. A voice sounded over the intercom, urgent but controlled. It was Angus McDonald, the flight engineer: "Skipper, engine fire, starboard inner."

Devon turned to Bacon. "Power back the engine and action the fire extinguishers." Devon was sitting on the right-hand side of the cockpit and had a clear view of the engine. Flames licked out from the cowling and a thin jet of smoke trailed behind the aircraft. There was a risk of a sudden, catastrophic explosion in the engine that would destroy the aircraft. Bacon's right hand was already on the throttle as Devon spoke; he pulled back the lever then immediately pressed the red button for the fire extinguishers on engine number three. Gases from the extinguishers formed a white cloud around the engine and the flames disappeared, to be replaced by more black smoke.

In seconds, the extinguishers were empty. Devon waited, hoping the fire had been put out. Suddenly the smoke stopped and he could see no signs of fire. Without being instructed to do so, Bacon followed his emergency training, closed down the engine and applied power to the starboard outer engine to provide extra lift.

Flight Sergeant James Ware, the navigator, came on the intercom: "Magnetic track to St Mawgan, sir, 080 degrees, 165 miles."

"Roger. Bacon, take up a compass heading of 085 degrees. Let's get back to Mawgan."

"Roger – 085 degrees." Bacon gently turned the aircraft to head for home.

Devon then called St Mawgan air traffic control and requested an immediate return. He tapped the clock on the instrument panel with the pencil he was holding. "About an hour away. Take it steady, Mike." The aircraft had four engines, so losing one was not a problem.

"Yes, sir."

Flying over Wolf Rock, to the south-west of the Isles of Scilly, McDonald spoke again. "Skipper, starboard outer is overheating. Could be a risk of fire there as well."

"Roger, stand by," said Devon. "Bacon, ease back on number four engine and increase the power on engines one and two."

Bacon's brow was knotted and his teeth gritted as he struggled to keep the aircraft straight and level with almost all the lift coming from the two engines on the left-hand side. The imbalance made the aircraft want to veer to the right, so to keep straight Bacon had to maintain pressure with his foot on the rudder; it was hard, tiring work.

"How's engine four, McDonald?"

"Unchanged, sir, still running hot. Could be we're losing oil – the pressure is dropping. Just reduce the power as much as you can."

Devon jabbed the press-to-talk radio button again. "*Mayday, mayday, mayday!* St Mawgan, Lion Three request straight in approach and landing. We have one engine out, second engine losing power."

"Lion Three, understood. You have priority. State your current position."

"Twenty miles west of Scilly, heading 075 degrees."

"Roger, Lion Three. Continue to land, runway in use zero eight."

Devon decided not to take over from Bacon; it would be a good test of his piloting skills and Devon would be able to intervene, if necessary, on the dual controls. He spoke on the intercom to all members of the crew. "Stand by for an emergency landing. Seat belts on."

Bacon was struggling to maintain altitude as the coast of Cornwall approached. They were down to 1,500 feet and descending steadily. If Bacon pulled up the nose of the aircraft too much, he risked stalling it and spiralling it into the ground. Devon estimated they should reach

St Mawgan with just enough height to spare. But as they passed over St Ives Bay, McDonald's strained voice came over the intercom again. "Sir! Oil pressure dropping, temperature in the red – we have to close down the engine before it seizes up."

"Pull back the power on number four, Bacon. And get all you can from the port engines. Distance to Mawgan, Ware?"

The navigator answered immediately. "Twenty-five miles, sir."

"Roger." Devon looked at the altimeter. They were down to 800 feet. His quick mental calculation of the distance, airspeed and rate of descent shocked him; they wouldn't make it to St Mawgan.

"Shit, this is going to be interesting," he mumbled. "Bacon, ease out 20 degrees north past St Agnes Point. We're going to have to ditch in the sea."

Again Devon called St Mawgan on the radio. "St Mawgan, Lion Three. We can't make it back. We're going to make a sea landing off St Agnes. Notify air sea rescue and the RNLI."

"Roger, that's copied, Lion Three. Good luck."

Devon pressed the aircraft intercom and told the crew to prepare for a crash landing in the sea. Bacon's face mirrored the anxiety that Devon was feeling. Their chance of survival was minimal. The rolling waves would make a controlled ditching very difficult. If the aircraft didn't break up on impact, it wouldn't float for very long, and it would be tough for everyone to get out and into a life raft, despite their emergency training.

"Remember, Bacon, full flap, make sure you keep directly into the wind, and kill the engines the moment we hit the water, not before."

They were flying at less than 600 feet and still descending steadily.

Then Devon leant across the cockpit and grabbed Bacon's arm. "Mike, cancel that! I've had an idea – we can go for a landing at Perranporth.'

"But, sir, it's disused – the runways can't be up to much."

"You're right, but it's got to be better than ditching. I think we have enough height to make it. Come back to an easterly heading – that should take us straight to the airfield." Devon pressed the intercom again. "Ware, give us a distance to Perranporth airfield."

"It's, er… eight miles, sir."

"Stand by, everyone, we're going for a landing at Perranporth."

Just two minutes later, the headland at Perranporth came into view. The airfield was situated on top of cliffs that were 300 feet high. Bacon was doing a great job of keeping the heading to the field steady but struggled to keep enough height to get over the cliffs and onto the airfield. The wind buffeted the aircraft, and a sudden strong wind shear forced them down another hundred feet. There was still more than a mile to the airfield.

"Sir, we're not going to make it!" Mike Bacon looked across to Devon.

"Yes, we are. Keep going. As we get to the cliffs, keep full power on and pull up just enough to get over – no more or we risk stalling and slamming in." It was too late to do anything else. Ditching in the sea was now out of the question; the cliffs loomed ahead, only a quarter of a mile away.

The last few seconds seemed to pass in slow motion as Bacon held his nerve and flew straight at the cliff face.

"Get ready, Mike," said Devon. The cliffs, their tops thirty feet above them, were only a hundred yards away. "Steady… steady – *now, Mike!*"

Bacon pulled back on the control column, the nose came up, and the wheels brushed the grassy top of the cliff. The aircraft managed its short climb, then lost airspeed immediately. They were about to stall and hit the runway. But Bacon had the wherewithal to gently push the nose down to keep forward motion but without crashing. As they were about to land, a gust of wind over the left wing made the Shackleton veer violently to the right, forcing the right-side wheels to hit the runway hard. The undercarriage couldn't take the impact: it bent and buckled, then collapsed. The wingtip struck the ground and the aircraft slewed across the runway. The screeching and crunching of metal was deafening, and the aircraft shook violently as the propellers smashed against the concrete runway.

After 200 yards the aircraft started to slow, but as it did the fuel tank in the right wing ruptured, and a trail of fuel streamed behind them. The aircraft came to a juddering stop and Devon ordered everyone out on the left side. The technicians scrambled out, followed by the navigator, the flight engineer and Pilot Eric Appleby.

"Well done, Mike, great flying. Time for us to go!" Devon called.

Devon and Bacon jumped out then ran to join the rest of the crew on the grass verge of the runway. As they ran, a shock wave of hot air nearly knocked them over. The fuel tank had exploded.

***

Hannah went downstairs from her office to answer the telephone. A junior aircraftman in the wing commander's office had taken the initiative to call her, and bluntly told her the aircraft had crashed and there was, as yet, no news of survivors. Hannah thanked him for the call, requested any updates and hung up. She had prepared herself many times for a call like this and knew she simply had to hold herself together, wait for news, be positive. But her hands started shaking as she stepped into the kitchen and vomited into the sink.

TWENTY-THREE

L ate on a Thursday afternoon, Fitzjohn was called to Macmillan's
office. He assumed it was for some final tidying up before the
PM and his entourage left for Chequers for the weekend. Very little
work was done at Westminster on Fridays as MPs returned to their
constituencies. He was shown into the Cabinet meeting room and was
surprised to see the Chief of the Defence Staff, Admiral Sir Adrian
Temple, there.

"Come in, Henry," said Macmillan. "You know Admiral Temple,
of course."

"Good evening, Prime Minister, good evening, Admiral."

Temple walked across to Fitzjohn and shook hands. "Good
evening, Henry."

"Do sit, please, gentlemen. I have asked you here to discuss the next
phase of our military initiatives to counter the Soviet threat. Henry, the
chiefs of staff have been working on the plans we outlined to them for a
pre-emptive strike. Specifically the plans for an invasion of East Germany,
Poland and Czechoslovakia. Before any significant advancement of that

plan, the chiefs need assurance from the government that it has the will to support the invasion and the subsequent occupation. We will also brief the Queen on our plans. This evening, Henry, I want you to outline to the Admiral how you see the political landscape."

"I see, sir. Well, what can I say? I sense that the public have had enough of the Cold War and the fear that 'the Russians are coming' has strained the population for long enough. Now they expect something to be done about it. Certainly nobody wants a war, but my feeling is that a rapid strike with relatively few casualties will be acceptable. And we can all live in peace, one hopes, thereafter."

"How, exactly, do you see the strike taking place in practice?" said Admiral Temple.

Fitzjohn held his hands out in front of him, palms up. "You're the head of the military. The role of the Minister of Defence is to direct military strategy towards the security of the country. It's not my place to suggest tactics."

Macmillan banged the table firmly. "Come on, Henry, you must have an idea of what would be acceptable to the people."

"I do indeed, but I'm not sure I want to share it with the chief. My views are political – isn't it up to the chiefs of staff to plan out the operation?"

"Certainly, but we don't underestimate the importance of public opinion," said Temple. "Just tell us, please, what would be acceptable and how it would work."

Fitzjohn stood up, went over to the antique roll-top writing bureau and opened the right-hand lower door. He knew there were some bottles and glasses in there. But before he touched them, out of respect he looked at Macmillan. "May I, sir?"

"Go ahead. I'll have a whisky with you. A rum, Adrian?"

Fitzjohn poured the drinks – large ones. It gave him time to choose his words. "The way I believe we will be able to overcome the Soviet defences is by following lessons learned from D-Day. A massive strike force and absolute secrecy over all our build-up. Only a very few people will know of the plans; the increase in our military capabilities will be disjointed, each service developing its plans, controlled by the supreme commander, who's yet to be named. The American public are known to oppose a massive land army operating in Europe – look how reluctant they were to join us in 1940. All that changed after Pearl Harbor, of course. But the fact remains: the Yanks will not join the party readily. We need to get Eisenhower on board with our plans, and quickly. I don't see a problem, as the threat to America by the communists is much more real to everyday Americans than the threat Germany posed in 1940."

Fitzjohn took a long sip of his whisky. "It will require swift action – shock troops, you could say – and an aerial assault that will destroy the Russian air force on the ground."

Macmillan nodded sagely, the trace of a smile on his face. "A radical plan, Henry, and very persuasive."

Sir Adrian Temple was clearly not expecting this; he got up from his seat and paced the room. "Prime Minister, I have great concerns about this strategy. The chiefs of staff still doubt the feasibility and wisdom of a massive ground attack with a front virtually from the north to the south of Europe – hence the limited campaign proposed. And there is always the risk of the Soviets using their nuclear weapons."

Fitzjohn cut in. "But we have the capability of shooting down their missiles, don't we?"

"I wouldn't rely on it 100 per cent – it only takes one or two to get through. Visualise an atomic bomb over London, if you will."

"Admiral, remember, if we do nothing we can expect a Russian invasion of West Germany and who knows where else, so you will have your ground war whether you like it or not. That's the key issue here. Look at the evidence: increased military activity in Russia and East

Germany, more spying, subterfuge and sabotage on our military bases. All designed to test us and ease the way for a Soviet attack. Classic signs of preparation for an invasion, are they not?"

Temple looked resigned to losing the argument. "Yes, indeed. Very well, Prime Minister," he said. "Let me have a month to develop the outline plans. I will say something now. If the Russians hear we are planning a pre-emptive attack, they will not hesitate to commence one of their own. The need for secrecy in this is absolutely paramount. You could say the very existence of Great Britain depends on it."

"Quite so, quite so. A month it is – thank you, Temple. Now, another rum?" said Macmillan.

Temple was halfway to the door. "No, thank you, Prime Minister. I will bid you both a good evening."

"Well, Henry, you have certainly set the cat among the pigeons."

TWENTY-FOUR

Three days after the crash, Wing Commander Louis Valentine entered the intelligence division's briefing room and stood behind the desk. Devon and all the operational pilots and crew were in attendance. Valentine explained that more work needed to be done on the burnt-out remains of the aircraft, but he wanted to apprise the team of the findings so far. His primary objective in the meeting was to deal with the speculation that had been circulating that the aircraft had been tampered with and Soviet agents were operating on the base. Fear of further attacks could undermine morale for the pilots and technicians.

The chatter quickly subsided and a still silence hung in the room.

"Good morning, gentlemen. Thank you for coming along. I know many of you have missions to undertake today, so I shall be brief. I am aware of the rumours circulating that some form of tampering may have caused the problems with the engines that led to the loss of the Shackleton, call sign Lion Three, on Monday.

"While the loss is regrettable, I want to assure you all that the evidence from the crash investigation team shows no signs of interference with the oil system. It is not impossible that the aircraft's engines were sabotaged, but leaks or mechanical failure are just as likely to be the reason for the fire and loss of oil pressure. You may be aware that the maintenance unit here at St Mawgan, plus extra technicians flown down from Scotland, have been working non-stop over the past two days to examine all the squadron's Shackletons, and no defects have been found on any engines. It would not make sense for a sabotage agent to interfere with one aircraft.

"The investigation team have also interviewed Flight Sergeant Bacon, Pilot Instructor Devon and Flight Engineer McDonald on the performance of the aircraft immediately before the fire and subsequent crash landing. Everything points to a mechanical fault with the oil system – the type that can happen at any time. So, gentlemen, I want to scotch the theory that we have Reds in our midst; we have enough to occupy us without misinformation. I'm sure I can rely on you all to avoid gossip. Now, any questions?"

Pilot Eric Appleby put up his hand. "Sir, if I may, we've noticed an increased presence of RAF Regiment guys on the airfield since the crash. Does this mean there are concerns about intruders?"

"Fair question, Appleby. It's belt and braces – the accident investigation team have given us their assurances, but we will also be increasing security for good measure. It's designed to prevent anyone feeling they can stroll in, including members of the press. Don't forget, everyone, you must not discuss the incident with reporters, on or off the airfield. That will be handled by our press office.

"If there are no more questions… Very well, please continue with your duties. Devon, would you stay behind."

After the room had cleared, Valentine and Devon were joined by Captain Peter Fuller from the RAF Regiment, in charge of airfield security.

"Devon, you know Captain Fuller, I believe. He's here to give us an update on the security risk on RAF stations. Captain Fuller…"

"Thank you, Wing Commander. Yes, the regiment is on high alert for intruders to air stations around the country after breaches of security on our bases at Laarbruch and Gutesloh in West Germany. Soviet agents have been arrested on three occasions and some minor damage reported. So far we have no reports of successful intrusions in the UK, but we are being extra-diligent. It is not beyond the realms of possibility that there have, in fact, been sabotage attempts on our bases."

Devon was almost dumbstruck by the captain's words, given Valentine's assurances in his briefing. "Let me understand this correctly: do you think my aircraft was sabotaged? What purpose would it serve to tamper with one aircraft?"

"In many ways the Russian secret services are testing us out – seeing how well they are able to breach our security. Their agents want to demonstrate to their superiors that security is weak. The initial examination of the wreckage cannot rule out that the oil lines were loosened before the flight. We just don't know. In the event of a war, the Russians would be confident of being able to plant explosives on our bases, to destroy aircraft on the ground. We have asked all senior officers to maintain secrecy about these activities, hence the briefing the wing commander gave."

"Thanks for the update – keep up the good work on security. As far as I can, as a civilian, I will make sure that none of my pilots or crew discuss the accident. Or the sabotage, if that's what it was," said Devon.

***

Over dinner at home that evening, Devon couldn't shake off the thought that they might now be legitimate targets of Russia, and the risk of war was becoming more heightened. He didn't want to worry Hannah more than she already was; she had barely recovered from the shock of the phone call from the airfield immediately after the crash. She had had several hours of fearing the worst.

"Are you alright, Adam?" Hannah said. "Is the crash still playing on your mind?"

"Yes, it will take a few more days for the shock to wear off. It could have been much worse. Bacon did a great job flying on two engines and landing at Perranporth. I wouldn't have fancied ditching in the sea."

"Have the people at the airfield found out what the problem was?" Hannah asked.

"They're still examining the engines. We know they had oil problems, which can happen, of course, but both at the same time? Very unusual."

"One of the mechanics is going to be in trouble if it's found that they made a mistake."

"Yes – if it was a mistake."

Hannah froze. "What are you saying? That someone nobbled the engines deliberately!"

"Oh, I'm sorry, I didn't mean to trouble you with this, but you might as well know now I've let the cat out of the bag. There have been breaches of security in RAF stations in West Germany. The intelligence and security people think it could be Russian agents at work." Devon tried to make light of the issue. "All a bit far-fetched, if you ask me. Engines are not totally reliable; they go wrong sometimes. We had a heavy landing of course, but no one was injured."

"Yes, but what if it was the Russians?" Hannah gently shuddered. "And what if they try again? What will happen next time?"

TWENTY-FIVE

In the planning room of the heavily fortified home base of the Soviet northern submarine fleet near Murmansk in the Arctic Circle, charts showing the waters around the British Isles were spread across a large table. Captain Fyodor Yegorov stood with his senior officers and listened to their plan to insert a special operations team onto the west coast of Scotland. In the back of the darkened room, two members of the Communist Party intelligence staff stood silently.

Major Alexi Petrov, the commander of the twelve-man operations team, tapped the chart with his index finger. "We need to be put ashore here, the bay at Labost, and be picked up six hours later here, at Fevig." He spoke firmly, implying an order. He was short, his pit bull frame tight in his uniform.

"And what is your objective, Comrade Major? There is nothing of military significance in the area you have chosen; it's a rocky, barren coastline."

"It is simply an exercise, Comrade Captain. We need our forces to be trained in land assault and extraction. On this occasion, we will be landing and staying under cover for the period of the exercise. Our senior commanders require us to be ready, should circumstances require it, to carry out special operations such as these. We train in the Soviet Union, but there is no substitute for experience on foreign missions."

Yegorov wasn't happy. He commanded the fleet's most powerful submarine, and its role was the destruction of enemy shipping, not a taxi service. But he also knew that special operations units had the support of the most senior military and political commanders. He sniffed loudly and thought for a moment. "Of course we can surface near the area you have indicated, but is this really the best use of the *Leninski*?"

Petrov bristled. He was not used to his missions and their purpose being questioned. "It is not for us to dispute, Comrade. This exercise benefits your crew and my team. Our orders, and your orders, are to be ready if and when the time comes for live operations. And please remember, that could be anywhere in the west of Europe, including the British mainland."

Yegorov was already aware of the increased need to be ready for action against the West: the European NATO countries supported by the Americans. He was being watched by the party officers. He had no choice but to cooperate. And to be seen to cooperate.

"What equipment will you be using to go ashore?"

"We will use two of the Z-16 six-man inflatables. I believe these can be stowed in the submarine and rapidly inflated with gas canisters as we leave. No heavy equipment – small arms only. When we are extracted from our rendezvous point the boats will be brought back with us, deflated and stowed in the submarine. We wish to leave no trace of the exercise."

"Yes, we can certainly accommodate your team and the inflatables in the *Leninski*. Do you have a date for the mission?"

Major Petrov stood up straight, his eyes level. "Yes, one week from today."

"But we have other exercises to complete before then – we have the northern fleet Baltic manoeuvres for the next month."

The older party member stepped out of the shadows. "Comrade Captain Yegorov, please do not worry. We have taken care of these exercises, and new orders will be transmitted to you. You will undertake this special mission, yes?"

"Certainly, Comrade."

***

As planned, within a week, the *Leninski* was ready for the assignment to the Outer Hebrides, with twelve operatives and two party officials on board. The exact location of the drop-off was kept secret; there was always the possibility of spies at the base. Once under way, the crew would carry out their orders and sail west initially, then south. Some crew members might have questioned this, since they expected to be heading for the Baltic Sea. But the Soviet navy did not encourage questioning.

The special operations team kept out of the way and had their own bunks and food. As the time approached for them to disembark, they gathered close to the conning tower ladders, dressed in black, with an array of personal weapons – guns, knives and gas containers – strapped to their torsos and legs. They pulled their masks up to their eyes; they didn't want to be recognised, even by the submarine's crew members.

Captain Yegorov ordered the submarine to surface. They were two miles off the coast of Lewis at Labost Point, a dangerous, rugged promontory. The night was dark, with no moonlight: low clouds scudded inland across the Atlantic rollers that crashed on the rocks. Major Petrov's team worked quickly and in silence, with only red-shaded torchlight to see by. Within minutes they had the two inflatable dinghies ready to launch from the bow. Petrov gave the order. The boats were boarded and launched on the landward side of the submarine.

Their small outboard motors purred, almost unheard against the sound of the wind and waves. Captain Yegorov ordered the *Leninski* to move away from land and dive as soon as possible.

Petrov directed his helmsman to steer towards a small beach at the head of the narrow bay. Both boats ran up on the shingle and all but one man in each boat jumped out. The teams pushed the boats back out to sea: the helmsmen's job now was to go down the coast, find the pick-up point and hide for the next six hours.

After scaling the low cliffs, Petrov's men pressed on through the darkness. Near the small village of Labost they found a disused bothy to serve as a hiding place for Petrov and five of the men. Petrov did not want the whole team to stay in the same place – that was standard practice. If they were compromised, then at least part of the team could continue with the mission. The remaining men were ordered to carry out a recce on the village.

Petrov's team patrolled the surrounding area as far as the main road leading down the coast towards Carloway. After four hours he sent word for the recce team to join him at the bothy. They all advanced towards the rendezvous point: a small beach at Fevig. He was pleased to see the two inflatable boats ready and waiting. A radio operator signalled to the submarine, and forty minutes later the boats had been deflated and they were on board.

Major Petrov sat down in Captain Yegorov's small cabin with the senior party official for the debrief. He was elated that the mission had gone entirely to plan: it had been an excellent rehearsal for any future action assigned to the team. No alcohol was allowed on board the submarine, but he promised he would buy the captain a drink back at Murmansk. He was unaware that two of his men from the recce team had broken into the village shop and stolen two bottles of whisky. The bottles had been handed round the team and finished off before the major returned from his briefing.

At 8a.m. Angus Ross opened his shop. Two minutes later he called the police station to report a robbery but, due to the important matter of it being Captain's day at Stornoway golf club, and the local constable was a keen golfer, no one was available to answer the telephone. No police investigation was made and Ross put the theft down to local teenagers. No report of intruders was filed and the opportunity of alerting the military was lost.

TWENTY-SIX

Fitzjohn disliked late sittings in the House, listening to mind-numbing debates that meant little to him. But as a minister he had to put the time in. He glanced at his watch: nearly nine o'clock. He relaxed. He was not due at Vanessa's flat until ten, and it would only take fifteen minutes to get there, at most. He had reserved a table at Stella's again: it was expensive, but the food and wines were excellent and the staff unobtrusive. He had never been recognised at the restaurant – at least, he had never heard anyone comment on the Minister of Defence being a regular diner.

After a superb meal, a shared bottle of champagne and large brandies with coffee, Fitzjohn was ready for London's nightlife. "What do you fancy, Vanessa, the Blue Angel or Imogen's?"

Vanessa, who was wearing a low-cut white chiffon dress, twitched her nose in a thoughtful way. "Er, the Blue Angel would be nice, Henry." Imogen's was her favourite place, but she knew that on a Thursday night Stephen Walmsley might be found there, possibly with Russian friends. Somehow Yuri Andreyevich had obtained her phone number and she'd met him for dinner at the Dorchester. But she refused to venture to other parts of the hotel with him and was home by 1a.m. She had no desire to progress their friendship any further.

"Are you sure, my dear?" Fitzjohn had picked up on her uncertainty.

She put on a broad smile. "Yes, of course, sorry. Shall we go now?"

The Blue Angel was packed, mainly with the younger set, up from Chelsea and Sloane Square. The dance floor was full, keeping Fitzjohn and Vanessa close together. After more champagne and dancing Fitzjohn had a pang of concern: he was due at a meeting at the Ministry of Defence at ten o'clock in the morning and it was nearly two now.

Vanessa noticed Fitzjohn glancing at his watch. "I've had a lovely evening, Henry, but shall we go now?"

In the taxi across London, Vanessa sat close to Fitzjohn and put her hand on his thigh. "You can stay tonight if you want to," she whispered.

He didn't hesitate. "Splendid, my love."

Fitzjohn took full advantage of her welcoming nature and keenness to please. Their vigorous session in the bedroom left him thirsty. Returning from the kitchen with two glasses of water, he found Vanessa sitting up in bed, the sheet up to her chin.

"Here, you might need this," he said, passing one of the glasses to her.

"Thank you, you're so thoughtful. Tell me, um…"

"Yes, what is it?"

"I just wanted ask… I mean, you're not married, are you?"

"Goodness me, what makes you ask that!"

"Well, as we're getting on so well, I was hoping that we might have a future together. Oh, I don't mean get married next week, but I'd be unhappy if there was anyone in your life who had a claim on you."

"You're right, we're not going to get married next week, but rest assured, my love, that you are very special to me. No, I'm not married, and I like things that way. Let's just enjoy each other's company and see where life takes us, shall we?"

Vanessa put her glass on the bedside table and wrapped her arms around Fitzjohn. "Oh, Henry, you are a darling, let's enjoy each other's company a little more, shall we?" she purred, trailing a hand across his shoulder and down his chest.

"Much as I'd like to, I think it's time I had some sleep. I have an important meeting in the morning. Would you set the alarm for me, please? Half past eight."

Vanessa drew away, pouting. "If I must. But why is the meeting more important than I am?"

"I'm afraid that work must sometimes come first."

"What is it you do, exactly?"

"I have my airline to manage down at Gatwick. But more importantly, I'm an MP – you know that."

She turned her back on Fitzjohn. "Very boring desk job, if you ask me, doesn't sound at all important. Not like Stephen – he's a famous architect and gets invited to all the best parties. And he's always very kind to me."

Fitzjohn was irked by being ranked lower than Walmsley. "Actually, I'm chairing a meeting of the Ministry of Defence chiefs of staff. If you must know."

"Meetings, meetings, meetings. Is that all you do?"

Fitzjohn's temper got the better of him. "No, you silly girl! I'm setting the strategy for a major action against the Russians. Something that could change world history." He was almost shouting. "Somewhat more important than designing a kitchen!"

Vanessa rolled back over to face him. "Henry, I'm sorry, I didn't mean to be rude. It's just that I don't really understand what MPs do. Please forgive me."

He calmed down. "Well, that's alright. I shouldn't discuss my work, but as the Minister of Defence I have to think about what our enemies are up to and do something about it before they do."

"There's not going to be a war, is there?"

"There could be – that's what I'm discussing tomorrow."

"Are you the boss of all those chiefs…"

"Chiefs of staff. Yes, essentially I set the strategy with the prime minister and the Cabinet's consent, and the chiefs of staff carry out the military operations."

"Goodness, you really are important. I'm so lucky to have such a special boyfriend!"

Her flattery struck home with Fitzjohn, who smirked.

Vanessa wrapped herself around Fitzjohn and gave him a lingering, passionate kiss. Despite the late hour, he couldn't resist responding in a way that satisfied them both.

TWENTY-SEVEN

April 1960

Wing Commander Valentine asked Devon to meet the intelligence officers to study a report sent down to St Mawgan from the RAF station in Kinloss, Scotland. Shackletons operating in the areas to the north and west of the British Isles had tracked a submarine, they thought, on its way south to the Atlantic.

Valentine introduced Squadron Leader Archie McDonnell, the senior intelligence officer. "For a short period the submarine was lost, somewhere off the west coast of the Isle of Lewis. Then there was further contact as it surfaced for two short periods. We think it then headed back to Murmansk. At first my intelligence team assumed that there must be some form of mechanical trouble requiring a return to base."

Valentine asked, "Have you or your technicians seen any similar behaviour in the approaches to the English Channel, Devon?"

"We have reported some submarines staying in one point as part of their tour of duty, waiting and watching. I don't recall a sudden return to base, as was the case here. I agree it's suspicious – it seems they simply abandoned their mission. I wonder what they might have been interested in on the coast of Scotland. Where exactly was contact lost, then re-established?"

An intelligence officer pointed to a chart on the wall, but the response was of little help.

"This area is more of a tourist attraction than a military target," said Devon. "It's curious that the second contact was a few miles away from where it was lost. What was the submarine doing during the time it was out of observation – over six hours?"

"That's a good question, but one we can't answer, of course. We've been in touch with the local constabulary, but nothing untoward has been reported."

Devon pondered the report from Kinloss. "When a sub stays in one place for a period it's usually on a reconnaissance mission, observing shipping movements. But a sub is not likely to see much more than a few fishing boats in this area."

"Even those are few and far between, and then mainly from Carloway, down here." McDonnell pointed to a village on the chart. "There might well have been a fault with the submarine that meant it had to return."

"Yes, there is that, or a sudden change to its deployment," said Devon.

Wing Commander Valentine had seen and heard enough. "Very well, thank you. Squadron Leader, I believe constant vigilance is the order of the day. We will ensure all our maritime pilots are briefed to look out for unusual activity."

"Thank you, sir. Good hunting."

Devon went to leave also.

"Stay behind would you, Adam?" Valentine said.

"Certainly, sir."

"Take a seat – and please, it's Louis when there's no one around."

"Of course."

"I wanted to update you on developments since the crash at Perranporth. Our engineers now believe there's a strong possibility that the two engines were tampered with. Nothing could be salvaged from the burnt-out engine, but the starboard outer has been examined and a loose oil connector found. That could be deliberate – either one of our own people who is perhaps being bribed or threatened by outsiders, such as the Russians, or perhaps more likely, infiltrators gained access to the station at night, sabotaging the aircraft."

"Actually, Louis, that was my thought exactly. I can't believe an aircraftman would risk the lives of his colleagues."

"Quite. But perhaps more concerning is that the intelligence types have reported increased activity in the pubs and clubs around military bases, notably Plymouth and Portsmouth. Strangers buying drinks, asking questions, that sort of thing. Some evidence of incursions into barracks and ports. In all bases around the country the military police, RAF Regiment and no doubt MI5 are stepping up their efforts.'

"Good to know. It's not a very warming prospect to think that your aircraft might have been sabotaged when you're 300 miles out in the Atlantic."

"Well, that's why I wanted to assure you that all air stations are now under extra guard. You should be perfectly safe."

"Thanks for the update, Louis – it's appreciated. I will be off now, if there's nothing else?"

"No. Have a good evening, Adam."

The two men stood and shook hands warmly.

***

When Devon arrived home, Hannah and Michael were having drinks in the garden. As the clocks had gone forward the weekend before, the sun shone into the early evening. Michael was thrilled to see his father and jumped up into his arms. Devon leant forward and gave Hannah a quick kiss.

"How has your day been?" he asked.

"Very nice. Michael and I planted some geraniums at the bottom of the garden."

He smiled. "Was that fun, Michael?" The boy gave a shy "yes, Daddy," and nuzzled his face into Devon's shoulder.

"It's getting chilly, let's go in. Dinner's almost ready, and I have some news." As they entered the kitchen, Hannah said, "Would you mind taking the chicken out of the oven, Adam?"

"Sure. And what's your news?"

"A letter arrived this morning from Val and Drake. They're going to be in Plymouth for two or three months and said they could come over at Easter and visit us. Val included her phone number so I called her this morning."

"Excellent – it will be good to see them again. Will they have Charles with them?"

"Yes. It will be nice for Michael to have someone to play with."

"What are the plans?"

"They're coming for lunch on the Saturday, staying over and returning to Plymouth Sunday evening."

"That's great. I wonder what Drake is doing now."

"Me too. And I gather that Val is back at work since having Charles. But things are never straightforward with those two!"

"That's true. They seem to find trouble wherever they go, but that's life in the secret services," said Devon.

TWENTY-EIGHT

From Point Saturn house, the view across the Fowey estuary took in the fishermen's cottages over in Polruan, the ancient blockhouse, and the blue-green expanse of the English Channel. As he waited for his guests to arrive, Sir Bartley Paget, containing his excitement, patiently watched a yacht sail slowly into the harbour. Not many visitors came all the way down to the house from London. He smiled as the bell from the front gates rang in the vestibule, and he heard Rufus running to open the door.

"Lovely to see you, darling." Paget kissed his daughter on both cheeks and squeezed her shoulders. "And welcome, everyone, to Point Saturn. I hope you have a very enjoyable Easter weekend. I believe we're promised some excellent weather. And help yourselves to tea and cake."

"Thank you, Daddy, it's lovely to be back in Cornwall. After tea, can Rufus take everyone's bags to their rooms? It's been such a tedious journey on the train. Slow running and packed with schoolchildren coming down for the holidays. Awful!"

"Yes, of course. Cook will be serving dinner at eight o'clock, with drinks in the lounge any time you're ready. No need to dress, we're very informal here. I'll see you all later." Ever willing and accommodating, Rufus scampered ahead, carrying four bags up the central staircase to the corridor on the east side of the house.

"Emily, this is your room; James, you're next door. And be good, you two." Vanessa was revelling in her role as hostess. She had got to know so many people in the plays and musicals she had performed in and had invited her best friends down to the house at Readymoney Cove. "Cecilia, you're across the hall there, and Auguste is at the far end. My room is upstairs."

***

Vanessa made sure she was up early on Good Friday to take breakfast with her guests. The group arrived downstairs sharp at 9a.m. "Daddy's weather prediction was perfectly accurate. It's already lovely and warm, and there'll be sunshine all day." She smiled. "I thought we could take the Bodinnick ferry this morning and do the Hall Walk. It's a beautiful route through the woods and along the river on the other side. We then come back to Fowey on the Polruan ferry and we can have lunch in town. There's a lovely pub called the King of Prussia right on the town quay. Then we can come back here in the afternoon or go down to Readymoney Cove."

Cecilia clapped her hands together in excitement. "Oh, Vanessa, it sounds such fun. I've never been on a country walk before. We will be just like the Famous Five!"

"Don't be silly, dearie, one of the five was a dog," said James, the oldest in the group at twenty-three – and therefore, he thought, the wisest. "I hope you brought good walking shoes and a sun hat. It's not a stroll along Bond Street, you know."

"Yes, James, I have my gym shoes and my old straw boater from school." Cecilia didn't like to be teased.

"Daddy has said Rufus will drive us into town, where we can get the ferry. Shall we leave at about eleven?" said Vanessa.

***

After the exertion of the walk and the unaccustomed fresh air, then lunch and a glass or two of the local cider in the King of Prussia in Fowey, the group had little inclination to take a turn around the beach and idled the afternoon away. In the early evening, the friends gathered on the patio, still warmed by the late sunshine, for champagne.

Dinner started with dressed freshly caught crabs served with melba toast, followed by turbot fillets, Cornish new potatoes and samphire. Sir Bartley was delighted that Vanessa seemed to be doing so well with her acting career and had made such an agreeable set of friends.

"Lovely strawberries," said Auguste. "And so early in the year."

As she passed around the bowl of clotted cream, Vanessa said, "And cream from our tenants' farms," with more than a hint of pride in her voice.

When coffee was being served, Sir Bartley managed to speak to Vanessa. "I don't think we have had such a happy time in the house since your mother died, my dear. I'm so glad you came down, and your friends are charming."

"Yes, they're good fun, Daddy. Thank you so much for putting on the spread – the food and champagne were very nice. I know how tight money is."

"Now don't you worry about anything in that department. Tin prices are picking up and we expect the mines to be back to profit very soon. I hope to let some of the properties in North Street for the tourist trade this year, so if there is ever anything you need, just ask. You seem to need very little income."

"I'm careful with money, Daddy, and I do earn some money from my acting." The blush in her cheeks as she felt the shame of her secret lifestyle, and how this kept her in the luxurious comfort she was unwilling to go without, went unnoticed by Sir Bartley.

The next two days were spent walking the coastal path, hiring a fishing boat and guide, and most exciting of all, Daphne du Maurier and her husband, General 'Boy' Browning visited Point Saturn for afternoon tea on Easter Sunday. The actors and actresses were thrilled to meet the author of *Rebecca*: they had all seen the film and fallen in love with Maxim and 'the girl'. They were mesmerised by du Maurier and talked afterwards about the mysterious Cornish coastline with its hidden bays and coves.

"Daddy is such a good pal of Boy; they were in the army together," Vanessa was proud to tell her friends later. "Daphne has always helped me with my acting career." Only a small white lie, she thought.

Before dinner there was a knock on her bedroom door. "Miss Vanessa, you had a telephone call while you were with Miss du Maurier. A Mr Walmsley."

"Oh, right, thank you, Rufus. Any message?"

"Yes, miss, he simply asked that you call him at your convenience."

"Thank you, Rufus." Vanessa's dreams of romance and adventure were abruptly ended and she was shaken back into the real world; she had a feeling she knew what Walmsley wanted. Before her friends assembled in the lounge, she went downstairs to the office, where she could make a call in private. She called the operator and asked for an immediate connection.

"Stephen, it's Vanessa."

"Dearest, how lovely to hear from you. How is Cornwall?"

"Very nice. Beautiful weather."

"Splendid. I hope you are suitably refreshed and ready to return to the delights of London later this week?"

"Yes, we are taking the train on Tuesday. Why do you ask?"

"Come now, Vanessa, you know how I miss your company. And I have to say, my good friend Yuri Andreyevich is also pining for you. I have suggested you might like to have dinner with him on Saturday and then go on to Imogen's." Walmsley raised his voice a touch, indicating he wouldn't brook any disagreement. "I hope you find that an exciting prospect."

Vanessa had been right about what Walmsley wanted. She wasn't keen. "I'd rather not, Stephen, if you don't mind. Yuri is not really my type."

"Nonsense, he is a very agreeable young man!"

"Not that young," Vanessa whimpered.

"Look, he is a very important client of mine, and I would be most obliged if you would entertain him. I'm sure you understand what I'm saying."

"He really isn't for me, Stephen. I hope *you* understand."

Walmsley lost his temper. "You will do as you're told, girl, if you want to stay in that flat and enjoy the luxuries I give you! I will call Yuri and let him know he can pick you up on Saturday evening at nine o'clock. Is that clear?"

Vanessa suppressed a sob and took a deep breath. "Alright, if you insist, I will go out with him."

"Good show, old thing. I'm sure you will have a wonderful time."

After replacing the receiver, Vanessa said quietly to herself, "Oh, Henry, I wish you were here, you would get me out of this mess."

TWENTY-NINE

"Good morning, Prime Minister."

"Good morning, Henry. Take a seat. We have an hour before Admiral Temple arrives, and I want to get the strategy clear between us. He will undoubtedly report that the chiefs of staff have rebelled against the idea of a full pre-emptive strike. Our job is to hear what they have to say and then steadfastly continue with our plans. Is that agreed?"

"Certainly, Prime Minister." Fitzjohn liked Old Mac's approach: he took no nonsense from the military types. He was the boss, after all. "I can summarise my plans as follows, sir. At the beginning of spring 1962 we commence our removal of the communist threat with the invasion of East Germany, Czechoslovakia, Poland and Hungary. These countries will quickly turn in our favour and help push the Russian armies back through the whole of the Eastern bloc. The attack must be on all fronts and through all arms: army, navy and air force. The plans must, of course, be supported by our NATO partners, particularly the Americans."

Fitzjohn expanded on his ideas, only vaguely aware that each time he discussed the plans he added more aggression to the West's attack, more radical measures to neutralise the Soviet threat.

Macmillan listened patiently. "If we are to get buy-in from the Americans, we need to be certain that we are able to counter the Soviets' retaliation. Can we assure the Cabinet that our interception systems will destroy incoming nuclear missiles?"

"The chiefs always remind us that no one can be certain, sir, but isn't that the point? With the Russians becoming more and more belligerent and developing new weapons we need to act now, and in a decisive way, to remove the threat. This may entail some risk, but not as much as doing nothing."

Macmillan sat up straight and placed both hands on the table, palms down. "I'm sorry, Henry, but I can't go along with this strategy if there is any chance of the UK being hit by nuclear weapons – any chance at all."

Fitzjohn was angry. This amounted to back-pedalling by the prime minister – and any sign of doubt about the strategy would be seized upon by Temple and would undermine his, Fitzjohn's, position. He *had* to force his plans through.

"As we know, Prime Minister, there is a real and present danger that the Reds will invade West Germany, possibly the Low Countries and France. Even the UK. I believe that my plan is our only solution to the threat."

"Very well. Then you will have to convince Temple. If you can do that, then you have my support."

Fitzjohn could clearly see that this moment could signal a seismic change in the relationship between himself and the prime minister. A change that he could make happen. If he didn't take control now, he would always have to kowtow to Macmillan's wishes. "Leave that to me. Let's remember why you appointed me Minister of Defence, at my age." Fitzjohn tapped an index finger on the table. "I'm the future of the Conservative Party and I'm the future of the country. That's the agreement we have, and that's what I'm taking forward. Are you still willing to back me personally if we have to ask for a vote of confidence in the Cabinet?"

They were interrupted by a knock at the Cabinet room door. A secretary entered and announced that Admiral Temple had arrived. Macmillan took the opportunity to avoid Fitzjohn's question.

"Come in, please," said Fitzjohn before the prime minister could say anything; a breach of protocol Fitzjohn didn't much care about. The secretary poured coffee and quickly left the room.

Fitzjohn continued. "Please sit, Admiral. I presume you have consulted with the chiefs of staff and are now ready to outline your plans for the attack?"

"Yes, Mr Fitzjohn." Temple turned to look at Macmillan, who looked away. "Prime Minister, we see certain merits in the pre-emptive strike that you have indicated the government wants, and we are willing to investigate the achievability of such a plan."

Fitzjohn responded, effectively cutting Macmillan out of the conversation. "Certain merits? *Certain merits?* Is that really all you can say in the face of the Red Army, not to mention their navy and air force, potentially on the brink of attacking us?" Fitzjohn was clearly trying to subdue his anger; he didn't need to shout, he spoke firmly, making rigid eye contact.

The admiral was made of stern stuff. He went on. "Mr Fitzjohn, please do not underestimate the chiefs of staff: they are concerned about the threat and our defence against it. We have substantial forces in West Germany and we are willing to use them – perhaps more so than you are aware yourself, if I may say, with respect. But a widespread pre-emptive attack is a different matter. We have considered your plans for the strike. We do not disagree that they would open for us a significant opportunity to defeat the Soviets, but…" The admiral hesitated. "The real danger lies, of course, in nuclear retaliation." He turned to Macmillan. "Prime Minister, we would do all we could to prevent Russian rockets coming our way. However, we cannot guarantee that we will intercept them all. You and Mr Fitzjohn must ask yourselves: how many nuclear explosions over the UK are you willing to accept? How many would the population accept?"

Fitzjohn again took the initiative. "Your job is to make sure that no missiles get through our defence systems. Let me say it again, we are facing immense danger from a conventional attack. Do you deny this?"

"No of course not." Temple hesitated. "So be it. I will consult once again with the chiefs of staff and come back to you. Good morning, gentlemen."

***

Ten minutes later, Fitzjohn left Downing Street and returned to his office in Horse Guards Road. He didn't notice Admiral Temple step from the private secretary's office back into the Cabinet meeting room, where Macmillan was signing a pile of letters and memos.

Temple closed the door behind him. "Prime Minister, may I have a few moments?"

"What is it, Admiral? Somewhat out of order this…"

"With respect, sir, I feel I must speak directly to you. The strategy that Mr Fitzjohn is promoting is dangerous warmongering and is likely to lead to catastrophic destruction and death in our country. I have been asked by the chiefs if you would dismiss his plans for the sake of maintaining peace."

"I am sorry, Admiral, but the future of the country will be in the hands of the next generation in very short order. I do not disagree that Fitzjohn has some radical plans, but I am not minded to interfere. And be assured I do share his concerns – all of our concerns – about the danger of the Russians attacking. That's all I am willing to say, Admiral."

"Very well, Prime Minister."

THIRTY

While she was making pastry, Hannah heard a car arrive. Quickly she took off her apron and hung it up. Drake Casey pulled up outside and opened the boot to take out their suitcases as Val lifted four-year-old Charles from the rear seat.

Casey – five foot ten, straight-backed and muscular – looked exactly like an ex-serviceman. His wartime role as an American paratrooper had set his attitude to life: work hard, be the best you can be, and stay fit for active service. After the war he spent five years assigned to the intelligence corps, seeking out and arresting Nazi war criminals. During his subsequent transfer to the CIA's Berlin operation, he had met and worked with Val Hetherington-Brown. They had fallen for each other and married in 1956.

Devon came round from the back of the house. "Drake, Val, great to see you, welcome to Cornwall!" He kissed Val and shook hands with Drake. "Hello, young Charles, nice to see you too. Come in, everyone."

Hannah was in the hall. "Val! How lovely to see you all – welcome. What is it, two years or so since we last met up? Far too long, anyway."

"Yes, something like that," said Val, "but it's a nice coincidence that we will be in the same area for the next couple of months."

"You look great, Val, as chic as ever!" said Hannah.

Val always looked good: today she wore a slim-fitting pale-green trouser suit, her hair up in a French twist. She had a film star's effortless style.

"You're looking great too – beautiful dress."

Hannah was pleased. She had bought the dress in Selfridges on her last trip to London. "Is it your work that has brought you down here?" she asked.

Val's smile faded. "Yes, I'm afraid so. Well, Drake's work. He has an assignment at the naval base in Plymouth. We can talk about that later."

"Of course. I'll make some tea and we can sit in the garden."

The two young boys ran around the garden all afternoon, to the delight of their parents, and by the time the sun went down they were ready for their evening meal, followed by a small Easter egg each. Soon afterwards, they were settled in bed for the night.

In the kitchen Hannah said, "We will start dinner with a prawn cocktail, and I've cooked a leg of lamb from the local butcher with more Cornish produce – some lovely potatoes, carrots and peas, and mint from the garden."

"You certainly live well down here," said Val.

"Yes, we're lucky to have so much local food."

"And beer!" Devon called from the living room. They all laughed. "Gin comes from London, of course. Hannah, Val – Drake and I are having a beer before dinner. What would you like? I also have cider, or perhaps a G&T?"

"Gin for me, please," said Val.

Hannah waved her hand at Devon as if she were saluting him. "I'll have the same."

The friends sat in the living room with their drinks and some cheese straws Hannah had made.

"Val, are you still working for MI6?" asked Hannah. "After the assignment to Berlin that we were involved in, you went back to Germany, but what have you been doing for the last couple of years?"

"Initially, more work to bring German and Soviet scientists over to the West. But when Drake and I got married and Charles came along, I asked to stand down from field work. I transferred to MI5, and I'm focusing on counter-intelligence at the moment. Pretty similar to the work Drake has taken on, but I work at a desk. I have a team of agents monitoring the Russians in London. They have increased the number of cultural attachés they have sent over – these jobs are, of course, covers for spies. The workload has increased enormously, so I'm recruiting more agents, but it's not easy getting the right people."

"Indeed. Such a testing time for everyone," said Hannah.

Devon was suddenly more interested in Casey's work. "Tell me, Drake, what mission are you on in Plymouth? Why are you Americans involved?"

Casey frowned. "It's aligned to the role you have in the air, Adam: seeking out Russian intruders. The British secret service asked the CIA to work with them to boost military base protection. Because of my US connection I have been assigned to Plymouth with my team. We have several navy ships in the harbour at the moment, scheduled to carry out exercises with the Royal Navy. We don't want any prying eyes watching us, and certainly no intruders in the base."

"Makes sense. But surely you're not going to be patrolling the base yourself at night with a torch and a gun?"

"No, no, we leave that to the British military police and security people. Some of my team are embedded with the servicemen and women, listening out for any evidence of agents approaching British or American personnel. If there is any contact, I want to hear about it pronto. We're keen to know what the Reds are doing before they do it."

"Good plan," said Devon. "You know about my Shackleton crashing, I take it?"

"I sure do, and that's just one example of the intrusions reported over the last three months."

"We are not 100 per cent sure that a Soviet agent tinkered with the aircraft, but the chances are that's the case. There's much more security these days at St Mawgan."

"That makes sense, buddy. The recon work you do is vital to our naval operations."

Val turned to Hannah. "Are you still working for our Israeli friends, Hannah?"

"Yes, rather like yourselves, we've had an instruction from Tel Aviv to increase our capabilities, but with Mossad we are more interested in the intentions of Arab countries towards the State of Israel and anti-Jewish movements generally." Hannah stood up. "Shall we take our drinks through to the dining room?" She was hoping they would not spend the entire weekend talking about work. "And we can decide what we do tomorrow. The weather forecast is good so we could go to a lovely beach we know, near Fowey."

"That would be great. I'd love to have a swim in the sea, and the boys will enjoy the beach," said Val.

***

The weather turned out to be warmer than expected, with hardly a breeze. The tide was almost fully in when they arrived at Readymoney Cove, but it soon retreated, exposing the sand and shingle beach. In the rocks on the far side Devon and Casey helped the two young boys search for crabs with their nets. Val and Hannah swam for a short time; the sea water was still cold in the early part of the year.

"There was quite a crowd of Americans here waiting for the go signal on D-Day," Casey said to Devon. "And lots of troop carriers hidden up the Fowey estuary. We saw a hell of a lot of ships as we flew over. Boy, what a day that was."

"That was before my time. I wasn't sent to an active Spitfire squadron until May 1945. Hence my being sent to Malaya, then Singapore and eventually Hong Kong."

"Hey, you know what? I've never heard how you got to meet Val back then," said Casey. "Hong Kong, wasn't it?"

"Yes, she was with the governor's office and I was with 28 Squadron – at least, that was her cover. She was still with MI6 there. We met at a formal dinner given for the squadron when we arrived. Hannah was working for the Israeli secret service, seeking to recruit Spitfire pilots for the Israeli air force. That all fell apart, but that's how we got to know each other. There were Egyptian agents operating there at the same time. Things got nasty, there was a shoot-out, but Val and her team intervened and saved Hannah."

Casey nodded. "And then there was Henry Fitzjohn, of course. Val told me about his mischiefs. He seems to have done very well for himself since he resigned from the RAF and returned from Hong Kong."

Devon laughed. "Yes, hasn't he? Minister of Defence – and you never met more of a rogue. And he's the main shareholder in a successful airline."

"He did a good job for us in East Germany in 1952. Got us all out of trouble," said Casey.

"He did indeed," said Devon. "Haven't seen him since – thankfully, as he's always trying it on with Hannah. And talking of which, here they are."

Val and Hannah had bought ice creams for everyone at the shop at the back of the beach. The long, warm afternoon would soon come to an end.

THIRTY-ONE

Vanessa Paget enjoyed her shopping trips to Harrods, especially since all her purchases were charged to Stephen Walmsley's account. She wanted a new dress and shoes that would be suitable for dinner and dancing at the Café de Paris, the most fashionable venue in London. Stephen told her not to worry about the expense. Choose something elegant and enticing, he'd said, and Vanessa knew exactly what he meant by that: sexy and sensual. He also said she should visit the lingerie department as they had a new collection just in from France, and she should stop by the Chanel consultants for advice on the latest make-up and perfumes.

The doorman carried all her bags to a taxi. On the ride back to her flat, she admitted to herself that she was now excited about her date with Yuri. She felt she was entitled to mix with stars, royalty and the aristocracy: after all, she was a West End theatre performer and the daughter of a knighted land owner. If Yuri was going to take her to the Café de Paris then she liked him all the more.

Vanessa had managed to dismiss Stephen's rudeness and his

insistence on her dating Yuri as due to tiredness and pressure in his extensive business empire. He was clearly a very successful architect, or how would he be able to afford her flat, the presents, the shopping trips?

As he liked to do when she was going to meet one of his friends, Walmsley came round to the flat an hour before she was due to leave.

"Stephen, it's very kind of you to come and make sure I have everything, and thanks for bringing the champagne." She would limit herself to two glasses; she didn't want to be tipsy over dinner.

"A pleasure, my dear. You are, after all, my favourite girlfriend. And you look fabulous in that dress – an excellent choice."

His compliments had more of an enlivening effect on her than the champagne. "I've been told that pink suits my complexion," Vanessa said as she twirled in front of Walmsley. The satin dress was off the shoulder, full length, with a split up to her thigh.

"Indeed it does. Now, I hope you enjoy your evening, and the rest of the weekend. I will phone you on Monday and you can tell me all about it."

***

Andreyevich had sent a chauffeur-driven Mercedes, one of the embassy's best cars, to collect Vanessa at 9p.m. He was waiting in the lobby of the Café de Paris and greeted her with a bow and a kiss to her hand. Very much the suave Russian.

"Oh, you are such a gentleman, Yuri."

"It's lovely to see you, Vanessa. Let us have a cocktail at the bar before we go to our table."

"Thank you, that would be nice." Vanessa was enthralled by the cathedral-like vaulted dining and dance floor area, the red and blue lighting and the slow rotation of the mirror ball. She revelled in the sophisticated styling, the elegant guests and the soft sound of jazz music. "Lovely place. Is this a regular haunt for you?"

"Not really. I have only been here a few times, but I wanted to ensure we have the best London can offer tonight."

"Well, it's certainly… Oh, thank you." A waiter placed a menu in front of Vanessa.

"I can order for us both, if you wish?"

"Would you, Yuri? That's so nice of you."

Andreyevich looked up at the waiter. "Bring us Beluga caviar to start, then the filet mignon. Peach Melba to follow."

After dinner, the lights were lowered and Matt Martin, in his soft baritone voice, performed a range of beautifully romantic ballads. Yuri and Vanessa danced and sipped champagne into the early hours, until Vanessa asked if she could be taken home. While she was powdering her nose, Andreyevich spoke to the concierge. The embassy car soon arrived outside. In the quiet streets of London, it only took fifteen minutes to reach York Terrace.

"Would you like to come in for coffee, Yuri, and a brandy maybe?"

Andreyevich said something in Russian. The chauffeur got out to open Vanessa's door for her while he got out the other side. The chauffeur quickly returned to his seat and drove off. Andreyevich took Vanessa's hand and led her to the lift.

THIRTY-TWO

After a second mission to drop special agents off from the *Leninski* onto the barren north-east coast of England, Captain Fyodor Yegorov was glad to find that his orders were to return to probing the British maritime defences. In the senior officers' quarters in Murmansk, there was increasing speculation about the potential for war against the Western alliance. The Soviet premier, Nikita Khrushchev, had made speeches vilifying NATO and denouncing it as an alliance binding together enemies of Russia who were building their forces, ready to attack. It was the duty of all Soviet military personnel, and those from all communist countries, to be ready to protect Mother Russia.

Captain Yegorov was a committed believer in socialism, and deep inside he feared that the West would seek to destroy the Soviet Union. That would be a tragedy and a disaster. He also fretted about his family, who lived on the outskirts of Murmansk, which was known to be a target for enemy forces. He would not fail to do his utmost to protect the homeland.

As the submarine was being prepared to sail on a mission in the Atlantic, Yegorov briefed six senior officers in his cabin. He warned them that all missions from here on must be treated as rehearsals for war; there would be no tolerance of sub-standard performance. He was pleased that all the officers nodded in agreement. Some muttered "*Da, da*" while others looked grimly determined. They were all experienced submariners and knew how vital their role would be in the event of war.

Yegorov gave the order to sail. At first they took a route west towards Iceland, then south, skirting the west coast of Ireland and heading out to the Atlantic. They had been ordered to patrol the approaches to the English Channel. In less than a day and a half they were on station. They detected several merchant ships and performed simulated attacks: everything that would have been expected in a real scenario, but without firing the torpedoes.

On the third day of the mission, they advanced towards Falmouth at the tip of Cornwall. Soviet spies had reported that the fishing and merchant ship repair yards were being used as a base for Royal Navy minesweepers. Yegorov wanted to find evidence of navy movements, and within hours he had found and tracked two ships.

All sightings and practice attacks were reported in the boat's log. That evening the same senior officers gathered for a briefing with the captain. There was an air of jubilation as they discussed the day's work. If they really had been on a war footing they would have created havoc among the British shipping, effectively closing off large parts of the Channel. Yegorov congratulated his men and ordered a small box of salted salmon from his personal supply to be opened before dinner, but as the sub did not carry alcohol he was unable to offer a toast to the Soviet Union with a glass of vodka. He disclosed that their next operation would commence in two days: observing British and American naval exercises.

***

Adam Devon arrived at St Mawgan soon after daybreak and went directly to the flight briefing room. Within minutes the rest of the crew arrived, together with the intelligence officers. Pilot James Braithwaite copied the flight plan, weather forecast, fuel requirements and radio frequencies onto his knee pad. It was his final training flight: if all went well, he would be signed off as a qualified maritime reconnaissance pilot. Devon was pleased to see that his usual worried look had been replaced by a more confident demeanour. Devon also spoke to the captain of the lead aircraft of the three that would be flying the mission, Flight Lieutenant Herriot, as well as the crew for a flight of three more aircraft: they were scheduled to patrol the Irish Sea.

Flight Sergeant Tim Harper, the adjutant to the station commanding officer, called the pilots and technicians to attention. Wing Commander Louis Valentine stepped onto a low platform in front of an air chart showing the southern half of the UK. "Gentlemen, you all have your flight plans and orders for the day ahead. You will be patrolling the Channel from Plymouth, west and north to the Irish coast. Exercise Sea Anvil is under way. It consists of manoeuvres involving fifteen Royal Navy ships and six from the US Navy. Our job is to watch for Russians. We can expect a surface and submarine presence. Any questions?"

"Do we have any reports from Kinloss on sightings, sir?" asked Pilot Robin McCoy.

"Good question, McCoy, but a bad answer, I'm afraid. No, there have been no reports of submarines, but we know they will be out there somewhere. Anything else?" Valentine looked around the room. "Very well, you are dismissed. Fly safely, gentlemen."

***

Captain Yegorov stood over the charts of the eastern Atlantic with his navigation officer, Lieutenant Andre Saranov. He ran his index finger over the chart from right to left then tapped a depth marker on the chart. "We will position ourselves here, Saranov, 120 nautical miles south of Land's End. Initiate silent running and advise me when we are five miles from the objective."

"Yes, sir."

"And send Lieutenant Panchenko to me."

"Certainly, sir." Saranov moved quickly to the bulkhead leading to the reactor and turbine rooms, where he would find the submarine's head of engineering.

The lieutenant presented himself to the captain and saluted. He had taken no time to change his working tunic; the smell of steam and hot grease wafted across the bridge and combined with sweat, made more pungent as Panchenko's nerves were rattled whenever he was called to speak to the captain.

"Report, please, Panchenko."

The head of enginering stood erect and looked straight ahead. "Reactor operating in normal temperature range, Captain. Turbines running at three-quarters power. Oxygen levels satisfactory. I can confirm that the electrical circuits are within required range, sir!"

"At ease, Lieutenant. You said that the electrical circuits are within range: do you expect them to be out of operating tolerances?"

Panchenko looked at his commanding officer. "No, sir!" The young officer coughed gently, conscious that reporting any problem that insinuated poor Soviet engineering design or a criticism of Russian shipbuilding skills would not be tolerated. "Sometimes they can overheat, so we have to reduce electrical usage." He didn't add that there had been short periods of power surges outside of tolerances – any more and the system would become dangerously overheated.

"Understood, Panchenko. Report any problems immediately they become apparent. Carry on."

As Panchenko saluted and left the captain's cabin, he gasped. His anxiety had got the better of him. He knew the electrics were running hot, but he was confident he could reduce the power demand and cool the circuits.

The whole crew had a strong sense of purpose in this mission: war had not been declared, but the assignment to simulate an attack on the enemy fleet was as close as they would get. They all knew it was vital to avoid the anti-submarine tactics of the RAF and Royal Navy. The danger levels were increasing, day by day.

As for Yegorov, his personal orders from the admiral of the northern fleet included not to be photographed, not to be captured, and not to fire upon any NATO ships.

***

A junior member of the crew spotted the smoke issuing from an electrical panel serving the turbine compartment on the *Leninski*. Panchenko and two men went to investigate. They quickly shut some circuits down in an effort to reduce electrical demand, but suddenly the automatic gas extinguishers detected the smoke and flooded the room with carbon dioxide, but only partly smothering the flames. The fire alarm sounded on the bridge and the order was given to seal off the compartment. An engineering officer on the lower deck called over the intercom to say that men were still in the compartment: did they have permission to rescue them? This could expose the whole submarine to fire. The reply came back from the command centre: no. Close off the compartment.

Panchenko and two other men suddenly saw the door close. They grasped the door wheel, desperately trying to open it whilst choking in the thickening smoke and CO_2. They banged their hands frantically on the door, their screams ending as they collapsed, suffocated.

Captain Yegorov ordered the bridge officers to stand by to surface, but he wanted to know more about the damage before giving the order. A confident young seaman, one of Panchenko's engineers, approached the captain and said without hesitation, "Sir, we have a problem with the electrical generator. A power surge caused the fire, and we couldn't cool the generator with the usage we currently have. We need to switch off as many systems as possible, including the air recirculation plant. Sir, with respect, I believe we should surface to cool the system and vent the turbine compartment."

Captain Yegorov nodded. "Lieutenant, emergency surface. You speak very plainly, sailor. What's your name?"

"Engineer Second Class Doski, sir."

"Well, Doski, I agree with you, and from here on you are an engineer first class. Now get back to your station and find a way to reduce the demand for power. And prevent any further uncontrolled surges. We will only stay on the surface for a short time."

Doski saluted and dashed away.

The risk every submariner fears: a fire on board. Yegorov looked at the chart. At least they were a good distance from the British and US ships, but he knew there could be submarines and aircraft hunting for them in close range. He ordered a rapid ventilation of the boat, cutting all power to the galley and half power to the accommodation areas. As they broke the surface, the door to the conning tower was opened and the officer of the watch, Lieutenant Saranov, went up followed by a four-man team, with four machine guns to be fixed on the mounts on the deck. They were followed by four others with ammunition boxes – standard precautions when surfacing. Two other crew members held long-range binoculars to their eyes and scanned the sea.

***

The three-aircraft flight of Shackletons detailed to patrol the south-west approaches separated. Keeping five miles between them reduced the risk of a collision and meant they could search the widest area. The technicians in the rear of Devon's aircraft studied their screens and listened intently on their headphones. The navigator spoke over the intercom: "Navy flotilla on a heading of 280 degrees, skipper, range eight miles."

"Roger, 280," said Devon, then spoke to Braithwaite, who was flying the aircraft. "Head directly west, James, we'll pass to the south of the ships."

Devon looked out of the window and saw the exercise in progress: two frigates in a tight turn, churning streams of white foam behind them, and a couple of miles ahead the American ships sailing directly towards them. A cat-and-mouse routine designed to test the ability of the hunter to pursue its prey – and the hunted to keep out of trouble. Other ships were manoeuvring to join the battle, with white flares being fired and black smokescreens flowing across the water behind them. Devon was mesmerised for several minutes as he watched more than twenty warships criss-crossing the sea at full speed.

The Shackleton flew on towards the far side of the patrol zone. After five minutes of steady flying, the intercom crackled, then there was silence for a second.

"…Donaldson to skipper, contact, sir! Heading 170 degrees, three miles, likely submarine."

Devon gave the order for Braithwaite to head south and descend to 1,000 feet. Within minutes they were overhead the area where they thought the submarine was, but they could see nothing.

"Any contact, Donaldson?" asked Devon.

"The contact is intermittent, sir. It was probably a sub on the surface, and it's dived."

"Roger. Keep watching, everyone."

Very soon Donaldson was back on the intercom. "I have it, sir! Approximately two miles, 120 degrees. A ship or surfaced sub."

All eyes turned to the south-east as Braithwaite gently banked the aircraft over to the left. After a few minutes an observer called over the intercom, "Target sighted directly ahead!"

"Break to port, Braithwaite," said Devon, then transmitted, "Technicians stand by to photograph."

The Shackleton descended to 500 feet and flew a curving pass 200 yards from the submarine. It then banked for another pass almost overhead. As the plane approached the sub, flashes of orange light could be seen on the deck and tracer bullet trails headed for the aircraft. Braithwaite shouted, "Bloody hell, they're shooting at us!"

***

"We must bring them down, Saranov," said Captain Yegorov. "They will have photographed the boat. We must not let them take any images back to their base. When they approach again, fire all four guns and make sure you hit them."

As the aircraft levelled out for its photographic pass overhead, the two nearest gunners started firing, far too early to be effective. The red stream of the tracer bullets now alerted Braithwaite to the line of fire, giving him a split second to bank away and avoid being hit. The second pair of guns had time to send a couple of rounds through one of the aircraft's tail fins, but without causing serious damage.

***

"Bloody cheek! I'm not going to be shot at without returning fire." Devon was livid, his fighter pilot background suddenly to the fore. In peacetime the Russians had no right to fire at them, but the Shackleton's crew did have the right to defend themselves. He now had no doubt that their crash had been caused by Russian infiltrators. He wouldn't let another attack on him go unanswered.

"Bring her round again, Braithwaite," said Devon. "And line up for a direct attack. Let's see how they like our cannon shells."

"But, sir, they will have a line on us now."

"Don't worry, Braithwaite. With any luck we can damage the sub and prevent it from diving. Bring her round – steep turn!"

The aircraft had forward-facing cannons in the nose. Devon was looking to make a low-level attack where the shells could damage the hull of the submarine. Braithwaite quickly got the message and flew in low and fast. Devon called over the intercom for one of the aeronautic engineers to come forward into the nose of the aircraft to fire the Shackleton's guns. As they lined up to attack, the cannons pounded their shells away, water spouts erupted in the sea ahead of the sub. As the aircraft climbed away, half a dozen of its shells hit the sub's conning tower. One of the men with the binoculars fell back, grabbing his shoulder.

Devon looked back from the side window to see the crew of the submarine piling down the hatch. Within seconds they were all below and the hatch was secured. The submarine was taking up speed, and Devon was acutely disappointed when he saw it dive.

THIRTY-THREE

After a sumptuous meal at the Amalfi restaurant in Victoria, Henry Fitzjohn eased himself into the seat of the taxi and slipped his arm around Amanda Spencer's slim waist. She rested her head on Fitzjohn's shoulder. "A wonderful night out, Henry. Thank you."

"A pleasure, my love. We can have a nightcap back at the Thames Vista. I've got some news for you."

Amanda knew better than to ask what the news was at that moment. The saying 'careless talk costs lives' was as relevant now as during the war.

In their suite, Amanda poured herself a brandy and a whisky and ice for Fitzjohn and switched on the coffee percolator. "Well, Henry, what is the exciting news you have for me?"

"Something of a coup on my part, I think you could say." Fitzjohn walked around the room with one hand behind his back, like a university lecturer, a whisky glass in his other hand. "I've convinced Mac that we should go ahead with the pre-emptive strike. At last Admiral Temple is on board and is now getting all the chiefs of staff in line. And this is the big one, something that will put us in the history books: we're going to make a rapid strike on the Eastern bloc, blitzkrieg style. I've drawn up the overall plan, Temple is looking at the detail. Spring 1962, less than two years away, we will hit them hard and fast on all fronts from the north to the south."

Amanda almost choked on her brandy. She managed to say, "That's crazy, Henry! They'll respond with nuclear weapons and we'll all get wiped out!"

"No, we won't. Temple has assured me that we can shoot down Soviet missiles before they get near the West. And they might not even resort to their nuclear arsenal, since they know we will do the same. The war will be done and dusted in a couple of weeks and we will be rid of the Soviet danger forever."

"Henry, please don't try to sell this idea as being a simple jaunt for our forces into the East, with the war being over in a few months. These things never work like that. You're a military man – you know that's true. And I'm surprised Temple and Macmillan have gone along with the idea."

"I've made it clear to Admiral Temple that he must do as he is ordered. Old Mac is happy to leave it to me; he has virtually handed over command to me. And it won't be long until he steps down and I am appointed prime minister. That's something you want, isn't it?"

"Ah, now I see where you're going with this. Rid the country of the communist threat and become the people's hero." There was cynicism in Amanda's voice.

"That's it exactly, and let's not forget, the Russians have become more belligerent recently under Khrushchev. If Mac doesn't agree to my plans, he might find he is the sitting prime minister at the time the UK is overrun by the Red Army. Not a very appealing prospect to have such a blight on your name in the history books. But with my plans he gets the credit for supporting the actions that will bring enduring peace to the free world."

Amanda's eyes widened as what Fitzjohn was saying became clear to her. "And after everything has died down, you become prime minister, and I get to take up residence in 10 Downing Street as your special advisor. Excellent!" She stood up, wrapped her arms around Fitzjohn and pressed her body against his.

"Well, er, yes, there is that." Fitzjohn kissed Amanda briefly then went over to the drinks tray and poured another whisky. Amanda waved away the brandy bottle. He had not really thought about having her as his consort, even though she had made clear her desire for them to be seen at Number 10 as a couple. A partner, or indeed a wife, would be nice to have, and clearly an asset, but that was something he could sort out at a later date. In the meantime, he would take advantage of Amanda's pleasing desire for him.

THIRTY-FOUR

On reflection, Vanessa was pleased to be offered a part in *Oliver*, even though it was in the chorus, but more than this she was excited that she would also be an understudy to Nancy. She felt it was jolly unfair that she should only be the understudy for the role, but she was confident that her career would take off this year in a big way.

After her bath she took a nap and then laid her clothes out on her bed. She couldn't decide which dress to wear; Henry had complimented her when she wore the black velvet cocktail dress, perhaps because of its high hemline, but on the other hand she had never worn the green satin strapless dress when she had been out with him.

She went through to the lounge, opened the drinks cabinet, poured herself a small dry sherry and looked at her watch. She had another hour to wait, so she sat down and read *The Stage* for a while before returning to her bedroom to dress and do her make-up and hair. Vanessa was looking forward to seeing Henry again: she felt a genuine connection with him – much more than with her other men friends. It would soon be her twenty-first birthday and after that it would be such fun to settle down and marry, if she could find the right person. Henry was a bit older than her, but he might very well be the one. She decided that this evening she would invite Henry down to Point Saturn for a weekend; it would allow them get to know each other better.

"My dear, you're looking wonderful. Absolutely stunning dress!" Fitzjohn kissed her on each cheek as he stepped into her flat, looking fitter than usual in his black dinner suit, white shirt and a new slimline bow tie.

Vanessa had chosen well. Green suited her and the slim cut of the dress flattered her figure. "Where are we off to tonight, Henry?"

"There's a lovely little Chinese restaurant near Shaftesbury Avenue, and then I thought we could take a table at the Blue Angel. Dance the night away and all that. How does that sound?"

"Perfect. I'll get my coat."

Vanessa returned wearing an oyster-white mink jacket. "Very nice. New, is it?" said Fitzjohn.

"Yes, I suppose it is," replied Vanessa, with all the nonchalance she could muster, and carefully buttoned it to hide the Russian fur house label.

"From a friend, no doubt – the wonderful Stephen Walmsley."

"Actually, no, a different friend."

"Oh yes, and what's his name?"

"Never you mind, Henry, it's not important. Now are we going out or not?"

"Of course. The taxi is waiting downstairs." Fitzjohn shrugged off the pang of irritation he felt when he was reminded that Vanessa had many male admirers willing to bestow luxuries upon her. He looked forward to an amusing evening that he hoped would go on into the night. He had no appointments in the morning, just a defence planning meeting in the afternoon.

After their meal, Vanessa returned from the ladies' room, sparkling in newly applied cherry-red lipstick and a dusting of face powder. "Henry, can I ask you something?" she said.

Fitzjohn was intrigued. "Certainly, what is it, my dear?"

"Are you able to take time off from your busy job in the government?"

"Occasionally, of course, depends on what's going on. And you know I'm extremely busy at the moment."

"Yes, I do, with all that war planning you do."

"Hush, girl! That's all confidential. Please never mention it in public, or to anyone else."

"Oh yes, terribly sorry. Silly of me to forget. But you see, I wanted to ask you if you would like to take a weekend away from London and come down to my family house in Cornwall. It's in a place called Readymoney Cove, near Fowey. With the weather being so nice, we could have a lovely time on the beach, swimming in the sea, that sort of thing."

Fitzjohn gave it no more than a second's thought. "Splendid idea! When exactly do you have in mind?"

"Any time, really, but perhaps the weekend after next? Certainly before the school holidays start and the place gets overrun with children."

"Let me think. Yes, that should be fine. I will telephone my chap at the airline tomorrow – I'm due to go down to Gatwick next week, but I can put that off. You'd better let me have the address and phone number of the house. I can drive us down to Cornwall if you wish."

"Oh yes, Henry, would you? It would make a nice change from the train."

When the couple arrived at the Blue Angel they were shown to a secluded table away from the stage, where they could talk. Fitzjohn ordered champagne then took Vanessa's hand and led her to the dance floor. He was becoming very fond of her and had no compunction about having a relationship with her behind Amanda's back. Amanda was, after all, amusing herself with Sir Robert Darnell. But he resolved not to get overly involved with Vanessa: he knew she was free with her affections and favours. He might be just another man to her.

Back at Vanessa's flat, she made coffee and poured a brandy and a Talisker that she had bought herself, knowing it was Fitzjohn's favourite. But they didn't linger long in the living room; soon Fitzjohn was stepping into the bathroom and running the shower in the spacious cubicle. It was Vanessa's favourite place to be. They removed their clothes quickly and held each other under the steaming water. Nothing was rushed. They spoke gently to each other, and as their closeness fuelled their passion, Vanessa said, "Oh, Henry, I love you."

***

In the morning Fitzjohn used Vanessa's telephone to call Richard Dunn at Granta Airlines' offices in Gatwick. "Good morning, old chap. How are things down there?"

"Morning, Henry. All in good shape, I believe. Bookings are going well – the tourist numbers going to Majorca, Spain and Italy are booming. The Viscounts are full on every trip. And the air taxi side is also doing well as business in Europe is picking up. How are things with you?"

"I'm fine, thanks, Dickie – the Westminster madhouse is keeping me busy. Pleased to hear Granta is going great guns. Small favour, if I may. As you know, I was planning to come down to Gatwick next week, but I need to put that off, if there is nothing urgent requiring my attention?"

"No, I can't say there is, but it's always good to see you and for you to see the operation."

"Excellent. Now, if anyone should enquire about my presence from Thursday, I want you to confirm that I'm in Gatwick but can't come to the phone, cannot be found at the moment, something like that."

"I think I understand, Henry. You're lying low for a few days, is that right?"

"Exactly, old boy, all in the cause of national security, you know. But I will call in over the weekend. In an emergency you can call Sian – she will have details of where I will be."

"That's fine, Henry. Have a good time, whatever you're up to. Don't leave it too long before you come and see us."

"I won't. Thanks again, Dickie."

The day before going to Cornwall, Fitzjohn called Sian into his office and explained he was going to be away on business for the weekend, gave her the Point Saturn address and phone number, and told her not to divulge his whereabouts to anyone – short of a national emergency, or if Richard Dunn called. She should certainly not give the details to Amanda Spencer.

THIRTY-FIVE

After Devon's radio call to the mission leader, Flight Lieutenant Herriot, advising him of the attack by the submarine, Devon was instructed to fly his aircraft back to St Mawgan immediately to check the extent of the damage. The patrol would be completed by the two remaining aircraft. Devon had handed back control to Braithwaite and told him to follow the navigator's instructions on headings to fly to make a standard approach to land. Despite all the excitement, Devon had a job to do, and that was to pass Braithwaite as a qualified Shackleton reconnaissance pilot. He had every intention of doing that; the man had performed well, even under stress.

Climbing down the stepladder out of the aircraft, Devon heard his name called. A military policeman and an intelligence officer wanted him to jump into their Land Rover. He was driven at top speed to the station commander's office. When he arrived he was not surprised to see half a dozen senior officers, including the head of intelligence, lined up in the office. He knew he was going to face some serious questioning for the attack on the submarine without direct orders.

Wing Commander Valentine spoke first. "Devon, you will be required to complete a full written report on completion of this meeting, but first I would like you to summarise the action this morning."

"Certainly, sir, but before I do that, could I ring my wife, please? News of action spreads fast, and I'd like to reassure—"

"No, you damn well can't, Devon." It was the intelligence officer, Perryman, almost shouting. "You're lucky you're not on an immediate charge for exceeding your authority in attacking the Russian sub. Just get on with the briefing, man."

Valentine nodded and Devon continued. "In simple terms, gentlemen, I was acting in defence of the aircraft. We were photographing the submarine, in accordance with standard practice, and without warning they opened fire on us with their deck-mounted machine guns. I ordered the pilot to go around again and had the gunner fire at the conning tower. I do not believe we caused serious damage, as the sub quickly dived."

"And how does that amount to self-defence?" said Perryman. "You could have simply flown away from the danger."

Devon took a moment to breathe; he needed to keep calm to avoid antagonising the senior officers present. "Well, sir, the way I see it is that if any British servicemen are fired upon, they have the right to return that fire." Devon looked squarely at Perryman and added more forcefully, "I'm not in the business of running away at the first opportunity."

"You could have endangered your aircraft."

"More danger comes from allowing the enemy to think they can fire upon us with impunity. For our safety and that of other aircraft, I believe it was appropriate to counter-attack. The Russians must know that if they attack us, all hell will fall upon them."

Perryman pointed an index finger directly at Devon's face. "Your personal opinions are not relevant here, Devon. You're not a dashing

Spitfire pilot anymore, and you must operate within your specific orders. This may well blow up into a major political incident."

"Well, sir, I wouldn't be sorry if it did. It's about time the government took a stand with the Soviets. And as I say, I feel all servicemen and women would object to being fired at and would shoot back at any aggressor. And for the record, I have never been ordered not to engage with a hostile force when on reconnaissance operations."

Perryman was becoming visibly annoyed with Devon. Wing Commander Valentine stepped in. "Gentlemen, I think the best way forward is to ask Devon to write out his action report in full and we can take it from there. We will also have the photographs later today, which will be very interesting. In the meantime, back to work, everyone."

Perryman wasn't satisfied. "But, sir, surely Devon is suspended pending an inquiry?"

"Certainly not. We need every aircraft and qualified pilot during these naval exercises. Any disciplinary measures may or may not come from the ministry. Thank you, everyone. Devon, stay behind please."

After the men had trooped out, with Perryman last to leave, glaring at Devon, Valentine took off his cap. "Take a seat, Adam. You've created quite a commotion today, but well done. I agree with you. If the Reds think they can just shoot at us and we will walk away, they should think again."

"Thank you, sir. Louis. I'll get on and write that report now."

"Right. Let me see it first before you give it to intelligence," said Valentine.

"Of course. One other thing you should know."

"Go ahead."

"I think the submarine was the *Leninski*."

"I see. So they're sending their best and newest submarine to test us out. No wonder they fired at you."

THIRTY-SIX

As the submarine passed to the west of Fastnet Rock, it surfaced again. Captain Yegorov supervised the burial-at-sea ritual for the three men lost in the fire: "Heroes of the Soviet Union," he announced, barely able to take his eyes away from the cannon-shell damage to the conning tower wall. He then ordered a rapid dive and a direct return to Murmansk and the debriefing meeting.

At the meeting, the four-man committee listened without any signs of emotion. Yegorov gave his reasons for opening fire: the need for secrecy over the *Leninski* was paramount and he knew that would always be a good defence. What caused the electrical fire would be investigated; this was not the time for anyone to doubt Soviet engineering. And Yegorov was confident that an inquiry would find that Lieutenant Panchenko was guilty of mismanaging the systems.

At the end of the briefing, Yegorov was dismissed. He was told to stay on the submarine and not to return to his home. There was to be no discussion about the incident; all matters related to the *Leninski* were top secret.

Later that day, in his cabin on board the submarine, the duty officer came in with the damage report. Yegorov was disappointed to read that, as well as damage to the conning tower, the outer skin of the hull had been peppered by shell fragments and required repairs. This meant the submarine would be out of service for two weeks. A potentially shameful blot on his service record, which had been impeccable to date.

***

Henry Fitzjohn's secretary, Sian Shelby, telephoned him at his flat at 11p.m. Not so unusual, as she worked all hours herself, keeping the Minister of Defence's workload under control. The prime minister wanted him to attend an emergency meeting first thing in the morning, she said. Papers were being sent to him by despatch rider to read ahead of the meeting.

"What's all the fuss about, Sian?" Fitzjohn grumbled.

"Not over the phone, Mr Fitzjohn."

"Oh, alright. Don't suppose I have any choice about the meeting, do I? I was hoping to go down to Gatwick tomorrow."

"It would not be wise to miss the appointment, in my opinion. Your car will be outside your apartment block at eight forty. The meeting's at nine."

"How very precise, Miss Shelby. I'll be there."

In fact, Lionel arrived at half past eight, in case his passenger decided he wanted to get to Downing Street early. And it was as well that he did, as Fitzjohn appeared just a minute later. "Stop off at the Kardomah in Piccadilly, would you, Lionel? I need to get a quick bacon roll and coffee. I'm sure we have time."

When they arrived at Downing Street, two other Jaguars were just pulling away. Fitzjohn could see several men in impressive military uniforms entering Number 10. The papers he had read were short summaries of the issue: a potential political controversy with the Russians over an incident in the Channel. No big deal. But he would have the opportunity to press the chiefs of staff on their preparation for the invasion.

Macmillan was already in the Cabinet room with his senior secretary, Sir Oliver Colton, by his side. When Mac took his seat, everyone else also sat down. Fitzjohn found himself at the far end of the table, his view of the PM obscured by a row of uniformed officers and a couple of grey-suited ministry strategists.

"Good morning, gentlemen," said Macmillan. "Thank you for coming here at short notice. I trust you have all read the briefing note in regard to the incident in the Channel. The question for us today is what, if anything, we do about it. Sir Thomas, sum up the situation, please."

Sir Thomas Park, Air Chief Marshal and head of the air staff, leant forward. Fitzjohn was intrigued. He liked Park: a former fighter pilot, a man of action and a skilful orator.

"The Soviet submarine was undoubtedly observing Exercise Sea Anvil when it surfaced. We can only speculate about why the captain surfaced at that time and place, but it's almost certain the sub had some sort of technical problem. As the maritime reconnaissance Shackleton circled to take photographs of the sub, the Russians fired upon the aircraft – fortunately, without causing any significant damage. The Shackleton fired back, hitting the submarine but not causing enough damage to prevent her diving – and good show to the pilot for having a go, in my view. What you have not seen are the photographs. We now have them, and they confirm the sub was the *Leninski*." Park paused and glanced around the table, to a mixture of looks of consternation and ironic smiles.

He went on. "We can call in the Russian ambassador and give him a rollocking if you wish, Prime Minister, but I'm fairly sure they would say that the sub captain thought he was under attack and fired to warn off the Shackleton."

"Do that in any event, Air Marshal – usual protocols in these circumstances. But, gentlemen, the more serious issue is that this type of incident is what our Minister of Defence has expressed deep concern about – the increasing belligerence of the Soviets, reaching a point where they fire upon one of our aircraft. Wars have been declared for less. It is not beyond the realms of possibility that the submarine surfaced with the aim of being attacked and giving the Soviets an excuse to respond in a major way. Another reason why we are building our plans for an action of our own in the next year or two."

Fitzjohn nodded sagely but remained quiet, Macmillan was doing his talking for him. He was pleased that the incident gave fuel to his argument. He noticed Park had a file with many photographs, reports and statements. He leant across and asked to have a look at the file. While Macmillan garnered the views of the senior military and civil service personnel present, Fitzjohn flicked through the papers. He found the pilot's report on the action.

"*What the hell?*" He gasped. All conversation in the room stopped. He looked around the table. "Apologies, gentlemen, something just caught my eye." Quietly, he said, "Adam Devon – well, I'll be a son of a…"

THIRTY-SEVEN

May 1960

Fitzjohn's chauffeur dropped off the Jaguar on Wednesday evening at the flat in Kensington, fully fuelled and checked, ready for Fitzjohn to drive to the West Country first thing in the morning. He would call at York Terrace to pick up Vanessa and they'd be on their way out of London by 9a.m. There was little traffic on the A30, and less when they took up the A303. Fitzjohn noticed Vanessa falling asleep as he pressed on westwards. As they approached Stonehenge he pulled into a roadside café – no more than a large shed on the edge of Salisbury Plain with a view of the monument, only three hundred yards away.

A slim middle-aged woman in a checked pinafore took their order: coffee and sausage sandwiches. There was no one else in the café.

"This really is so exciting, Henry. A whole weekend ahead of us, and there are so many things I want to show you in Fowey and Readymoney Cove. There will only be the two of us plus Rufus and Cook. Daddy will be away down at Redruth, visiting the tin mines and farms we own. The house is right by the beach so we can swim and sunbathe if the weather's good enough. And we can walk into town for a drink, and perhaps take a boat out."

"Excellent, I'm very much looking forward to it." Fitzjohn eyed Vanessa, dressed in a cream trouser suit and blue shirt, hair brushed back in a ponytail. She wore a little foundation and pale-pink lipstick. He thought she was more attractive like this, in her understated, relaxed clothes, than she was in glamorous evening dresses. She was only twenty but had the poise and manner of someone more experienced. He wondered for a fleeting moment how she would look stepping across the threshold of 10 Downing Street, as the wife of the new prime minister.

"What?" she said, conscious of his gaze.

Fitzjohn snapped out of his reverie. "Oh, sorry, my love, just thinking how wonderful you look today."

Vanessa took his hands in hers. "And you do too. You are such a handsome man, Henry." They kissed gently, then sat back quickly when the woman brought their breakfasts, a knowing smile on her face.

***

After dinner that first evening at Point Saturn they took their coffee and brandy into the drawing room and watched the last of the sun's rays illuminate Polruan, across the estuary.

"Polruan the sunny side, Fowey the money side," said Vanessa with a smile.

"Is that the way it is? Looks a lovely village from here."

"It is – much quieter, despite the big ship repair yard. There are lots of ex-workers' cottages, now largely holiday lets. Have a look at the houses in Fowey and Readymoney when we go out – there are some lovely properties. There's Fowey Harbour Hotel and Place House: it's like a castle right in the town. You'll be impressed."

"I shall look forward to the guided tour, my dear."

Vanessa put on a record and they danced until tiredness following a long day overcame them and they took the stairs to Vanessa's bedroom. They enjoyed each other slowly and quietly: their lovemaking reflected the silence that surrounded the house, apart from the low murmur of the sea on the rocks below.

***

The early morning sun shining into the front windows brightened the bedroom by 7a.m. Fitzjohn felt the urge to get up and head down to the beach for a swim while Vanessa slept on. He found his shorts and a towel and went downstairs. Rufus was opening the French doors to the garden. "Mornin', Mr Henry. Lovely day it is too."

"Good morning, Rufus, it is indeed. I thought I might have a little swim before breakfast."

"Yes, sir, come through 'ere." He pointed to the garden. "Them steps on the right lead straight down to the beach. Take care, sir, the tide's on its way out."

"Will do, thanks."

Fitzjohn was inspired. The bay was a perfectly secluded spot, with the waves from the English Channel reduced to a low swell as they entered the cove. He left his towel on the black rocks at the bottom of the steps and waded into the sea up to his waist before diving forward. The rush of cold water electrified him. A naturally strong swimmer, he swam out to the headland below Point Saturn. Across the bay he could now see the grey granite blocks of St Catherine's Castle and beyond that the open sea. He swam towards the right-hand side of the cove and looked up at the curious layering of enormous, fractured rock sections that had formed small horizontal caves. Then he felt himself being carried out to sea into the Fowey estuary and realised Rufus was right:

the tide was taking him away from the beach. Time to swim back, have a shower and check on Vanessa. With any luck, he thought, she would still be in bed.

After they had had breakfast, Fitzjohn sat down with the newspapers, just delivered from Bodmin. He skimmed over speculation in the editorial on the risks of war, studied the cricket scores, and was pleased to see Jack Brabham's Formula One win. He started the crossword but was restless and suggested to Vanessa that they go for that walk into town and hire a boat.

"Lovely idea, Henry, I'll get my cardigan. And my sun hat – it looks like being a lovely day again."

On the walk along Esplanade, Fitzjohn asked her, "Did you grow up here?"

"Yes, but I was sent away to boarding school in Truro. After that I went to performing arts school in Bristol. I love Cornwall, but as an actress my future is in London."

"Yes, I see. I've never asked, do you have any brothers or sisters?"

"No, it's just me and Daddy now. Mother passed away three years ago. And there's my uncle Tristan and two cousins who live near Padstow. Uncle has properties of his own in the town: a hotel and a couple of apartment blocks on the harbour front."

Fitzjohn realised that Sir Bartley Paget's wealth would at some point pass to Vanessa. Quite an estate: Point Saturn, tin mines, farmland and properties. Her husband would marry a beautiful, charming young lady, but would also become very wealthy indeed in time. He knew he had to settle down at some point and had thought it might be with Amanda, despite the age difference. But Vanessa would be a real catch. He already knew that he was falling in love with her, and she was fun and smart, without being overintelligent. But it troubled him that she was so free with her affections back in London. He wondered if she would be happy with married life.

"The boat hire is along here, Henry."

They turned the corner and dropped downhill from Esplanade into Town Quay, passing a group sitting with their morning coffee outside the King of Prussia pub. Fitzjohn saw a huge industrial ship coming slowly up the river and was intrigued. "Hell, I wouldn't have expected a ship like that to come up here," he said.

"It's going to the china clay works. The harbour is very deep, which allows ships to come right in. She will probably stay at the docks along the river until tonight. She'll be out of sight in a few minutes."

Fitzjohn paid the boatman sufficient for the whole afternoon and the couple trod carefully down the harbour steps and into the open rowing boat. Ten minutes later they were passing Bodinnick and heading upstream into the calm waters of the Fowey river. Fitzjohn was enjoying the effort of rowing, finding time to admire Vanessa's long, slim legs as she lay back on the cushions at the front of the boat. They travelled almost as far as Golant before turning back, curving round into Pont Pil, weaving through the moored yachts and slowing a couple of times to enjoy the views. Fitzjohn found a small secluded bay, with overhanging trees – an ideal place to take a rest from rowing and enjoy some physical activities with Vanessa in his arms. Then, as the afternoon passed, Fitzjohn saw Vanessa yawn. He headed back to Fowey.

***

They sat on the front terrace of the King of Prussia for a glass of cider before going back to the house. Vanessa had her cardigan over her shoulders. The temperature had dropped and the air was crystal clear.

"It will be a beautiful night – moonlight and stars, very romantic," said Fitzjohn.

"Henry, you are a dear. After dinner, perhaps we can have our coffee outside this evening?"

As soon as they arrived back at the house, Rufus passed a slip of paper to Fitzjohn. "The telephone is in the office, off the main hall."

Without hesitating, Fitzjohn excused himself and found the telephone, closed the door behind him and dialled the number. Sian Shelby answered immediately.

"What's up, Sian?" said Fitzjohn.

"Macmillan wants to talk to you first thing in the morning. I told his secretary where you are, so he agreed that if you can't be there in person, then you can call on a secure phone. If you can get to a military base with a high-security connection, that would work, and save you from having to come back from Cornwall overnight."

"Any idea what it's about? No, scrub that, you couldn't tell me on this line even if you did know."

"Indeed," said Sian. "One option is for you to drive over to RAF St Mawgan or the naval base at Plymouth. Which do you prefer?"

"St Mawgan is much nearer. Will you call them and tell them I'm coming?"

"Yes, straight away. I'll call you back to confirm."

"Splendid, thank you, Miss Shelby. I wouldn't fancy a drive back tonight."

"My pleasure."

In less than an hour, Fitzjohn had been authorised to attend the airbase and to ask for Wing Commander Valentine.

THIRTY-EIGHT

While Henry Fitzjohn was spending the afternoon caressing Vanessa, with the rowing boat tied up against an old jetty out of sight of other river users, Stephen Walmsley was insisting that he pick up the tab for lunch with Yuri Andreyevich. But his dining companion would hear nothing of it. He had invited Walmsley to the Dorchester, and he would have the bill added to his account.

Walmsley pleaded with him but knew when to accede graciously.

"It is the least I can do to thank you for the introduction to Vanessa, Stephen. She is a most charming girl."

"My pleasure, Yuri. I'm glad you are getting on so well with her. She is a favourite of mine but remember, I have other lady friends I can introduce to you, one or two somewhat younger, should that amuse you—"

"Ah, no. Vanessa is very attractive and good company. I would like to see more of her, if possible. I have made the bank transfer to the account you nominated to cover your expenses in the introduction, and more is readily available, should she and I continue our relationship."

"I'm certain that can be arranged."

"I hope so. I asked her to dinner this weekend but she is away at her family home in Cornwall, she told me."

"So I gather, but that is a rare event," said Walmsley.

"You do, of course, have a very wide and important set of clients in your business. Being an architect, I mean. But tell me, Stephen, is Vanessa in a relationship with anyone else in your circle of friends, or elsewhere?"

"She may well be. I couldn't say," Walmsley lied; he knew she had several boyfriends. "Would it trouble you if she was?"

"Not at all. It's just that sometimes it is valuable to me, and to my comrades, to gain insights into British affairs through people who are high up in society. This is how we develop our cultural appreciation of the countries we have relations with, you understand. But the embassy insists on strict confidentiality about the business and pleasurable activities of its staff, and so some enquiries have been made about Vanessa."

Walmsley felt affronted. He didn't appreciate his young ladies being observed or spied upon. But such was the price of doing business with foreigners, especially the diplomatic types, who were always scared of their own shadows.

"And are you happy that she mixes with all the right people?" asked Walmsley.

"Certainly. Your friends and contacts are the most engaging people. Financiers, medical men, landowners and politicians."

Now Walmsley was flattered. He was intensely proud of the network of clients, of all types, that he had built up over the years. "Yes, indeed. The best of London society, I think you'll find."

"And who would you say are her best friends, her special friends, so to speak?"

"I have no doubt she has many close friends from her work in the theatre, but that's her business, nothing to do with me. She has occasionally had dinner with my good friend Andrew Marston, Lord Valley's youngest son, then there's Arnie Colhoun, the West Indies cricketer, lovely chap. She has met Henry Fitzjohn and Simon Braedon – both have senior government positions, of course. She is a popular girl but not tied to anyone in particular."

"That's good to know. I wonder if she is free next weekend. It would be such a pleasure to have dinner."

"Vanessa will be at a cocktail party I'm hosting at my flat on Saturday. Why not come along, have a few drinks, then take things from there? I'll tell her – I mean, ask her – to make herself available. Come along any time from 9p.m. Here's the address."

"That would be excellent, thank you. I accept your very kind invitation."

THIRTY-NINE

Flight Sergeant Harper escorted Fitzjohn through to a room in the intelligence office, with a desk and the telephone ready. An armed guard from the military police stood outside while Fitzjohn made the call. He had sensed the tension on the airbase the moment he reported to the security gate: they were clearly conscious of the risk of unwanted visitors and were on high alert. Fitzjohn looked out across the airfield at a group of six Avro Shackletons about to depart on patrol. He wondered if Devon was in one of the aircraft and felt a degree of envy: he would love to be flying today, rather than being tied up in the tangles of politics.

The operator put the call through.

"Thank you for calling in, Henry. I have Admiral Temple here with me as well as Colton, my secretary."

"Good morning, gentlemen."

"The reason for having this urgent discussion is that we have been receiving reports from the secret services on Russian intrusions at our military sites, both in the UK and Germany. Admiral Temple here believes they are assessing our strengths. Admiral…"

"Indeed, Prime Minister. I'm very concerned to advise you, Mr Fitzjohn, about a break-in at the headquarters of the British Army of the Rhine. Papers were taken, but we do not believe they were significant. But this means that our planned increase in the capabilities of all of our services will become more and more difficult to hide. Certainly we can explain the mobilisation of the army in West Germany as being part of joint NATO exercises, but sooner or later the Soviets will realise we are building a much greater force than before. Recruitment into the armed forces has been scaled up, orders have been placed with aircraft manufacturers, shipyards and munitions firms, and these cannot be hidden for long."

Fitzjohn interrupted. "What are you saying? That we should pull back from our plans?"

"No, not necessarily. It's the timing we should look at. We have planned to attack in the next two years, perhaps spring 1962, but I think we should consider bringing this forward to early summer of next year – almost a year earlier. We are drawing up the logistical plan and will have this ready for your approval later this week, when you return to London."

"Understood. I look forward to seeing the plans. And by the way," said Fitzjohn, "I hope you now see my point about the threat and the need to get going with our own attack plans. When will they be ready?"

"At a high level, Thursday next week."

"Very well, I will see you then."

***

Vanessa was bored. It wasn't the best way to spend Saturday morning, sitting around, waiting for Henry to return. Luckily she had brought her lines from *Oliver* with her, so she decided to rehearse in the garden, dancing and singing her part, much to the amusement of Rufus and Cook in the house and the gardener on the lower lawn.

As soon as Fitzjohn got back they took the steps down to the beach, both dressed to swim. Vanessa was also a strong swimmer, and they crossed the cove and climbed onto the sun-warmed rocks below the castle.

"Why did you have to go to St Mawgan this morning, Henry?" asked Vanessa.

"I had to make a phone call. Just government business."

"But you're not in the RAF. And why didn't you use the house phone?"

"It had to be a secure phone – I was calling 10 Downing Street."

"Really! How exciting. I know you are very important and will make sure there is no war – it worries me sometimes."

"Well, I can't guarantee there will not be a war in the next year or so."

"Against the Germans again?"

Fitzjohn laughed. "Ha, no, they're on our side now, mostly. No, it's the Russians we have to be worried about. You have probably heard on the news the concerns about communism spreading – the Russians might invade West Germany or even more countries."

"Like they did in Hungary three or four years ago? They just invaded like stormtroopers."

Fitzjohn was impressed by Vanessa's awareness of Russia's military suppression of the so-called uprising against communism in Hungary in 1956. "Yes, something like that, but on a much bigger scale. They could try to take over all of Europe."

"I'm really frightened by the Russians, but our army would stop them, wouldn't they?"

"They would certainly try." Fitzjohn was fired up by Vanessa's simple comments: if she could concern herself with the Russian threat, then he would do his best to protect her and the country itself. "But my plan is to take the initiative: attack the Russians before they can do anything. The news I received today is that we must accelerate our plans, not wait two years, more like one. Within a year the communist threat will be gone."

"Can you really do that?"

"Well, not me personally; I will only direct the action to be taken by our armed forces. But look here, my dear, all this is strictly secret – I shouldn't be burdening you with this information. You're not to discuss my job with anyone else."

"I know that, Henry. I haven't even told Daddy what an important boyfriend I have." The sun had turned round the headland and cast a shadow over them. "Now, shall we swim up to the beach and sit in the sun?"

"Yes, good idea. And we can have a cup of tea and some cakes from the shop. Jackie knows me – I will owe her the money. Let's race!" Vanessa slipped off the rock into the sea and with an expert front crawl headed for the beach. Fitzjohn laughed and followed her in, but found he had little chance of catching her. He ran after her up the beach and wrapped his arms around her waist. He didn't take any notice of the two women sitting on a picnic blanket with their young children.

FORTY

"Are you alright, Hannah?" asked Diane.

"Oh, yes of course. Sorry, just had a bit of a shock, that's all. Shall we take Alice and Michael down to the water and have a paddle?"

"A'right, my luvver, if you feels OK. You've gone white. What has shocked you?"

"Well, it's silly, really. I've just seen someone from my past, not someone I wanted to see again." Hannah turned to look up the beach. "You see that couple outside the shop? The man is Henry Fitzjohn. I knew him years ago when I lived in Hong Kong, and then we met again in 1952 in England. Not a nice man at all."

"Henry Fitzjohn – isn't he an MP?"

"Yes, he is quite high up in the government. Minister of Defence. He was in the RAF when I first met him in 1949. He was in the same Spitfire squadron as Adam in Singapore and Hong Kong. Unfortunately, and this was before Adam and I got together, Fitzjohn tried to have his way with me. I had to fight him off. I was really frightened of him, and that fear comes back to me from time to time, especially if I see him. Such a coincidence he is here in Cornwall."

"That's awful, Hannah. Did he, I mean, were you able to…"

"Yes, I managed to get him out of my house. He had been making advances towards me but I had to see him as part of my job. This was with the bank I worked for." Hannah left out her role at the time with the Israeli security services. "I was terrified that he might return and try to attack me again. That never happened, but the dread I felt has never quite left me. I hope he doesn't see me here."

"That girl he's with, that's Vanessa Paget. She used to live in the big house up there, Point Saturn, before going up country. She comes back with friends every now and then. Otherwise it's just her old dad in the house with the staff. He owns tin mines and land."

"She looks very pretty, and they seem to be getting on very well. Trust Henry to be among the money."

"That he might be, but times are tough for them mine owners and I wouldn't bank on the Pagets having the money they used to. Tin prices have dropped, and the cost of running the mines has gone up. Some mines are closing. Old Paget may have other income to help him along, but it's more likely that Vanessa would gain from being part of Fitzjohn's family rather than the other way round."

"Poor Henry!" They both laughed.

"Come on, let's have that paddle and forget about old times," said Diane.

***

Hannah struggled to shake off the upset she'd felt at seeing Henry again. When Devon returned home that evening she served dinner as soon as he arrived. After they had cleared things away, she decided to speak to him about Fitzjohn.

"Adam, I went to Readymoney Cove today with Diane and the children."

"Excellent, did you all have a good time?"

"Mostly, but something happened." Hannah stared at the floor.

"Tell me, darling, what was it?"

"I saw Henry Fitzjohn on the beach. He was with a girl from the big house on the cliff, Point Saturn. They swam for a while then came up the beach to the shop."

"I know the house. Did he speak to you?"

"No, he didn't see me, thankfully."

"Well, I guess he was just visiting. On holiday, perhaps?"

"Yes, that's what Diane thought. All I know is that I want to steer clear of him. I won't stop going to Readymoney; I'll just keep an eye out. It was a bit of a shock."

"I can imagine. You never know who you are going to bump into. But make sure if you see him again, you keep well away."

"I certainly will. Now, how has your day been?"

"The usual: a recon flight out to Wolf Rock and down to the Channel Islands. Unfortunately, nothing spotted."

"Don't you mean fortunately? Isn't it a good thing if there are no Russian submarines prowling about?"

"Well, I suppose so. But our concern is that they are out there and we can't see them. The one piece of luck we've had, with the sub that surfaced, was probably down to it having mechanical trouble."

"Have you heard any more about that? Are they going to reprimand you or fire you from pilot training?"

"No, no, they won't do that. It's all settled. With the backing I have from Louis – I mean, Wing Commander Valentine – I think my job is safe."

"That's good. Are you still enjoying your role and living down here?"

"Yes, absolutely, no question. It's great to see the pilots progress and get signed off for operational work. Heaven knows we are in desperate need of maritime pilots. In fact, all members of the aircrew are needed, with the heightened threat we're facing. And you're happy living in Cornwall, aren't you?"

"Oh yes, I love it here. Despite what happened at the beach today."

FORTY-ONE

It was unusual for Amanda Spencer to arrive at Henry Fitzjohn's parliamentary office without calling first. Sian could see the determination in her face and didn't even try to stop her as she walked straight through and into Fitzjohn's office.

"Amanda! How nice to see you," said Fitzjohn. "I didn't know you were calling in."

"Very nice to see you too, Henry." She shut the door behind her and sat down. "I've been trying to get in touch with you for nearly a week."

"Yes, sorry. Sian did give me a couple of messages, but I've been so busy here in the ministry and down at Gatwick with Granta. Is there something I can help you with?"

Amanda was peeved. She wasn't used to being ignored, and now he was talking to her like a member of his constituency asking for a favour. At the back of her mind was always the awareness that Fitzjohn could tire of her and find other things, and other girls, to entertain him. Could this be happening now? With his promotion to ministerial level and the possibility of him being appointed prime minister, this was the wrong time for their special relationship to end. She still wanted to achieve her life's ambition and enter 10 Downing Street.

"No, it would just be nice to see you, perhaps have dinner."

"Exactly my thoughts, my love. This Saturday evening, if you are free?"

"I think I am."

"Splendid. Will you be staying at the Thames Vista? I could pick you up at, say, eight thirty?"

"That would be lovely, thank you." Amanda stood up to leave. "I will see you then. Before I go, tell me, where were you over the weekend?"

"I was with Dickie Dunn at Granta. He's doing a great job with the airline but needed me to meet a couple of new pilots and go through the business plan. And I'm pleased to say, everything is going extremely well."

"Good to hear, Henry. See you on Saturday," said Amanda, smiling happily as she left the office.

Fitzjohn sat back in his chair, musing. He had to admit that he did not want to upset Amanda. He cared for her hugely and knew that if he wasn't careful he could lose her. He thought little of her relationship with Sir Robert Darnell; he couldn't see that Darnell would divorce the beautiful Anthea for Amanda. But Amanda had her pride, and Fitzjohn knew she would readily distance herself from him if he treated her uncaringly, and that included being in a relationship with someone else.

He reflected that he had had a wonderful time with Vanessa in Cornwall and wanted to see her again as soon as he could, but not at the expense of shunning Amanda. Fortunately, Vanessa had said she was unavailable this coming weekend – she was going to a party with some of her acting friends – so he decided to make a special effort for Amanda.

He called out to Sian.

"Yes, Henry?" she said, walking into his office. "Coffee, tea?"

"Coffee, please, and could you make a booking for this Saturday for two at the Ritz for nine and then a table at Imogen's."

"Got it. That's dinner at the Ritz, dancing at Imogen's. She's a lucky girl."

"You think?"

"Sure. How many girls get taken out to such lovely places? I don't."

Fitzjohn looked at Sian. She was tall and slim, with fair hair that Fitzjohn thought could be called strawberry blonde, a broad smile, a fine straight nose and blue eyes. Altogether a great-looking woman and as sharp as ninepence. But he knew nothing about her private life. He resolved to ask her one day if she had a husband or partner.

"By the way, thanks for looking after things last weekend," said Fitzjohn.

"My pleasure. I hope you enjoyed your visit to Readymoney Cove."

"How did you know – oh yes, the phone call."

***

Fitzjohn was pleased that the evening had gone so well. A lovely meal and dancing at Imogen's to a new four-piece band of mop-haired youths playing what the compère called the Liverpool sound. Back at the Thames Vista, they enjoyed a quick romp in bed then, exhausted, they both fell into a deep sleep.

In the morning Fitzjohn awoke refreshed and without a trace of a hangover and thought about taking Amanda out to lunch. He picked up the phone and ordered coffee and toast from room service and asked them to make a reservation at Claridge's for 2p.m. When Amanda surfaced, he poured her coffee. "Good morning, my lovely. How are you?"

"I'm fine, thanks. It was such fun last night, wasn't it?"

"Splendid indeed. And if you have the energy, I have booked lunch today at Claridge's."

"I say, I am honoured; you're throwing your money around."

"Only the best for a special girl…"

Amanda sat up in bed to drink her coffee, dishevelled, half asleep and with no make-up. She looked wonderful, thought Fitzjohn.

"Do you have a busy week ahead, Henry?"

"Yes, a meeting tomorrow with Admiral Temple at the ministry offices. He wants to give me the full details of the new plans. Then we will go to Macmillan on Thursday for his approval. Not that I need it, but you have to go through the motions, don't you?"

"What do you mean, new plans?"

"Oh, right, I haven't told you, have I? There's huge concern that the Russians are increasing their intelligence-gathering efforts and will see our increases in manpower, equipment, etc. There's a strong feeling they are brewing up to carry out their own pre-emptive strike on West Germany before we hit them. So, Temple has said we need to get a move on. He and the chiefs of staff think we should go next spring instead of the year after. I'm all for this, but he will have to convince me that we have all our ducks in a row before I agree. Or before Old Mac and the Cabinet agree."

Amanda felt a bolt of anguish in the pit of her stomach. All-out war was getting nearer, becoming a realistic probability, rather than a theoretical idea. "This is quite a radical development, Henry – why haven't you told me about this?"

"Do I need to, my dear? I have no wish to burden you with all the tactical aspects. I've spent many hours planning out the detail; it just wouldn't happen if I wasn't driving it. I'm sure you're not all that interested."

"Not in the detail, but if the war is successful and you become prime minister then I'm very much interested."

"Don't worry. If I get the job, war or otherwise, you're coming with me."

"Is that a promise?"

"Certainly is, sealed with a kiss. Now come here…"

FORTY-TWO

When Amanda arrived home early on Sunday evening she called Sir Robert Darnell. She knew that as Chairman of the Conservative Party he would be coming into central office for his Monday briefing and it was a chance to meet him. In fact, she wanted to have dinner with him; it had been some time since they had spent time together. He had mentioned that Anthea would be away for two nights as usual, visiting her elderly parents in Marlborough. Amanda was open-minded about the prospect of an overnight stay, but business always came first: she wanted to find out what Darnell knew about Fitzjohn's military plans, and whether he supported them.

Amanda arrived at the Capri, the small, select Italian restaurant in Soho favoured by Darnell, especially as no one else in his political circle frequented the place, to find he was already there, a bottle of champagne opened, perhaps half consumed.

"Ah, Amanda, lovely to see you. And you're looking stunning as usual." They kissed.

"Are we celebrating something, Robert?"

"No, just the pleasure of your company, my love. I haven't seen you for a couple of weeks and have missed you terribly, so I thought we should treat ourselves."

Amanda wasn't sure why she felt uncomfortable. He was always a lovely host, and she cared for him hugely, but he was overdoing it. Something didn't feel right; he was trying too hard. The waiter poured Amanda a glass of champagne and topped up Darnell's.

"Well, cheers, here's to us," said Darnell.

"Yes, happy days. Mmm, very nice." Amanda replaced her glass. "I wanted to have a quick chat about Henry."

"Fine young man, doing a great job."

Amanda wasn't sure if he was being sarcastic or serious. "Glad you think so."

"I do indeed. Very popular with the grassroots party members, good with the press. Mac loves him. Altogether a great recommendation of yours, Amanda."

He was indeed being serious, and the glowing report was more than she could have hoped for. "That's good to hear. But there is one particular point I wanted to raise."

"Are we going to talk about Fitzjohn all evening, my dear?" Darnell reached out across the table and took Amanda's hand in his, his eyelids half closed and his lips in a lewd grin. "You know how much I've been looking forward to seeing you again, and I know you desire to be with me. So why don't we get the meal out of the way and make the most of the evening back at my flat? Seeing you reminds me of the favour you owe me for my support of Fitzjohn."

Amanda shivered. Yes, she enjoyed Darnell's company, and he was sensitive and kind in bed. But she wasn't going to be used as his side piece forever based on his backing of Henry. She had believed that he cared for her and their relationship was a romance, not a business deal. She didn't feel she owed him anything. Tonight she was seeing a different side to Darnell: he was an unpleasant, lecherous drunk, trying to take what he thought was due to him. She felt used, a touch disgusted with herself. She knew she would never go back to his flat again.

"There's no hurry, Robert, and this champagne is too good to rush. Let's look at the menu, shall we?"

"Very well, if you insist."

The waiter hovered nearby. Darnell sent him away to get another bottle of champagne.

"What is it you wanted to ask?" said Darnell.

"It's about Henry's military plans, those he has agreed with Macmillan." She kept her voice low. "And the question of the Russians."

Darnell looked at her searchingly but said nothing as the waiter returned to take their order.

"Right, I see why you're interested. Yes, there are some quite extreme plans being considered."

"A pre-emptive strike on East Germany and elsewhere? Does the Cabinet support this plan?" asked Amanda.

"Yes, I would say so. Certainly there has been no dissension. The threat from the East is growing all the time, and most believe there's a good chance the Russians will invade West Germany. Mac is an old campaigner himself, you know: had an excellent Great War, wounded on the Somme, and all that. No wonder he supports Fitzjohn's gung-ho approach."

"I see, so the country is going to war in less than a year, is that what you're saying?"

"I'm not predicting anything, but if it is left to Fitzjohn, there's a good chance that might happen."

Amanda was satisfied. Henry had told her the essentials of the plan, and she was happy that he had been truthful. Of course, if the war should come about, or even without a war, in the next few years he would be one of the most influential members of government and in a good position to be a future prime minister.

"Thank you, Robert. The spaghetti Bolognese was excellent – how was your raviolo?"

"Very nice, thank you. Now, perhaps a coffee and a grappa? And then I'll get the maître d' to call us a taxi."

"I will take my own taxi, Robert. Thank you for a lovely evening."

Sir Robert couldn't contain his surprise. "What do you mean?"

"I mean I'm going home."

"But you said you would spend the night with me at the flat!"

"No, I didn't. You simply mentioned that Anthea would be away for a few days."

"Oh, come on, old thing." Darnell took her hand again.

She pulled it away. "No, forget it, Robert."

Angry, and slurring, he said, "I suppose you prefer the delights of a younger man. I'm not good enough for you, am I? Something else you might like to know about your precious Fitzjohn. He's not the boy scout you think he is."

Amanda was tired; she wanted to go home. "What are you talking about, Robert?"

"A very good friend of mine told me that he's associated with Stephen Walmsley and his entourage. Seems Fitzjohn has a very close relationship with one of Walmsley's lady friends."

Amanda felt the jolt in her stomach and knew it could mean only one thing – a high-class society hooker. "Are you sure?"

"Certain. It has been brought to the attention of the security services. We like to keep our senior politicians safe. But since he is doing nothing illegal, I'm willing to let sleeping dogs lie, if you understand me."

"If you're lying…"

"Why should I? Make your own enquiries, ask Henry how he is getting on with the lovely Vanessa Paget. I hear they have really hit it off. They're often seen together in the most exclusive joints. She's brunette, well shaped, only twenty. Just right for a man of Henry's standing." Darnell laughed and held up his wine glass. "Do you want to reconsider your plans for this evening?"

"Certainly not."

"Well, your good health. Goodnight, Amanda!" Sneering, he laughed again.

Amanda pulled the strap of her handbag over her shoulder, stood up and threw her napkin on the table. "And a good night to you too, Robert!"

FORTY-THREE

Stephen Walmsley had excelled. This time the party at his flat had all his best clients – or friends, as he called them – with the added benefit of three new debutantes. Some of the wealthiest property owners in London drank his champagne, danced to his exclusive and almost-well-known lady singer, and enjoyed the delights created by the cordon bleu chef in the kitchen. They all went home charmed by the evening, some of the men with a deb on their arm.

Walmsley had spent much of the party with Yuri Andreyevich and Vanessa. He wanted to make sure she was not distracted by anyone else and that she gave all her attention to Yuri. He was not disappointed in her; he had instructed her before the guests arrived that she should be attentive to his best client and enjoy his company to the full.

But while Vanessa was powdering her nose, Andreyevich took Walmsley to one side. "Wonderful party, Stephen, but there is one guest I was expecting who is not here."

Walmsley was curious, and a touch piqued. He felt that anyone who was anyone was present: he had invited all his best friends and couldn't recall who out of the very few declines might interest Andreyevich. "Oh… may I ask who that person is, Yuri?"

"The English politician, Henry something. I don't remember. Tall, big man, with brown hair."

"Ah yes, that would be Henry Fitzjohn. I'm afraid he had a pressing engagement preventing his attendance tonight. Is he a friend of yours?" It was one of Walmsley's stock questions; he didn't believe for a moment that Fitzjohn and Andreyevich would have anything in common.

"No, no, it's just… No, it doesn't matter."

And from that comment, Walmsley understood that the Russian was playing games: he knew Fitzjohn's name well enough, and it mattered a lot to the Russian to know more about him.

Walmsley was delighted that he could give an impressive answer. "He's the British Minister of Defence – rather a long way from your interests on the cultural side, Yuri."

"That's true, but as you know, my job is to promote Russian music, the arts and culture. I wondered if Mr Fitzjohn was interested in music and theatre… or in any particular actresses."

"I believe he is very keen on the theatre, but as to whether he favours anyone special, I'm not sure."

"You see, it would not concern me if Vanessa was a good friend of Mr Fitzjohn's, offering him special favours – for example, inviting him to her father's house in Cornwall."

The comment took Walmsley aback. How did Andreyevich know this? These diplomats love their spying and intrigue, he thought, and realised that Andreyevich must be having Vanessa watched. Who else, including himself, had a raincoat-wearing agent following them around London? But as usual his thoughts went to the substantial sums Andreyevich was paying him for Vanessa's company.

It was time to stop bluffing.

Walmsley noticed that Vanessa had returned to the room and was talking to her old friend Penny Vaughan-Hart and a couple of Lord Valley's son's young friends. He decided to leave her; she would return to Yuri within a few minutes, he was confident.

"Well, I am aware she has dined with Fitzjohn and he spent the weekend at her family home. I'm not sure that will happen again, as the musical she is in starts soon."

"And Fitzjohn himself, what of him?"

"What can I say? He's single, ambitious, very much in favour with the prime minister, it seems."

"He has a lady partner, Miss Amanda Spencer. They seem to spend a lot of time together."

For the second time, Walmsley felt blindsided by the Russian. He realised that he knew little about Spencer and her relationship with Fitzjohn. But he wanted to show his support for Andreyevich. "I think the important thing, Yuri, is that Vanessa enjoys her time with you. She will soon lose interest in Fitzjohn, I'm confident of that."

"I dare say you are right. But please do not forbid her from maintaining a relationship with Mr Fitzjohn. I think it's important for the young lady that she mixes with the good and the great in society, wouldn't you agree?"

Walmsley wasn't sure he knew what Andreyevich was getting at, but he quickly replied, "Certainly, I like to think she is a well-rounded person."

Vanessa arrived back, with a bright smile on her face, and she fluttered her eyelashes at Yuri. Walmsley glowed inside. This was going to be a very lucrative pairing.

FORTY-FOUR

In an office in the Murmansk naval buildings, Captain 1st Rank Fyodor Yegorov sat with a group of senior naval officers and two KGB men – they were no longer sitting in the background – and pored over their plans for an exercise in the Atlantic. Yegorov was in his shore-based uniform. His dark-blue jacket had gold epaulettes and five gold buttons on the front. The KGB officers wore plain grey suits, white shirts and similar dark-grey ties, just as much a uniform as Yegorov's. Products of the newly formed secret service, the men had little military experience but carried the power of a state that would not tolerate any dissention or disagreement.

The target for their next operation was the British aircraft carrier HMS *Hermes*. Soviet spies on the ground in England had discovered that the ship would be sailing from Plymouth with an escort of three destroyers and four frigates. They were to link up with two further destroyers and four minesweepers from the French navy and undertake exercises in the Bay of Biscay. The battle group was supported by three British and two French submarines, which would be seeking out enemy submarines and shipping. The *Leninski's* task was to infiltrate the fleet and simulate a torpedo attack on the aircraft carrier.

Yegorov was inwardly pleased that again his boat had been selected for one of the most challenging and dangerous tasks. This was what the *Leninski* had been built for. He drew a line across the chart with a blue chinagraph pencil, taking the submarine on a curving track round Ireland and out to the eastern Atlantic Ocean and then south from Brest. The KGB men seemed satisfied with the plans. One almost smiled for a moment and assured Comrade Captain Yegorov that the successful completion of the mission would be well received at the highest level in the Kremlin. They did not outline the consequences of failure.

The *Leninski* was prepared for sailing and was ready to leave port in less than two days. This time there were no special forces operatives to carry; it was a training exercise for the submarine's crew, the officers and their weaponry. The now familiar journey past Iceland, skirting to the west of the Outer Hebrides and into the Atlantic, was uneventful. The captain called the senior officers to his cabin to plan the attack. It would be a classic exercise in cat and mouse: they would approach the fleet, stop and observe, advance again, get closer. When the captain was certain of having achieved a theoretic kill, he would withdraw and return to base, taking a different route home.

Thirty-six hours later the cameras fitted to the submarine's periscope recorded the image Yegorov had been hoping for: the *Hermes* in his torpedo sights. Yegorov felt like a wolf at a kill when he knew he could press the button to fire the torpedoes. But this was an exercise, successfully delivered. Two of his officers slapped him on the back, a familiarity that could result in a charge, but on this occasion Yegorov just smiled. In a real war, the aircraft carrier would at least have been damaged, but the captain knew it would most likely have been fatally wounded below the water line – either sunk or immobilised, unable to fly its aircraft. Job done.

Yegorov ordered the submarine slow-ahead to quietly disengage from the attack. He felt certain that the British and French submarines would have picked up soundings from the *Leninski*; he would now torment them with his tactics. He ordered a period of absolute stillness and silence resting as deep as he dared go, almost hiding in plain sight. No signs of discovery or sudden closing in by ships or aircraft on their position emerged from the submarines and reconnaissance aircraft protecting the fleet.

When the enemy battle group moved further away on their exercise, the captain directed the navigation officer to plot a route back to Murmansk. Comrade Captain Yegorov was exhilarated with what they had achieved on the mission and for once was looking forward to reporting the success to his admiral, and to the KGB men.

***

The same secret intelligence operation that had discovered the plan for the *Hermes* was also making headway with its spying on UK government ministers. Telephoto cameras captured pictures of ministers whenever they met their mistresses, and tiny spy cameras copied secret documents. The development of miniature microphones by the KGB had allowed them to listen in to discussions in the offices of several senior people. Fortunately MI5 was alert to the threat and regularly carried out sweeps of offices and homes of officials holding high office – and of course, the military chiefs.

But the KGB still preferred the old-fashioned spying techniques of following and watching targets, in some cases twenty-four hours a day. As Henry Fitzjohn occupied the most senior government position on defence, he was naturally afforded the honour of constant observation.

Fitzjohn's eagerness to enjoy the delights of London's West End gave the Soviets plenty of scope to monitor who he was with, and where.

The senior KGB staff laughed at the naivety of some of their targets, especially Fitzjohn. Only occasionally did he avoid the attentions of the less experienced Russian footpads and was able to dine and dance unaware of the rare temporary privacy he had achieved.

It was easy for the Russians to bribe politicians, captains of industry and civil service dandies who were discovered to be engaging in extramarital affairs.

But Fitzjohn had no wife at home, wondering where he was. The woman he spent most of his time with was his constituency campaign manager, a role the Russians barely understood. They dismissed any real wrongdoing by Fitzjohn, and some questioned whether he really had a romantic relationship with the woman in question – someone his mother's age.

When the KGB in Moscow decided to send Ilya Zarnov to London, they needed to create a cover story that would be foolproof. He was a retired Red Army colonel so could not be the military attaché, but he would pose as a specialist in Russian arts and culture, seeking to promote Russian music, theatre and historical events in Britain. His cover was easy to structure: he had a genuine interest in Russian ballet. His mother was a dancer, and he had spent time after his military service studying engineering, and perfecting his English, in the USA. The final part of his cover had been to change his name to Yuri Andreyevich.

Before Zarnov, or Andreyevich, left Moscow, he was given time to study files on the main players in British society. He was attracted to Stephen Walmsley, as previous agents working in London had seen his entourage at the best restaurants and nightclubs. Soon after arriving in England, Andreyevich ordered full-time surveillance on Walmsley and requested weekly reports on his activities. It soon became clear that Walmsley was operating a network of high-class prostitutes and making a substantial income from fees paid to him, as well as the money and gifts given to the women. His client list was exceptional, with the leaders of society enjoying the services he offered.

Andreyevich established himself on the London scene by concentrating on bringing the Moscow String Quartet to Cadogan Hall, with all expenses paid by the Russian government. His aim of being accepted as a worthy supporter of the arts was easily achieved, and after accepting invitations to concerts at the Royal Albert Hall and sponsoring a room of Russian art at the Summer Exhibition at the Royal Academy, it was time for Andreyevich to establish and exploit a relationship with Stephen Walmsley.

FORTY-FIVE

July 1960

Hannah had spent the morning going through reports from her network of contacts. One agent was certain there were anti-Jewish activists in his trade union at the electronics manufacturer where he worked. Hannah asked the agent to closely monitor activities and obtain details of the suspects, including their full names, dates of birth and addresses, for submission to Mossad's central intelligence team, based in London.

As well as reports from her British network, Hannah received summaries of Nazi-hunting work and subsequent arrests. More than fifteen years after the end of the war, the number found was diminishing steadily, but there was nevertheless a steady stream of Nazis who had taken on new names and identities. Some were even living in the UK, largely because they had married British women immediately after the war. Hannah wondered if the women knew the true details of their husbands' role in the war, as SS officers, concentration camp guards, or members of squads that rounded up Jews to be taken as forced labour. The time that had passed also meant that fewer Jewish people came forward with information about war criminals, but the source had not entirely dried up; occasionally in a street in France or Germany, a Nazi would be spotted by someone who had suffered at their hands. It was Mossad's aim to provide somewhere where survivors of the Holocaust could go and trust that the war criminal would be brought to justice.

But Hannah's work was taxing. It brought frequent reminders that her parents and wider family had been murdered in a concentration camp. She had a few letters from her parents, written when she had first arrived in England in 1938, and just one photograph of her parents with Hannah and her brother, which she had taken with her when she left Germany. She managed to control her bitterness at what happened to them and was as determined as ever to help Mossad identify antisemitic activities that, unchallenged, might lead to a new form of nationalism and hate towards Jews.

But when Diane Trenwith arrived at her door in the early afternoon with Alice, asking if she would like to go for a walk with the children, she was very glad of a break from her work. Diane suggested they take a short drive and park at Cardinham Woods, where they could walk the forest trails. They had done this before, so Hannah knew it would make for a lovely afternoon out. There was a tea hut there that looked like a NAAFI canteen, but it sold cakes and sweets so was a favourite with the children.

As Hannah parked the Land Rover she said, "This is a beautiful place, Diane. Thanks for coming to get Michael and me. I was deeply tied up with work and needed to get out of the house for a while."

"My pleasure, m'dear. It's great to get the children out and about in the first week of the summer holidays. You know you shouldn't work too hard – that's what your man's for, isn't it?"

Hannah laughed. "Yes, sometimes I think that, but overall I enjoy the work. Shall we start by walking up that hill? The forest opens up near the top and we might get some sun."

"Good idea, and it will tire the children!"

After nearly two hours of walking, often carrying Michael and Alice, they arrived back at the tea hut, thirsty and hungry. Diane insisted on buying the drinks, along with bright-yellow Cornish saffron cakes, cut in half and buttered.

"You know, Diane, I might think about giving up work. If we have another child, I really don't know how I would fit it all in."

Diane nudged Hannah's arm. "You planning to have more, my luvver?"

"I wouldn't say we're planning *not* to have more children, if you see what I mean…" Hannah looked thoughtful. "I have to be honest – it's not something that Adam and I talk about much. If it happens, it happens."

"Well then, how do you know what Adam really wants, if you don't ask him? My Terry and I want to have three, but little 'uns are expensive items. Dreckly he gets promotion to site manager we will get to it."

Hannah laughed again. "Diane, really! But it sounds like a good plan – what are you, only late twenties?"

"Twenty-seven, but Terry, he's coming up for thirty-five. Hope he still has it in him!"

On the drive back, the children fell asleep and Diane was quiet. Hannah reflected on their discussion and realised that she had been hoping for a second child. She resolved to talk to Adam. She needed to know his thoughts. Diane was right, she should ask him.

FORTY-SIX

With little free time due to rehearsals for *Oliver,* Vanessa had a genuine reason to resist Yuri Andreyevich's invitations to dinner. But Stephen Walmsley's call, late on a Friday, persuaded her to make herself available the following evening. Walmsley had booked them a table at the Loire restaurant, just off Piccadilly, for half past eight. He had asked Vanessa to wear her black satin cocktail dress and double strand of pearls; Andreyevich had said how much he liked her in this outfit.

She arrived a little early but was pleasantly surprised that Yuri was already there; so often her male companions kept her waiting until it suited them to arrive. When they ordered, Yuri displayed his usual self-assurance, ordering the most expensive items on the menu and wine list. She knew she had to show she was impressed by his good taste, and said so, but inwardly felt he was unsophisticated and simply wanted to show off his money.

After dinner, Yuri asked Vanessa if she wanted to join him on the small dance floor at the back of the restaurant, or go to a nightclub.

She was happy with the Loire: it was modern, tastefully decorated with murals of châteaux and paintings of vineyards and rolling green hills. She had never been to France but hoped one day to go shopping in Paris and visit the Folies Bergère.

The restaurant became quiet after eleven, and by midnight they were the last couple dancing. Vanessa invited Andreyevich back to her flat for the usual coffee and brandy. He didn't hesitate to accept. Vanessa liked the man well enough, and was physically attracted to him, but in the bedroom she felt herself wishing that they had the kind of relationship where they cared for each other, and took the time to please each other. She was warmed by the thought that the only man who gave her those things was Henry.

Neither of them were especially tired. Vanessa made more coffee and brought it into the bedroom, dropped her silk dressing gown to the floor and slipped between the sheets. Andreyevich was sitting up, running his hand through his thick black hair.

"You looked wonderful tonight, Vanessa, quite the English rose," he said. "And I would like to see more of you – two or three times a week."

"Thank you, Yuri, you're very kind. But you know I'm very busy at the theatre at the moment."

"So I understand. But you make time for your regular boyfriend, Mr Fitzjohn, don't you?"

"How do you know about Henry?"

"He is a high-profile man in British society, is he not? And you have been seen with him at various establishments in London, so it's no secret. Mr Walmsley even mentioned you had taken him to your family home in Cornwall, a pleasure I have not enjoyed."

Vanessa was annoyed. Walmsley acted like he owned her, bossing her around and telling her who to go out with. "Well, it's my business who I see, Yuri. Yes, I admit it, Henry is very special to me, as you are, of course, and he has a very important job in the government. I know you are high up in the Russian embassy with your cultural things, but Henry's job is much more important."

"What does he do that is so special?"

"He's the Minister of Defence – tells the army people what to do."

"Ha, really? I thought all the decisions were made by the military people. What could someone like Fitzjohn do? He's an office worker, at best."

Andreyevich's goading was already starting to work.

"Well, if you must know, he is trying to prevent you Russians from starting a war. I'm not supposed to talk about it, but you're a cultural person so you wouldn't understand. What you don't know is that we're all worried that the communists will try to take over the whole of Europe, including us. It's in all the newspapers, this Cold War business."

"It is a concern to us as well; no one wants a war. You're right, I'm not a military man, just someone who loves Russian art and music. But how can we trust the British and Americans not to attack us?"

"I'm sure Henry doesn't want a war either, but you have to admit that the only way to stop the communists is to have a strong army of our own, and if you don't watch out, we will be over in East Germany sending you all packing."

"And is that what Mr Fitzjohn is doing, building up an army in West Germany to attack us? Seems a foolish thing to do."

"Henry is not foolish, thank you, Yuri, he's a very intelligent man. He is the one driving the chiefs of… something, to be ready. He's the brains behind all the plans. He's telling the army people what they need to do. I'm sure they would do nothing if it wasn't for Henry. He's the best thing this country has had since Winston Churchill."

"I did not mean to insult your boyfriend, Vanessa, forgive me." Andreyevich used his most consolatory voice.

"Well, alright. But the important thing is that we all live in peace together, isn't it, Yuri? What good would a rotten war do us? What's the point in shooting at each other?"

"Yes, you are right. Such a bright, beautiful girl." Andreyevich slipped his hand around Vanessa's waist and rolled her towards him. She smiled, and her eyes gently closed. Why not? he thought. He might as well take advantage of the benefits of his work.

FORTY-SEVEN

Wing Commander Louis Valentine had made sure the whole air station was in immaculate condition, all aircraft neatly parked and every serviceman and woman's uniform clean and pressed. It was rare for the head of the air force to visit the station, but when he did, Valentine wanted him to go away with a high opinion of the operation. What had brought Air Chief Marshal Sir Thomas Park to St Mawgan was explained in a speech he delivered to the officers and senior service personnel in a hangar on the edge of the building complex.

His message was clear: the risk of war was at the highest level, and the role of maritime reconnaissance was key to the security of naval and commercial shipping. The base should expect the arrival of another squadron of fifteen Shackletons, called back from Singapore, within the month, along with experienced transport pilots to retrain on hunting enemy submarines and shipping. After the air chief marshal's aircraft departed St Mawgan back to Biggin Hill, Valentine called his senior officers and Devon into his office.

"Gentlemen, as you heard, the pressure is building. I'm perfectly satisfied that our role to date has been expertly delivered, but now we can expect longer and more frequent missions, possibly a greater number of Soviet intrusions and an increase in naval exercises, including with foreign navies. Devon, I would like you to draw up a list of the student pilots who are nearest to completing their training to be prioritised on operations in the next few days. Let's get as many through the course as we can, as soon as possible, to make room for the next intake."

Devon raised his hand. "I will do that, sir, but in regard to the squadron coming to us from Singapore, do we know if they are all qualified maritime pilots, or are there some students?"

"Good question." Valentine looked across to Flight Sergeant Harper, as he had the paperwork. "What do we have, Flight?"

"Thirty qualified pilots will be coming, sir, plus five still in conversion training. They do not intend to bring their instructor, so the burden will fall to Mr Devon."

"Very well. Please add these men to your training roster, Devon."

"Yes, sir."

Another pilot, Braithwaite, said, "Sir, if I may, are we authorised to fire upon any Soviet ships or subs we come across?"

"Only when it's self-defence – either of your own aircraft or one in your flight. Is that clear, everyone?"

A round of 'yes, sirs' rang round the office.

"No other questions? Very well, continue with your duties."

***

Yuri Andreyevich took his notes into the meeting room in the Russian embassy in the exclusive district of Kensington Palace Gardens in London. Two operational KGB agents were present, as well as the new head of intelligence, Comrade Colonel Valery Kupovsky, recently arrived from Moscow. He was an old friend of Andreyevich, but now his superior officer.

"Ilya, good to see you again, you're looking well. Enjoying life in London, no doubt?"

"Thank you, sir, I am indeed. And in London I am Yuri. As you know, my cover is cultural attaché, but today I have some information that you might find interesting on an important British politician. My team have been observing him for several months, and I have been able to build a contact that is close to him."

"So I understand, Ilya – Yuri, I should say. And have you made good progress with this contact?" The head of intelligence had been given a file before the meeting and had seen a picture of Vanessa and Andreyevich's own notes. Kupovsky raised his eyebrows and smiled a knowing smile. The two KGB officers did not smile; that familiarity would get them disliked, and possibly assigned to another country, probably in central Asia.

"I believe I have, sir. I understand that Mr Henry Fitzjohn, the Minister of Defence, is the prime mover in a potential attack on East Germany, maybe other bloc countries, and on from there towards the Soviet Union. My source is close to him. He is apparently in frequent meetings with the chiefs of staff and the prime minister. I believe Fitzjohn is planning the attack."

"I see, but do we have details of the plans the British have for such an extraordinary adventure?" Kupovsky's grin was cynical.

Andreyevich read the signs and knew he had to take care with his new boss when expressing his view that Fitzjohn was a threat to Russia and to communism, if he wasn't to seem paranoid in his interpretation of the intelligence. "It is of course just rumour, sir; we have no hard evidence of Fitzjohn's ambitions or the extent of his influence. But we can indeed be sure of his motivation to become the next prime minister."

Kupovsky laughed, as did the two KGB agents, more quietly, showing their support for their senior officer. "Yes, I understand he has high ambitions – not surprising for a man of his age who has had rapid advances in his career to date. But tell me, Yuri, what do you need from me to assist you in your work?"

Andreyevich was on the spot and in danger of being ridiculed by Kupovsky, something that could ruin his career. But his instincts told him that there was more than an element of truth in Vanessa's words. "Look at the increase in military build-up in the West. Ask who is driving this – is it Macmillan, is it Temple, the head of the military? Could it be Fitzjohn? And if it is, how can we obtain information about the plans? My source is good, but not detailed."

Kupovsky wasn't smiling now; he looked worried. "They are good questions, and we need answers to them. How do you suppose we might be able to do that?"

"Increased surveillance, sir, phone tapping, planting a mole in the minister's office, if we can."

"Please go ahead with these measures without delay. I'm not sure how successful you will be with the phone tap. There might be another way… I will discuss with Moscow and come back to you. In the meantime, I'm sure it would be beneficial if you maintained your… relationship, shall we say, with Miss Paget."

"Yes, sir, understood." Andreyevich looked at the two KGB agents, who were making notes in their standard-issue black leather notebooks. "We will put the field operations in place immediately."

"Excellent, Ilya. Now, where do you keep your best vodka? It's so hard to get a good drink in London."

***

The next morning Colonel Kupovsky's assistant set up a call to Moscow on the most secure connection to the Kremlin. He ensured a senior KGB official would be on the other end of the line: one who could make a decision or, more likely, bring together the right committee to consider the proposal. After Kupovsky explained he had a key proposition on national security, he was told to call again at 6p.m. UK time. Kupovsky's plan was radical, dangerous for relations between the United Kingdom and Russia, but enticing for the Soviet leadership. It could result in a significant advantage over the NATO alliance. Kupovsky would make sure his masters understood it was his idea, his vision that would lead to such a masterful coup. He was going to spell out the risk to the Soviets of this man, this warmonger who was driving the commanders of the British forces to take on a war footing. He would request permission to kill Fitzjohn, perhaps late at night as he left one of his favourite venues. His lively socialising would make him an easy target for an unfortunate random robbery and knifing on the streets of the capital. An inevitable occurrence, given the lawlessness of the United Kingdom.

But Kupovsky's plan was thrust back at him. His leaders in the Kremlin were impressed with the idea; it suited their practice with any enemy of the state. Poisonings, shootings, knifings were all stock in trade for the KGB.

But this time they wanted a different approach: they instructed Colonel Kupovsky to have Fitzjohn kidnapped.

FORTY-EIGHT

September 1960

After Yuri Andreyevich had been briefed by Comrade Valery Kupovsky, he set in motion the plan that he had agreed with his old friend and superior officer. It was good to be working together again, and he hoped the successful outcome of the mission would give his career a major boost.

Andreyevich telephoned Stephen Walmsley to ask to meet urgently – that evening, if possible. He wanted a favour and said he was willing to pay a generous fee for a small piece of architectural work. Walmsley knew this meant something to do with his social life and the girls he had introduced to Andreyevich and sensed he could gain another substantial reward for doing very little work.

Walmsley suggested they meet in the champagne bar in Harrods – a touch of luxury that was intended to show Andreyevich he had excellent style and taste. Walmsley arrived early for their six o'clock rendezvous, found two stools at the end of the bar and asked for a bottle of Mercier 48 to be brought up and placed in an ice bucket, ready to open when his guest arrived.

Andreyevich shook Walmsley's hand with both of his in an 'old pals' style that was just showmanship. After some jovial banter about the rich young women sitting at the little round tables in the bar, the waiter filled their glasses for a second time. Andreyevich turned serious. He asked after Vanessa's health: was she still very busy with the theatre? Was there a chance she could be available on Saturday evening?

Walmsley felt deflated; he had expected something more interesting and lucrative than fixing a night out with one of his girls. "Well, I would have to enquire, Yuri. As you hinted, she is very busy."

"Of course. If you could arrange this, I would be in your debt. And then I have another request that I would be most obliged if you would consider."

Now Walmsley's interest was roused. "I will try my best for you."

"I will have some special guests visiting from Russia next week: my wife and her parents and some friends. I shall be taking them to the best places in London: Imogen's, Café de Paris, perhaps here to Harrods. I would not want us to inadvertently bump into Vanessa – you can understand why, of course."

"Indeed I do."

"So, it would be most convenient if she takes a few days' holiday. Down to her father's house in Cornwall seems most appropriate. She has mentioned to me how much she enjoys being there. I know Mr Henry Fitzjohn is a good friend, so I suggest she invites him, so she won't be lonely."

"I couldn't possibly say if Mr Fitzjohn is free and keen to go, but I can ask her to enquire."

"No, Stephen, you must *insist* that Vanessa invites him, and she must ensure he accepts. This is important. I am concerned that she might decide not to go, or might come back early. This is unlikely to happen if she has a companion, don't you agree?"

Walmsley did. He thought Andreyevich was being very shrewd: he could readily see his point and understood exactly why he would not want to come across Vanessa while his wife was in town. "I see, Yuri, very astute thinking."

"I know how time-consuming this would be for you, so I would be very pleased to let you have this bank transfer if you could make this arrangement." Andreyevich smoothed out a slip of paper on the bar.

Walmsley almost gasped when he read the amount, but he was good at maintaining a poker face. Slowly, Walmsley said, "That should cover my time and expenses, Yuri. I will go to Vanessa's flat tomorrow evening and endeavour to persuade her of the benefits of a few days enjoying the sea air – and, of course, dinner with you on Saturday evening. I will call you in a couple of days."

***

Vanessa was feeling the strain of her dual roles at *Oliver*: her chorus work and learning the part of Nancy as an understudy. But she had an excellent singing voice and the natural ability to memorise her lines and learn choreography. She had been looking forward to a quiet evening in, something she tried to do at least once a week, when Walmsley phoned her to tell her he would be calling in. She made a simple omelette and put her coffee percolator on. At 8.30 there was a ring at the door.

"Come in, Stephen."

Walmsley kissed Vanessa on each cheek.

"Can I get you a drink?"

"Yes, thank you, a G&T would be good. Easy on the ice."

"How has your architect work been?"

"Very busy, delighted to say. Demand never stops."

There was a short silence. "What brings you here tonight, Stephen?"

"I had a call from the show director, Angela Robinson. She tells me you are overworking yourself in your preparation for the musical. She thinks you should have a rest." It was a lie. Walmsley had in fact telephoned the director of *Oliver* and expressed his concern, as a good friend of Vanessa's, that she was unwell and needed a break. Angela was on the fringe of Walmsley's sphere of influence and knew she should tread carefully: a wrong word from him could cost her her own position. She relented quickly and agreed a week off for Vanessa.

"I'm not that tired, Stephen, thank you. I enjoy having a busy life."

"Quite right too – that's my girl. But I'm afraid Angela is insisting, and I have to say I think she has a point. You want to be in great shape for the opening next month, don't you?"

"Yes, and there's no reason why I shouldn't be." Vanessa frowned.

Walmsley took a firmer stance. "Well, I'm sorry, my dear, but that's the way it is. Why don't you go to Point Saturn next week, come back refreshed and raring to go? But first, I've arranged for you to have a night out with Yuri on Saturday – I know how you enjoy evenings with him."

"But, Stephen, it will be so boring for me there on my own. Daddy is always away at the mines and old Rufus and Cook are no fun."

Walmsley was delighted that Vanessa had fallen nicely into the trap. "Well, what about inviting Henry Fitzjohn to go with you? You enjoy his company, do you not?"

"Well, yes, I certainly do, but he is always so busy."

Walmsley put his hand in his jacket pocket and took out a small box with a padded royal-blue leather cover. "Here, try this on. I think it would suit you very well. If you can persuade Henry to accompany you to Cornwall, think how he will admire you wearing this. You have beautiful hands, you know."

Vanessa opened the box and her eyes widened. A three-row pearl bracelet with gold couplings sat in the box, cushioned in a satin lining.

She took it out immediately and extended her arm for Walmsley to fasten it. "Oh, Stephen, it's beautiful. Thank you so much!"

"Now, now. It is indeed yours, but only if you can get Fitzjohn to go with you to Readymoney Cove. Now, do you think that can be arranged?"

"I will try. I will call him when you've gone and ask."

"No, do it now. Time is of the essence."

"OK, but let me do it from the bedroom. I don't want to be embarrassed by you looking at me."

"As you wish. I will stay here."

Vanessa didn't think, but of course she should have known that Walmsley would step up to the bedroom door to listen in to her call.

"Yes, I know it's short notice, but the theatre insist I take time off to rest, and I will need you with me or I'll be so unhappy. I think I will go nuts if you're not there."

There was a short pause, from which Walmsley could have guessed that Fitzjohn had not taken a huge amount of persuading as Vanessa continued. "That's wonderful, Henry. Yes, I'll be ready at nine on Tuesday morning. It will be so lovely – thank you, my love." Vanessa returned to the living room, smiling and looking at her new bracelet. Walmsley was at the drinks tray, refilling his glass, trying to contain the smirk on his face. "And…?"

"He said yes. He'll come here Tuesday morning, first thing, to drive us down there."

"Splendid, my dear, splendid. Just one more thing: do be hospitable to Yuri on Saturday, he is such a nice chap."

"I really don't want to, Stephen. He's a nice enough man, but I'd prefer not to see him again."

"Look, you know how important it is for my business that you entertain the most important people in my circle of friends."

"I do, but can't you find someone else?"

Walmsley took Vanessa's upper arm in a vice-like grip, digging his fingers into her flesh. "You will damn well do as you're told, girl, if you know what's good for you."

"Stephen, you're hurting me!"

He squeezed even harder, making Vanessa wince with pain. Her knees started to buckle, and she gasped.

"I will hurt you if you give me any trouble." Walmsley pulled her up, let go of her, and patted her arm and kissed her cheek. "Now, now, let's not fall out over this. Yuri is very fussy. He doesn't want to see any of my other female friends; he only has eyes for you. You are so beautiful, after all."

Vanessa didn't want to antagonise Walmsley any further. She sighed. "Very well, Stephen. I will do anything to help you."

FORTY-NINE

Comrade Captain Fyodor Yegorov was irritated by his new orders. Once again his task was to land special operations forces on the coast of Great Britain for an exercise. He was told to ready the submarine and stand by for orders. This time the location was still to be agreed but would be somewhere along the south coast, the busiest shipping area in the English Channel. He had hoped to be given orders to seek out and destroy – unfortunately, in theory only – enemy shipping. He was getting an itchy trigger finger.

Major Alexi Petrov would lead the landing party, this time with one inflatable and a group of five men. Yegorov would be advised of the final destination and purpose of the exercise once they were at sea and within a day of the target. The usual two KGB men were to be on board, plus a new officer by the name of Comrade Karl Rimsky, who had orders direct from Moscow, Yegorov was told.

Five days later, they were given the order to depart. The route chosen was circuitous: out to Iceland, across to within 200 miles of Greenland, then south. They were also to be part of an apparent exercise, accompanied by three other submarines and several surface ships, which would detach themselves and carry out manoeuvres in the Atlantic. With less than twenty-four hours until their arrival at the western approaches to the Channel, Captain Yegorov was called to a meeting with Petrov, Rimsky and the navigation officer.

Rimsky spoke first. "Comrade Captain, you have been given the honour by the highest level to carry out a mission that is most significant to our national security. This is no longer just an exercise." He turned to the chart on the table. "You are to take the *Leninski* into these waters, surface, and allow Comrade Petrov and his team to go ashore." Rimsky used his index finger to draw circles on the map over the words 'St Austell Bay'. "The mission will take place at around 0900 hours on the day in question. We are uncertain when exactly that will be – probably two or three days from now. Assuming you can surface close to land, the team will be off the submarine for no more than an hour, Captain."

Yegorov choked out a short laugh. "But that's impossible! When we surface, we will be seen immediately. Why are we not doing this at night?"

"Because," Petrov spoke this time, "we are going to capture someone who will only be available to us at this time – he takes his morning swim in this bay. It's called Readymoney Cove."

"You mean we will kidnap him?"

"Call it what you will. Our orders are to seize the individual, a British government official, bring him back to the submarine and depart without any interference from the Royal Navy or RAF. It will be done quickly with the minimum manpower, hence only one inflatable."

"Why not take him from his house or somewhere else on land? I'm sure you have agents that are more than capable of achieving that. It's quite common in East Germany, is it not?"

"Perhaps, but we want him to disappear so that his family, the police and his employer all believe he got into difficulty swimming and was carried out to sea. Very sad: minister drowns on holiday, body never found. It is vital that there is no hint of a kidnap: no breaking into a house and, most importantly, no hint of Russian involvement."

Yegorov shook his head. "Who is this person that is so important that we place the Soviet Union's best submarine at risk?"

Rimsky responded, "You do not need to know his name, but the position he holds in the British government is key to their military ambitions. Our intelligence people in Murmansk will interrogate him once we have handed him over. I say again, Comrade Captain, this mission is of the highest importance."

"Very well, Comrade Rimsky, I understand." Yegorov felt a rush of adrenalin as he focused on the chart, revelling in the prospect of a live operation. "I will give orders for the preparation of the submarine, including, of course, plenty of ammunition for our guns as we have to surface."

Colonel Kupovsky directed the operation from London. He had agents booked in to the Fowey Harbour Hotel, an elderly man and his wife, who liked to take an early morning walk every day and have coffee at the Readymoney Cove shop. From there they monitored Fitzjohn's movements and the woman used the telephone box to send updates. For the first two days the code words 'the fish are swimming today' were all she said, but that was enough to let Russian intelligence agents know that Fitzjohn was in the sea. This news was radioed to the *Leninski*.

Captain Yegorov took advantage of the submarine's nuclear power to charge the propulsion batteries and remain submerged, stationary and silent. They heard no search vessels above them; the captain was confident that they had approached undetected.

Then on the third day of the target's presence at Readymoney Cove, after the woman had called, they received the order to carry out the mission. Yegorov went to the ladder up to the conning tower and shook Petrov's hand, then shook the special agents' hands. Yegorov felt emotional at the idea of being central to an operation that would benefit Mother Russia and keep his homeland safe from attack by the West.

FIFTY

After Adam had left the house to go to the airfield, Hannah telephoned her mother. She tried to do this every Monday or Tuesday and realised it was two weeks since they last spoke. She just didn't seem to have the time, with her work for Mossad increasing every day. It was no longer a part-time job but a major commitment. More agents had been assigned to her, enthusiastic and diligent investigators producing huge amounts of intelligence on suspected anti-Jewish activists. She knew her work was important in today's dangerous world and never complained to her boss.

"Hello, Mum, how are you?"

"My dear, how nice to hear from you – such a rare event these days."

It was no more than Hannah expected. "Yes, sorry. I have so much to do. But are you well, and Dad?"

"Yes, we're fine, thank you. Your father is spending much more time in the garden, but he's meeting his old friends from the college for coffee in Cambridge this morning. They do that twice a week these days, so he's happy."

"Sounds nice. And you, what are you up to?"

"The usual – still taking the dogs to Parker's Piece every day. I just got back, actually. Otherwise, not a lot. What is it that keeps you so busy? Playing with Michael, perhaps?"

"Of course, he is such a devil, always running around. But he loves going to nursery and has made lots of friends. And there's work, of course."

"Right, that's nice…"

Hannah felt a pang of guilt. She knew her mother was waiting for a long-overdue invitation to visit. She also missed her parents. "Mum, would you like to come down here for a few days? It would be so nice to see you and Dad. Maybe next week?"

"That would be lovely, darling. I'll let Father know. If we get the midday train from Paddington on Saturday, can you meet us at Bodmin station?"

"Yes, of course."

"Thank you, my dear. I will confirm our train booking, but otherwise look forward to seeing you all next week."

"Thanks, Mum. Have a good day."

***

With her parents visiting and Adam at home every evening, Hannah was on the go from dawn until late each day. It was great to see her parents and to go to Cardinham Woods with the whole family, but by Thursday evening she felt stressed and weary. She needed time to herself, time to relax, away from her work and household chores. Before going to bed she spoke to her mother; she had an idea.

"Mum, would you mind terribly if I went off for the morning on my own? I just need some time to relax, if you and Dad are happy to look after Michael. I'll take myself off to the beach with a book, and maybe have a swim. It would be so nice to have a break."

Mrs Shaw was a realist: she knew there were times when a parent needed to have time to themselves to recharge. "Yes, of course. We would love to have Michael to ourselves for a few hours."

Making the arrangement had an immediate uplifting effect on Hannah: she felt inspired, released from domestic life and her work commitments, but perhaps a little guilty at handing Michael over to her mother. She went upstairs and told Adam her plans.

"Great idea, the break will do you good. When will you leave?"

"First thing after breakfast, so I'll see you before you go to work."

"Good, but don't overdo it at the beach. You seem to have been a bit under the weather these last couple of weeks."

"Really, have I?"

"Well, yes, just a touch. Having a morning to yourself will do you good."

***

The next day dawned bright and sunny. Hannah walked down the steep road to Readymoney Cove. There were surprisingly few people on the beach, but it was early. A steady swell was coming in, and the sea was a clear, pale blue. A couple sat outside the shop with coffee in tin mugs, and a dog walker was throwing a ball for her spaniel, calling '*fetch it Smudge!*' and laughing as the dog charged across the beach to retrieve the ball. Hannah looked at the lady, absorbed in her relationship with the dog, seemingly without a care in the world. She was delighted that she had decided to come to the beach, to swim in the sea, people-watch and not think of work.

As she placed her towel on the stone flood protection wall at the back of the beach, she noticed a man walking down the steps from the big house – Point Saturn, Diane had called it. It took only a second for her to recognise Fitzjohn. She sat down and waited and watched; she had no intention of letting him see her. She was wearing her swimsuit but kept her shorts and cotton shirt on.

Fitzjohn jumped the last few steps onto the sand, ran to the sea and dived straight in. Hannah decided to kill time by taking a walk up to the ruined St Catherine's Castle, allowing Fitzjohn to have his swim and leave the cove. She jogged up the flight of steps from the beach onto a rough, steep path towards the headland. Turning a corner, she saw the entrance to the castle grounds and the last few steps up to the circular tower. She ducked her head and walked through the ancient doorway into the circle of dry, dusty earth, then stepped onto the ledge of an arched window, enjoying the view of the Fowey estuary and the English Channel.

Then Hannah noticed an inflatable boat approaching at high speed on the west side of the bay, coming round from Gribbin Head. The boat slowed down and hugged the water's rocky edge, directly below the castle. Hannah could see five men hunched in the boat, with another man at the back operating the outboard motor. She was curious. These were not fishermen or boys out for a bit of fun; she thought they looked like Royal Marines on an exercise.

The boat stopped before entering the mouth of the cove, out of sight of anyone on the beach or swimming in the shallows. Hannah walked carefully back out to the path and, kneeling in the bushes, instinctively not wanting to be seen, stretched forward to look over the cliff. What were the men going to do? Fitzjohn was unaware of their presence, swimming purposefully across the bay.

Hannah suddenly crouched down, her face almost in the undergrowth. Two of the men had scrambled out of the boat and were climbing up the cliff. She could see them more clearly now. Each had a pistol strapped to their thigh and carried a small sub-machine gun, slung across their backs with a leather strap. They had canisters, a knife and a radio attached to their ammunition belt, and they wore black balaclavas, showing only their eyes. They wore knitted hats and tight-fitting black leather gloves. They were strong climbers, and Hannah knew that she would be discovered within minutes. Her heart raced. She resisted the urge to get up and run; they would immediately see her and might attack her. Hannah pressed her body into the long grass. As she waited, desperately hoping that they wouldn't see her, she heard a voice call out below, in what she guessed was Russian, and saw the boat come slowly into the cove. Two of the men had their machine guns in hand, pointed at Fitzjohn, who was still oblivious to what was going on.

The two men squatted and looked towards the back of the beach. One man slapped the other on the shoulder and sped off down the path, hiding himself at the top of the steps to the beach. His companion had been left to watch from the castle side. He went down the path a few yards, found a rocky ledge to crouch on, took his machine gun off his shoulder and watched the sea.

Hannah shuffled backwards and worked her way round behind the Russian agent. If he got up to go, he would hardly spend time looking behind him. She almost cried out as Fitzjohn saw the boat, stopped swimming, and started to tread water. She suddenly realised that the boat was heading directly for him, about to run him down. Two of the crewmen leant over the side and grabbed Fitzjohn's arms, but he shook them free, then dived under the waves. The inflatable flew over him, grazing his shoulders and back. He made off at the best speed he could, heading for the beach, unable to see the agent kneeling in the gorse, his pistol at the ready.

The boat circled and slowed down. Fitzjohn was trapped. Hannah knew she had to alert him, had to call out to tell him of the danger of the agent on the beach. But the man in front of her would cut her down in seconds. She looked around and saw a jagged piece of rock: could she hit the man on the back of the head and knock him out? The rock seemed too small to use as a weapon, but she had no alternative. She had to make the first hit count. She got to her feet, still crouching, then pounced and smashed the rock against the back of the man's head. He staggered forward, almost falling over the cliff edge. Hannah raised her hand to hit him again, but he had recovered from the shock and swung his machine gun towards her. She dived at him and knocked him back, and they rolled together towards the edge. Hannah could not compete with his brute strength, and he threw her off, scrambled to his feet and stood up. He clicked off the safety catch and fired a four-round burst. But too late, his shots zipped high over her head, Hannah had found the rock again and a split second earlier thrown it at his face. It hit his left eye, and he staggered back on the loose stones and earth on the cliff's edge. His feet slipped from under him and he fell off the cliff. He slammed onto a rocky ledge sixty feet below and lay motionless. Hannah screamed out to Fitzjohn. "*Get away! Get away!*"

The four Russians on the water heard the gunshots and turned the boat round to see what had happened. They saw their comrade on the ledge and were shocked to see a woman standing at the top of the cliff. One man spoke into his radio. Immediately the agent who had gone to the beach started to run back up the steps. Hannah went to the edge of the cliff and picked up the sub-machine gun the dead agent had dropped. She didn't recognise it, had never fired one of its type before. She dashed to the cover of the bushes and waited.

Fitzjohn also heard the shots, then saw the boat stop. He took the opportunity to turn back towards the steps up to Point Saturn – a tough swim across the bay, but a safe refuge if he could make it there. The boat started to head again for the beach, until the crew seemed to realise they had lost Fitzjohn. They frantically swept the boat across the bay to the castle side and then back towards the centre and saw him.

From her position Hannah could see they were heading for Fitzjohn. Calmly, she looked at the Russian gun, the magazine, and the sights on the barrel. She got up, pulled the stock of the gun hard into her shoulder, took a breath, held the pistol grip firmly and opened fire. Spouts of water shot up behind the boat. She fired again, this time aiming ahead. The rounds ripped through the front left-hand side of the boat.

She spun around to look for the agent from down the path and was stunned to see him coming up the slope, no more than thirty yards away, pistol in his hand, advancing cautiously, his shoulders hunched. When he got closer he spotted Hannah, stopped for a moment, then took the pistol in a two-handed grip and raised it, knees bent. Hannah read the classic signs: he was positioning himself to shoot. Hannah stood up, pulled the machine gun into her shoulder and pushed her weight forward onto her left foot, her right foot behind her.

She fired at him as he fired at her. Hannah heard two rounds slam into the rocks beside her. He fired again. Her own shots went high, so she aimed lower and fired a short burst. She saw him jump backwards, clutching his face, blood oozing through his fingers. A burning pain seared Hannah's right arm and she realised she had been hit. She dropped the gun and staggered back towards the cliff edge. She knew her momentum was going to take her over, to die next to the man on the ledge. She took her only chance and jumped forcefully out towards the sea, clear of the rocks below.

Hannah felt the shock of cold water as she landed and fought her way back up to the surface. She gripped her injured arm with her left hand and kicked her legs, trying to swim to the other side of the bay. Blood flowed from her arm, colouring the water a reddish-brown. She rolled onto her back and saw the Russian boat limping out of the bay, sea water cascading over its left-hand side. As she turned to head for Point Saturn she saw Fitzjohn on his hands and knees on the steps, looking exhausted. Faintness was overwhelming her, despite the searing pain in her arm, but she was determined to stay conscious. She lifted her left arm behind her head, pulled at the water and kicked her legs.

It seemed hopeless: she couldn't get any momentum, could barely keep her head above the waves, but she struggled on.

Hannah's strength was ebbing away quickly. As the sunlight dazzled her eyes she thought of Adam and Michael, she thought of Mum and Dad at home, how she loved them all, how sorry she was for getting into this silly situation. Strangely, as blood seeped from her, a warmth flowed through her body and she stopped trying to swim. Water splashed her face and she gasped for air but sank lower below the surface. She knew this was where it was going to end and saw pictures in her mind of Michael running and laughing. Her last thought before darkness came was that Adam would be a good father to her lovely boy, and in time they would be happy again. She relaxed, felt the warmth of the sun and smiled, before falling unconscious.

***

Fitzjohn at last recovered his self-control. Shocked by the apparent attempt to kill him, and near exhaustion, he made an effort to stand and get up the steps to the house. He grabbed the rusty handrail and pulled himself forward. After ten steps, he had to stop to rest. He turned and looked back down at the bay. Floating out to sea was a woman's body. She was clearly dead. Fitzjohn looked up to the house. Not far to go.

But he couldn't move. A jolt of anger shot through him. Those bastards, whoever they were, had shot the girl. She had called out to him, helped him, and he didn't want to let her body be washed away. He clambered back down the steps and staggered into the sea. Perhaps more at home in the water than running up flights of stairs, he swam towards the woman. He was shocked when he stopped next to her. *Hannah!* He recognised her, even though it was some years since they had met. He put his arms under hers and attempted to tow her back towards the beach. Her arm was bleeding badly: a bullet had passed right through her. Progress was agonisingly slow as her dead weight sank in the water. But Fitzjohn kept her head tilted back and suddenly she coughed, choked and vomited sea water. Fitzjohn was delighted – she was alive! He was instantly energised. He kicked harder and pulled like hell with his free arm to get himself and Hannah to the shallows.

Suddenly, a shadow was cast over them. At first he was terrified and kicked even harder. Had the black inflatable returned? But it was the Fowey lifeboat that had arrived alongside them. Two crewmen leant over to pull Hannah aboard. Then Fitzjohn was bundled into the boat and immediately covered with a blanket. A crew member was gently slapping Hannah's face and encouraging her to talk to him, while another pressed wound dressings to her upper arm and wrapped round a bandage.

Fitzjohn sat up. "Thanks, chaps. How the hell did you know we were in trouble?"

The crewman said, "A woman on the beach with her dog heard gunshots and saw this lady fall into the sea. She alerted Jackie in the shop – there's a phone in there. Jackie called us." He turned back to look at Hannah. "She has a nasty wound. We will head straight across the bay to St Austell, where an ambulance will take her to hospital. Ross here's an ex-army medic, went over on D-Day. He knows how to treat bullet wounds, but she's lost a lot of blood. It will be touch and go whether she makes it."

"Right, do your best. She's a special lady – saved my life. Her husband is Adam Devon, he's a pilot at RAF St Mawgan. Can you get a radio message through to him?"

"I'm sure we can do that. Adam Devon, you say? Just a moment." The man spoke to the skipper, who went to the wheelhouse and picked up the radio transmitter. He called the lifeboat station to tell them they were going to St Austell and asked them to call St Mawgan. He turned back to the casualties and was delighted to see Hannah's eyes flicker open.

FIFTY-ONE

After the nursing staff had cleaned up his back, Fitzjohn was discharged from the hospital. Rufus and Vanessa had driven over from Readymoney Cove and were ready to take him back. He wanted to see Hannah, but after surgery only close family were allowed to visit. He showered and dressed in the clothes that Rufus had brought him. Before leaving, he was requested to give a statement about the incident to a police officer. It was short: Fitzjohn could only say that an inflatable boat had run him down and the woman, Hannah, had shouted to him, then fired at the boat before being shot herself. He saw the damaged boat heading out to sea before the lifeboat arrived. Fitzjohn was traumatised but got a further shock when the officer said that two bodies had been found in the cove, and they appeared to be Russian military agents.

Fitzjohn was allowed to use a phone in a ward sister's office. He called Sian Shelby. "Sian, have you heard what happened?"

"I have indeed, Henry – the police called me. How are you? Were you badly injured?"

"I'm fine, just some scratches across my back. I'm still at the hospital in St Austell but will be back at Point Saturn in a couple of hours. You have the number there, don't you?"

"I do."

"Good, now there's something I want you to do in the meantime. Get on to Admiral Temple. I want to know if the RAF or navy have arrested the intruders. The inflatable boat they used was damaged by Mrs Devon's gunshots – the lady on the cliff. It must be out in the Channel somewhere, assuming it hasn't sunk. This was a planned attack: these sods must have known I would be in the bay having my daily swim. Someone tipped them off, so please make a list of everyone who knew my whereabouts."

"Right, I'll get on the case. Who did you tell you were going to be in Cornwall?"

"Let me think. Obviously Miss Paget, as I have been a guest at her father's house. I told Richard Dunn, down at Granta Airlines. Lionel, because I drove myself and gave him time off while I was away. That's it, I believe."

"And who did Miss Paget tell she was entertaining such a high-profile... friend, shall we say, in Cornwall?"

"No idea. I hadn't thought of that." Sian's no fool, thought Fitzjohn. She seemed to know a lot about his private life. That's what made a good executive secretary.

"I dare say she would have mentioned it to some of her theatre pals. She would have explained why she was going to be away, wouldn't she?"

"Yes, good point. I'll call you later," said Fitzjohn.

"Before you go, I'm assuming you didn't tell Amanda Spencer where you were going, and who with?"

"Ah, no. Better that we leave her in the dark for the time being. If you could call her late tomorrow morning and tell her what's happened, I will see her as soon as I get back from Cornwall. The press will be all over this; there's no point in trying to disguise where I was when the attack happened."

"Right, will do. Bye for now."

After Fitzjohn had hung up, he looked around the office. The usual array of pens, papers, files and used teacups were scattered across the desk. A cork noticeboard was overloaded with medical updates, a staff holiday list and several thank-you cards. He reminded himself to send one too. Or at least get Sian to do it. He sat back in the chair. Who could have betrayed him? He couldn't think of anyone.

Except Vanessa.

FIFTY-TWO

Major Petrov looked behind him to see if any of the remaining assault team in the boat had been hit. Four or five rounds from a machine gun had torn through the rubber on the left side of the boat, forcing him to abandon the kidnap attempt and head back out to sea for the pick-up.

His number two powered the outboard motor. The other three men instinctively crouched down, out of the wind and spray, as they headed into the heavy waves of the English Channel. Petrov was anxious: the air was purring from the bullet holes and the boat was listing hard to the left; they could flounder and sink at any moment. The boat was only being kept afloat by its undamaged sections. He said nothing but pointed his arm south-west, towards the Falmouth Roads. The boat seemed to be faring well as they got further away from land.

Petrov clicked on the radio fixed to his jacket and opened up with a simple contact message to the submarine: "Petrov to Grey Seal, come in."

"Grey Seal to Petrov, pass your message."

"Mission failed. Two men down and target escaped. Boat damaged and sinking, returning to pickup point."

"Stand by, Petrov."

Minutes passed with no further transmission. Petrov gave the order to slow the engine.

On board the *Leninski*, Captain Yegorov stood at the periscope, one of his officers scanning the surrounding sea. He knew he was going to lose his temper in front of his crew, but that didn't matter. His job was not just to protect the submarine, but all personnel on board, including the special service agents.

"Comrade Rimsky, we must surface."

"No." Rimsky's face was red and furious. "They have failed in their duty! We must not expose the submarine to further danger. I order you to remain submerged and make a course for home."

"I don't take orders from you when we are at sea – the safety of all crew is my responsibility." He turned to his senior officer. "Surface, *immediately*."

Rimsky punched a fist into his open hand. "Captain, you will be dismissed from the service for this!"

Comrade Captain Yegorov was pleased. In his heart and mind he knew he was taking the right action; he had no time for Rimsky's threats. He did not lose his temper. Instead he smiled and stood over the chart showing their position.

***

Petrov directed his agent to take the boat to where the *Leninski* was expected to surface. He noticed in the distance two large aircraft approaching the area at no more than 1,000 feet. It was going to be a race against time to get on board the submarine, and he hoped the captain didn't order his gunners to shoot at the aircraft: they would undoubtedly return fire and that would mean the submarine would dive, leaving him and his men to be captured, or perhaps they would all drown if the inflatable sank.

The two aircraft separated, one turning to the left, the other to the right, and made wide circles over the sea. Five minutes later, Petrov estimated he and the team were over the right area and ordered the engine to be pulled back. Suddenly, about half a mile away, he saw the grey bulk of the *Leninski*'s hull begin to surface. The inflatable now powered towards the submarine, but water was swamping the boat; it would only be minutes before it sank. Petrov was confident that if they could just cover the last few hundred yards, they would be safe.

Two seamen were sent to open the hatch to the conning tower. One officer followed, focusing on the sky above them. He trained his binoculars to the west and saw, less than a mile away, a Shackleton levelling out from a steep turn and heading towards them. He looked down at the sea and saw Petrov's inflatable limping towards the submarine. Four more men came onto the conning tower and fixed a machine gun to the rail, ready to shoot at the aircraft as it approached. A message came through on the officer's headphones: "Do not shoot unless we are attacked."

As Petrov came alongside the submarine, ropes were thrown out for the agents to use to scramble up the curve of the hull and across to the conning tower. As the two seamen tried to recover the boat, a series of waves crashed it against the submarine. The inflatable split in two and compressed air sprayed water in the air. The boat sank in twenty seconds. At the same time the men ran below. The submarine was already making headway and would dive in less than a minute.

Wet, shaken and downcast, the special agents were taken straight to the captain's quarters, where Rimsky, his KGB colleagues, the submarine's intelligence officer and Captain Yegorov waited. Petrov pulled off his balaclava and gloves. "We were ambushed – they had people on the cliffs waiting for us. Ivanov was shot and fell off a cliff, and I think Savkin was also shot. They opened fire on us, hitting the boat. We tried to get the target, but he swam away. I heard more gunfire so I ordered a withdrawal before we were all killed."

"You left the target! A man having a leisurely swim in the sea was too much for you, Comrade Major?" Rimsky shouted.

Petrov had no time for desk-bound action men, regardless of their superior rank, and shouted back. "I had no choice! The boat was punctured and sinking; we only just made it back to the pickup point. As I said, they were waiting for us. But how did they know we were coming?"

A seaman came into the quarters. "Sir, the officer of the day would like to speak to you."

Captain Yegorov said nothing and followed the man through to the control room. Whatever debate was to be had with Petrov, the submarine still had to be sailed. "What is it, Lieutenant?"

"Sir, we are being tracked by the two Shackleton aircraft. They would have seen us on the surface and will vector anti-submarine ships towards us. Request permission to make maximum speed and depth onto a westerly heading."

Yegorov knew that the British would now be aware of their attack on Fitzjohn, one of their people, in their own country, and would view the *Leninski* as a hostile invader. They needed to get out of UK waters, out into the open Atlantic where no foreign navy would dare to attack them. He assented to the rapid escape, but, guessing the British would assume a direct route home, instructed the officer to set a heading south-west, down towards France; they would skirt the Brittany coast before taking a northerly passage back to the Arctic sea and to Murmansk.

Confident that they would avoid the ships and aircraft undoubtedly hunting them, Yegorov left the control room and went back to his quarters. Major Petrov was sitting, writing out his report; Rimsky and his two KGB agents stood over him.

"Comrade Captain, when Major Petrov has completed his report, you are to secure him in the boat's brig. He is under arrest."

FIFTY-THREE

Amanda Spencer was tormented. Unable to sleep, she decided to get up again and pour herself a glass of milk. She made the mistake of sweetening it with a large brandy, which did little to take away the frustration in her mind; it simply exaggerated her thinking and stoked her anguish. She felt she was being made a fool of. She paced the living room, tried to read a book, stood looking out of the window at the black night sky. The news Sir Robert Darnell had delivered had hurt her, struck to her heart. Yes, she had half prepared for the day when her bond with Fitzjohn would change. Always hopeful of an enduring, loving relationship, enriched by the success of his career, now she had to deal with the threat of it all breaking down and her life falling into ruin.

Only she knew why she had a burning desire to get to 10 Downing Street. Her father had favoured her two older brothers, sending them to private schools while she had to fight to get to grammar school. There she flourished. She was slated to go up to Cambridge to study history and politics, but at the last minute her father withdrew his financial support, and she had to go to the University of East Anglia to study journalism. On graduation, she joined the *Cambridge Independent* to train as a junior reporter. She longed to show her father just how well she could do, and this continued even after his death. She knew it didn't make sense, but she couldn't shake off her ambitions.

Amanda thought about how she would confront Fitzjohn. She could not pretend she had not heard the news, or bury her emotions; she was the type to face up to problems. But if she overreacted he might leave her, might go off with this girl, or decide he liked the freedom he had tasted, and want more.

This business of Fitzjohn driving the potential war against Russia troubled her. Did he genuinely want this, or was it a ploy to get noticed? She doubted the chief of the defence staff would go along with his plans if they didn't have some credence. And did Fitzjohn have the influence over Macmillan that he claimed?

The press have really gone on about the Reds threat, and not without reason, she thought. Wars are started by megalomaniacs and Russia had had plenty of those, but was Khrushchev, a fanatical communist, one of these? Was he an aggressor, or was he a global peacemaker?

Amanda took her drink back to bed and sat up, contemplating what to do next. She remembered the night at Imogen's when Henry had wanted to be introduced to Stephen Walmsley. She could easily imagine Henry being attracted to the glamour, the nightclubs, the parties, the admiration he'd find in Walmsley's circle. And if what Darnell had said was true, he would easily fall victim to the attractions of one of the beautiful young women Walmsley had available.

She put the cup down on her side cabinet and suddenly knew exactly what she would do. She would not challenge Fitzjohn straight away; she would take her time and find the right moment to speak to him. She would, however, bring Walmsley down. She would seek revenge for his part in the pain she was suffering. She planned to contact one of her journalist friends and find evidence of Walmsley procuring prostitutes and living off immoral earnings. A prosecution would follow and he would go to prison, she would see to it. That would be the end of Walmsley's society status.

Having resolved her plan of action, Amanda felt drowsiness come over her. She turned off the light and fell into an untroubled sleep.

***

For the third time, Wing Commander Louis Valentine read through the intelligence reports that had come through overnight from Kinloss. One of their Shackletons had spotted a group of three Russian submarines and five warships sailing in convoy south of Iceland. After passing to the west of Ireland the submarines disappeared, presumably below the surface, but the ships continued south in a loose formation. Valentine ordered Adam Devon's flight of three aircraft to take off at first light. They were detailed to fly past Cork, find the submarines and track their course.

Two hours after departure, they commenced their reconnaissance structure of crossing and recrossing the search area, watching and listening. Devon had given control of the aircraft to one of the new student pilots, Pilot Officer James Hyde. Devon was planning the next steps in the search: when to change to a new area, what height to fly, time on station, but his thoughts were interrupted when the radio burst to life.

"St Mawgan to Lion Three, come in, over."

The aircraft's radio operator replied, "Mawgan, this is Lion Three, go ahead."

"You are ordered to return to base immediately, making top speed. Please acknowledge, over."

Devon wondered what could be wrong but, before responding, pressed the aircraft's intercom and asked the navigator for a heading to fly back. He then called St Mawgan. "Lion Three returning to base, full speed. What's the problem?"

There was a moment's hesitation before St Mawgan replied. "Lion Three, Wing Commander Valentine here. Details will be given when you land. Just get back as soon as you can."

Devon was puzzled. The station commander must have been standing over the radio operator and taken the microphone from him. This must be something very out of the ordinary.

Less than an hour later, after Hyde had completed an excellent approach and landing, he taxied the aircraft direct to the airfield buildings. Devon could see Valentine standing outside so quickly gathered his logbooks and flight plans and climbed out of the aircraft.

"Come in, Devon. My adjutant, Flight Sergeant Harper, is in my office."

After the bright sun of the morning, it took a moment for Devon's vision to adjust to Valentine's dim office.

"Good morning, Harper." Devon turned to Valentine. "What's the problem, sir?"

"There has been some kind of incident over at Readymoney Cove on the south coast. I'm afraid it has involved your wife. She has been injured and is in St Austell hospital. Devon, sit down, please." Valentine walked round and sat at his desk. "Look, it seems she has been shot. It's not—"

"*Shot*? How the hell could that have happened? Do you know how serious it is?"

"No, I'm afraid I have no other information. It's not life-threatening, apparently; she has been in surgery. You're given immediate leave. Harper here has a car and driver ready to take you."

"Right, sir, I see, thank you. I'd better get going, but I'd prefer to drive myself, if that's OK."

"Of course, if you feel up to it. You've had a bit of a shock."

"No, sir, I'm fine. Can I get going now?"

"Certainly. And please telephone me or speak to Flight Sergeant Harper when you have some news." Valentine walked Devon to the door, shook his hand and patted his shoulder. "Good luck, Adam, old chap."

"Thanks, Louis. I'll give you a call as soon as I can."

***

The wing commander was right: the effects of shock were brewing inside Devon and he struggled to concentrate on driving. He couldn't get out of his mind that the incident, whatever it was, had to be linked to her work with the Israeli secret service. He dreaded the thought that she might be targeted for the work she did.

The Rover 90 powered effortlessly through the Cornish roads, some single-lane, then the A30, a major trunk route that allowed Devon to get a move on. Soon he had crossed the hills of central Cornwall, driven through the industrial china clay mining country and dropped down into the town of St Austell. He found the hospital and parked, adrenalin racing through his bloodstream. He ran to the entrance and up to the reception desk. "Good afternoon, I'm Adam Devon, here to see my wife, Hannah."

"Oh yes, we've been expecting you. One moment, please." The receptionist nodded to a figure behind Devon. He turned to see a smartly dressed man in a suit, white shirt, tie and trilby hat, holding a gabardine raincoat over his arm.

"Would you come with me, please, Mr Devon? My name's Detective Inspector Clive Thompson, Cornwall CID. We have a room just along the corridor."

Devon couldn't have known that Fitzjohn had used the same ward sister's office just a few hours earlier.

"The doctor has promised to let us know when you can see your wife. He shouldn't be long. In the meantime, I'd like to ask you a couple of questions."

"Certainly, but first tell me what has happened."

"Well, we understand that an attempt was made this morning to either kill or kidnap a senior politician. Mrs Devon intervened, and in the process was wounded by a gunshot to the arm. She ended up in the sea, and the Fowey lifeboat brought her to St Austell. The doctors have assured me that she will make a good recovery."

"Well, that's a relief. Who was this politician?"

"Mr Devon, I understand you are a civilian pilot with the RAF."

"That's correct."

"Then you are subject to the Official Secrets Act. What I am going to tell you requires you to maintain absolute confidentiality."

"I understand."

"We believe that Russian agents came ashore in an attack on the Minster of Defence, Mr Henry Fitzjohn. He was staying in a house in Readymoney Cove and having his regular swim in—"

"*Fitzjohn?* That's nuts! I know Fitzjohn – we were in the RAF together."

"Yes, so I gather. You will also know him as a senior member of the government."

"Indeed I do."

"I interviewed him before he was released from hospital. Seems he also knew your wife. It was he who went in to rescue her, before the lifeboat pulled them both out of the sea."

"That's good to hear. I can see he would be a target, famous politician and all that, but why should these Russians shoot Hannah?"

"We are still investigating all the events that occurred. Mr Fitzjohn has given us his statement and we are waiting to interview Mrs Devon once the doctor gives us permission. Clearly her account of the incident is critical to our enquiries. MI5 is sending a team down here, and no doubt they will also want to talk to her. Two men were found dead in the cove. One was shot; the other seems to have fallen off a cliff. We have recovered a machine gun at the scene and, when we are able, we will take Mrs Devon's fingerprints for analysis. Tell me, has Mrs Devon served in the forces? Does she have experience of firearms?"

"Yes – well, a certain type of experience, but can this wait? I would like to see her."

"I need to know Mrs Devon's role in these deaths, and how she came to be injured. And whether she fired the machine gun that killed the man."

"What are you insinuating? That she was culpable in his killing?"

"I'm not suggesting anything. We are certainly not planning to arrest Mrs Devon, given the fact that the man was a Russian enemy agent seemingly on a mission to kill or kidnap a British citizen. But we do need to know what happened."

"And so do I…"

There was a knock at the door. A nurse entered and asked Devon to go with her, his wife was awake. He didn't even look at the policeman but hurried out of the door and followed the nurse.

Devon was taken to a private room, where he was shocked to see Hannah lying in bed, looking pale and exhausted, with her arm and shoulder in bandages, a drip in her forearm and a heart rate monitor beeping steadily. A doctor in a white coat stood with his hands deep in his pockets. Hannah was barely awake.

Devon rushed to her side.

"Mr Devon, I'm Dr Penhale. I'm pleased to tell you that your wife has responded very well to the operation to repair the bullet wound. But please do not tax her; she is still very weak from her exertions in the sea and the effects of the anaesthetic. She will need a few hours before she can speak coherently. Please be patient."

"Yes, of course, Doctor. Thank you so much. Hannah, darling." Devon took her left hand and squeezed it gently. Hannah opened her eyes and looked at Devon for a moment, then her eyelids fluttered closed and she quickly, happily, went back to sleep.

"Leave her now, please, Mr Devon. There's a tea room in the garden annexe if you would like to go there, or return later, perhaps? She will need two or three hours' sleep."

"Is there a public telephone I could use? I need to call Hannah's parents; they are staying with us in Cardinham. Also the station commander at St Mawgan – I will have to ask for special leave."

"Under the circumstances, please use the telephone in the sister's office. I believe she will be on duty in the wards this afternoon, so you shouldn't be disturbed."

"Thank you, that's very kind. I will then wait in the tea room; it's not worth driving home."

***

After speaking to Hannah's mother, and a quick update with Wing Commander Valentine, Devon found the tea room. He picked up some old copies of the *Cornish Times* and *Western Gazette* but could only flick through the pages, unable to take in the awfulness of his wife's injury. He went outside for a walk in the gardens to pass the time and stretch his legs. After a second cup of tea, he had exhausted all the activities to occupy his mind and just sat, waiting. After an hour, the café door opened and the nurse called Devon to go with her. He jumped up and followed her.

"How is she, Nurse?"

"Awake and in good spirits. Excellent, actually – she's a tough lady. Dr Penhale is with her now. Mr Devon, the doctor has a colleague with him, Dr Andrews." As she led the way along the corridor to Hannah's room, the nurse looked over her shoulder at Devon. "Just to let you know, Dr Andrews is an obstetrician," she said and, without pausing, opened the door.

FIFTY-FOUR

At noon the day after her dinner with Sir Robert Darnell, Amanda's phone rang. She was working on a plan for a series of party supporter meetings in Sudbury in a couple of weeks' time, and her concentration on the task was such that she had put all thoughts of Fitzjohn's cheating out of her mind. She was surprised when she heard Sian Shelby's voice.

"Good morning, Amanda. Have I caught you at a good time? It's Sian."

"Hello, Sian. No problem, how can I help?"

"There was an… incident yesterday, with Henry. Did you hear about it?"

"No, what's happened?"

"It's all under wraps at the moment, but the press will soon get hold of the story. He was in Cornwall, visiting a friend. He went for a swim early in the morning and a group of men in a boat tried to kidnap him. It's believed the perpetrators were Russian agents. Two of them were killed before the rest escaped." Sian paused.

"My God – is Henry alright?"

"Yes, he was taken to hospital but only has some minor scratches. A woman who happened to be on the beach was not so lucky; she was shot. We think she was the one who dealt with the Russians, but she is under sedation and can't be interviewed this morning. She is recovering in hospital, but she should be OK, I understand."

"That's good to know. Where is Henry now?"

"At the hospital, but he should be back at the house later. It's in Readymoney Cove, near Fowey. He will be driving up to his London flat this evening, escorted by a Special Branch car, who are placing a 24-hour watch on him."

"Were these Russian agents trying to kill Henry?"

"Possibly. They hit him with their inflatable dinghy – that's what caused his injuries, but as far as I know, they didn't shoot at him."

"Sian, tell me. The lady who assisted, the one who got injured – was she the… er… friend that Henry is staying with?"

"No, it was someone else. You might as well hear it from me as read it in the newspapers tomorrow. Henry is staying with Vanessa Paget. Daughter of Sir Bartley Paget. The lady who assisted seemed to be a holidaymaker."

"Incredible that she was able to see off Russian agents. Was she actually with Special Branch?"

"No, we don't think so. But that's all we have for now."

"Right, thank you. Have you spoken to Richard Dunn at Granta Airlines?"

"No, I'm planning to call him now. But you know, he really runs the airline on his own so he won't miss Henry for a week or so."

"That's true. I will try and call Henry this evening. If anything else emerges, will you let me know?"

"Of course. Goodbye for now."

Amanda sat back and blew out a long breath. "How about that?"

she said to herself. She was relieved that Henry was not seriously injured, but sickened by the thought that he could have been killed.

She telephoned Henry at his London flat in the evening, but there was no answer. He was no doubt still driving up from Cornwall so she decided to leave it until the morning.

***

Amanda had set her alarm for an early start. She showered and dressed, ready to leave her flat with a moment's notice. The row with Sir Robert Darnell rattled around in her mind. Over coffee she thought about the situation. Stephen Walmsley had pulled Henry into his web of parties, society events, nightclubs and wealthy young socialites. Vanessa, the young and lovely daughter of a landowner, had become his favourite, it seemed. Amanda's outrage blended with a sense of loss, loneliness, indignation and sadness at hearing of Fitzjohn's duplicity. And it was all down to Walmsley. She resolved to get to know more about him, to find out how he operated and how he made his money. She would need help. She thought about going to the police, but she knew they would want more hard evidence of criminal wrongdoing. Having a circle of wealthy and glamorous friends wasn't an offence, and there were only rumours and whispers about Walmsley's parties, his girls, and the rich men he befriended. She knew he controlled and ran a high-class prostitution racket. Proving it would be a different story.

Then an idea came to her.

FIFTY-FIVE

When Devon entered Hannah's room, he was delighted to see her sitting up in bed, her hair brushed and a rosier tint to her cheeks. She held a cup of tea, and she placed it back on the tray that sat on her lap and reached out to Devon. "Oh, darling, I'm so sorry. I should never have got involved."

"Never mind that. How are you feeling?"

"Not bad, really. Tired, my arm is sore, and a bit nauseous – apparently that's normal, given the amount of sea water I swallowed." Hannah squeezed Devon's hand. "There's something else, Adam. Dr Andrews here told me that they carried out various tests when I was admitted. All routine for a trauma injury. But, it seems we're going to have a baby, my love."

"You're pregnant! That's wonderful." Devon turned to the doctors, suddenly fearful. "But could my wife's injury and being in the sea have caused any problems?"

Andrews stepped forward. "There is a risk that a shock such as this could result in the termination of the pregnancy, but your wife has recovered well, and all the vital signs with mother are normal. Dr Penhale would like to keep Mrs Devon in hospital until her arm wound has largely healed, and this will give us the opportunity to keep an eye on her condition. It could be a couple of weeks."

Dr Penhale added, "In hospital, we will be able to monitor Mrs Devon for any signs of delayed shock or infection."

"Of course – as you wish, Doctor. We have a three-year-old son, but Hannah's parents are staying—"

Devon stopped as the nurse came in the room. "Mr Devon, there's an urgent telephone call for you. You can take it at the hospital reception."

"Who is it?"

"He wouldn't say."

"Go and take the call, Adam," said Hannah. The two doctors said they would return the next morning and left the room.

"I shouldn't be long. I think I can guess who it is. Are you alright to leave on your own?"

"Yes, of course. I'm going to have to get used to being here for a while. When you're back we can have a chat. I think it might be time for me to think about giving up work, if that's OK with you?"

"It certainly is, if that's what you want."

"It could be. Now hurry along."

***

"Devon speaking."

"Ah, Adam, it's Louis. How is Mrs Devon?"

"Much improved since I called you, thanks, Louis."

"We're on an open line here, so I will keep it simple and to the point."

"Understood, go ahead."

"The two colleagues you left on duty when you were called back have now filed their paperwork." This meant that the two Shackleton pilots in his flight had completed their intelligence reports. "Right, that's good to hear."

"They reported spotting our old friend off the Cornwall coast, not far from Fowey. They picked up some men in a small boat then made their apologies and disappeared fast. We're putting together every one of our resources for an operation at dawn tomorrow. Will you be able to join the party?"

"Tomorrow? No, I'm afraid not, Louis. Hannah needs me. You understand she has been badly injured and almost drowned." He didn't feel inclined to mention her pregnancy. "Can I call you first thing in the morning with an update?"

"That would be fine, thank you. I wish her well."

"Thank you, sir. Goodbye."

***

Devon walked quickly back to Hannah's room and found her awake. "Was it the wing commander?" she said.

"Yes. There's going to be a big operation tomorrow morning to try to track the submarine involved with Fitzjohn's kidnap. One of the Shackletons saw the sub surface off the coast, picking up the agents who came ashore. The ones who were left, of course. They dived and are probably near Iceland by now."

"Will you have to join them?"

"No, I'm staying here with you. I will call your mother and ask them to put Michael to bed."

"I hope they can visit the hospital over the next few days. It would be so nice to see Michael… yes, tomorrow." Hannah's eyelids drooped, and soon she was asleep again.

He sat by the bed, pondering all that had happened. He realised he had taken the news of Hannah's pregnancy as a matter-of-fact report from the doctor, and now he was hit by excitement and happiness. He glowed with love for her and longed to talk to her when she was fully awake, so they could discuss the news together, privately.

He looked tenderly at her, breathing heavily, her face pale. He took her hand: his immediate concern was her recovery and the well-being of the child she was carrying.

FIFTY-SIX

Barely a word was said in the Paget Rolls Royce when Rufus drove Fitzjohn and Vanessa from the hospital in St Austell back to Point Saturn. Fitzjohn was still in shock: his efforts in the sea and the painkillers for his scrapes had made him drowsy. Once at the house, Rufus said that Cook would prepare steamed fish and mashed potatoes: a light dinner suitable for an invalid. Fitzjohn said he would like something to liven him up and decided on a large malt whisky and ice.

After dinner, when the staff had disappeared, Fitzjohn asked Vanessa to come into the main living room. He poured her a port and lemon and another malt for himself.

"Quite a day, my dear."

"Oh, Henry, I was so worried. When you disappeared this morning I was frantic, thinking you might have got into trouble swimming. Then when we heard you were in hospital I was relieved but also so frightened. I didn't know how badly injured you were."

"The police and my own security people will be investigating who the villains were – and how they knew I would be in the sea this morning. The local police think it might have been a kidnap attempt."

"Kidnap! You mean they planned to hold you for a ransom?"

"Could be, or worse."

Vanessa held trembling fingers to her lips. "What are you saying? That they might have killed you?"

"Possibly – who knows? But it's all over now and I'll be returning to London tomorrow. You can travel up with me; we will be accompanied by a Special Branch car."

"Tomorrow? No, I can't go with you. I have to stay here."

"Why? What could possibly keep you here? Your father is away and Rufus will look after the house."

Vanessa stood up and went to the window. "I've been told I have to stay here all week… I'm sorry, Henry."

"Who the hell by?"

"Please don't be angry. You know I have to be helpful to Stephen – he is so generous in allowing me to use his flat in London."

"What are you saying? *Walmsley* told you to stay here?"

"Just for the week, and it was his idea that I should invite you down here to keep me company. But I wanted to anyway; you know how much I enjoy being with you. That's the real reason I asked you down."

"But why for the whole week? What does it matter to him? No, we'll go back tomorrow and to hell with Walmsley."

Vanessa spun round, suddenly laughing and wide-eyed. "Yes! To hell with Stephen Walmsley – he has been kind to me at times but he is such a bossy person, getting me to do things I don't want to do, such as go out with people even if I don't really like them. He can keep the flat. Now I have such a good part in *Oliver*, I can afford somewhere of my own. And I don't want to see any more of Yuri, either." Vanessa quickly turned her back again on Fitzjohn, realising what she had said, and looked out of the window, her neck and cheeks blushing a deep rose-pink.

"And who is Yuri?"

"It doesn't matter."

"Tell me." Fitzjohn walked over to Vanessa, put his hand on her shoulder and gently turned her round. He could see tears forming in her eyes. "Just tell me, my dear."

"Oh, he's a friend of Stephen's, a nice enough man. He bought me dinner a couple of times… and…" Vanessa trailed off.

Fitzjohn knew what that meant. "I see. And has Yuri had the pleasure of your attentions for long?"

"No, he only arrived in London a year ago. He's Russian, but he came here from America. He looks after cultural things at the Russian embassy. Cultural attaché, that's it."

"*What?* You have been seeing a Russian government official? Of course he's a cultural wallah – they all are!"

"Oh, please don't be angry. He was just a friend, not special to me like you are. I told him that. He was always trying to seem big and show off, but I told him you had a really important job, stopping the war and telling the chiefs of – you know – what to do."

Fitzjohn's heart sank as a sense of cold realisation washed over him. "I need to use your telephone. What's this man's full name?"

"Yuri Andreyevich," Vanessa stammered.

Fitzjohn dashed through to the office and dialled Sian Shelby's home number. "Sian, it's Henry. I've got an urgent task for you. I want you to get on to MI5 – I need some information on one Yuri Andreyevich, said to be a cultural attaché in the Russian embassy. He could well be more than a supporter of the arts. Could be connected with my little incident today. Ring me back here at Point Saturn as soon as you have anything."

"Will do, but it could take some time – it's nine o'clock now. I'll make sure I ring you with an update first thing in the morning."

"Great, thank you." Fitzjohn leant forward, both hands on the desk. "I've been a bloody fool," he muttered. "That stupid girl! She probably told him the plans for the pre-emptive strike."

Vanessa was standing in the hallway, tears streaking her cheeks. Fitzjohn stopped and looked at her. He thought how wonderful she was, so beautiful and desirable. He couldn't remain angry with her; she was an innocent pawn in the game, heedless of the trouble she had caused.

"Hey, don't worry, there's no need to get upset. Come on, clean yourself up and have another drink." He put his arm around her waist and pulled her close to him as they walked back into the living room. She found a cotton handkerchief and dabbed her face.

"Will you really do what you said and move out of the flat? You know Walmsley has been controlling you in return for money."

"Yes, of course, I'll get my own flat, believe me. I might share with one of the other girls in the theatre company. And I'll never see Yuri or any of Stephen's friends again." Vanessa ran to Fitzjohn and took his hands. Laughing lightly, she said, "Oh, Henry, I do love you. For you, I will do anything."

Fitzjohn's heart went out to her. "No, you silly thing, you must do these things for yourself – not for Walmsley, not for me. It's time for you to stand on your own two feet."

"But I want us to carry on being special friends. Please say we can."

"Yes, of course, but it must be something you want to do, not something you do for anyone else."

"My darling, you are so kind." Vanessa pressed her cheek to Fitzjohn's shoulder and wrapped her arms around him. Kissing him gently, she failed to notice his agonised expression as she squeezed his wounded back.

***

When Fitzjohn and Vanessa were having breakfast in the dining room, Rufus came in and said there was a telephone call for him, a Miss Shelby. Fitzjohn went through to the office and closed the door behind him. "Morning, Sian, what do you have for me?"

"Mr Andreyevich, real name Ilya Zarnov, once a colonel in the Red Army, has been of interest to MI5 since his arrival here. They got some information from the CIA, who have also been watching him. They suspected him of being a spy during his time in the US."

"What has he been up to since arriving?"

"Well, curiously, quite a lot on the cultural side. Art exhibitions, ballet, etc., getting his credentials established. He also likes to socialise and has frequented most of the top nightclubs in London. Often in the company of Stephen Walmsley, the architect and every debutante's favourite party host. I wouldn't be surprised if Walmsley had set him up with one of his girls, if you see what I mean."

It was painfully obvious to Fitzjohn what this news meant: Vanessa had been sleeping with a Russian military agent and was being kept by Walmsley. His temper was rising when Sian said, "Hang on, Henry, Mea has just come in with a note. Let me look at it."

Sian laughed. "You are going to love this, Henry. It's a report from an MI5 agent at London Airport: *he's skipped!* Andreyevich took the early flight to Moscow."

"Ha! He was probably recalled – his mission to have me kidnapped failed. He will have a new job come next week. Such a shame."

"Indeed. And Henry, I had a call late last night from Sir Oliver Colton, Macmillan's private bulldog. Mac wants to see you tomorrow morning, 8a.m. sharp at Number 10."

"That's fine. Please let them know I will be there."

FIFTY-SEVEN

Fitzjohn stopped at an Italian restaurant in Earls Court at the end of the long, tiring drive from Cornwall. After the meal, he dropped Vanessa off at her flat and continued on to Kensington, closely followed by the Special Branch car. After a hasty discussion, the agents were replaced by another car with two new occupants, parked opposite his apartment block. Inside, he found an unopened bottle of Talisker and poured himself a small one: something to help him sleep but not enough to dull his wits in the morning.

He reflected on his relationship with Walmsley. He knew in his heart of hearts that Walmsley was a schemer, a user and a money-grabber. It was no surprise to Fitzjohn that Amanda had warned him off associating with him, and now he had to face the fact that one of Walmsley's circle of friends – or clients – was a Russian agent and had picked up enough information from Vanessa for the Russians to try to kidnap him. Fitzjohn was aware that only he knew all the details; the only civilian who had the complete picture of the attacks planned for the following year. If the kidnap had been successful, what would they have done with him? Something very painful to get him to talk, before a single shot to the back of the head. He also saw why the attempt had been made at Readymoney Cove: many people get into trouble swimming in the sea off the Cornish coast and are never seen again.

***

Sian had arranged for Lionel to pick Fitzjohn up at 7.30a.m., but as usual he was early and said a few words to the agents, who had been on duty all night. Lionel was a retired army officer and understood the hard life the agents had to endure.

Fitzjohn had showered and breakfasted in good time and selected his best charcoal-grey suit and Conservative-blue tie, with a matching silk square in his top pocket. He was looking forward to the meeting, hoping that more information had been gathered on the attack, and the villains in the boat.

In the Cabinet meeting room, Admiral Sir Adrian Temple was helping himself to coffee. Sir Oliver Colton was sitting, head down over a handful of notes, his two assistant secretaries waiting silently.

"Good morning, gentlemen," said Fitzjohn.

The men murmured greetings. Without lifting his head to look at Fitzjohn, Colton said, "Mac will be a few minutes late – he's on the telephone with the Home Secretary."

Fitzjohn poured a coffee, walked to the window and looked into the gardens of Number 10. Clearly, none of those present felt like idle chat. They only had to wait ten minutes before Macmillan swept in, defying his years, and took a seat at the head of the table.

"Gentlemen, I have just come from a call with Peter Titheridge. I have instructed him to coordinate MI5 and Special Branch in our immediate response to the attack on Mr Fitzjohn. We are rounding up all the suspect spies, informers, agents and no-goods that have been plaguing our military for the past couple of years, here in the UK and our bases in West Germany. I've just about had enough. Any Russian nationals who can't justify their diplomatic role will be expelled. Others will be held in custody under special powers as enemies of the state, and ultimately deported."

Fitzjohn was shocked by the fury in Macmillan's voice, and he must have looked it.

"Yes, Henry, an attempted kidnapping of a British politician is not something this government will tolerate. I have called in the Russian ambassador for a 9a.m. meeting and will give him a message for Mr Khrushchev: if the abduction had been successful, we would consider it an act of war, and we would retaliate. As it is, we are contemplating what actions we will take, in addition to the round-up I mentioned. We will have a full Cabinet meeting at noon to discuss the issue. Admiral Temple, what is the state of our armed forces?"

"I have given orders for all arms to move to twenty-four-hour readiness, sir. Our nuclear armed aircraft are on fifteen-minute take-off standby."

"Right. Colton, are we expecting a full house at the Cabinet meeting today?"

"Almost, sir. Anderson from Education is unwell at his home in Edinburgh and Jameson from Colonies is on a visit to Ceylon."

"Good. I am expecting full support for diplomatic actions that pressurise the Soviet Union into deconstructing their spying network in the UK. I want them to *cease* and *desist* their harassment of our bases and their seaborne incursions, *open talks* on the security of Berlin, and *agree* the *neutrality* of Eastern European states." Macmillan banged his hand on the table for emphasis of every key point.

"A tall order, Prime Minister," said Colton.

Macmillan now banged down both hands on the table. "It's the bare minimum, Colton! There's no way we are going to live any further under the threat from the Soviets! If they don't comply with my requirements, I will order the invasion we have been discussing."

Everyone in the room was stunned and silenced at the invective in the PM's voice. No longer Old Mac, his fury came through loud and clear. Eventually he said, having regained his composure, "Thank you, Admiral, thank you, Mr Fitzjohn, that will be all for now. Please return for the nine o'clock meeting. Colton, remain."

***

In the short time he had available, Fitzjohn telephoned Amanda Spencer from a private office. "He is absolutely livid – I never would have expected this of him. The Russians crossed a line with the attempt on me, and Mac is not going to let them get away with anything less than a significant expulsion of phoney diplomats and secret agents. And he's determined to end the hostilities and intrusions we've been enduring of late. We've pussy-footed around for long enough."

"But they will respond by sending home some of our people from Russia in reprisal."

"Macmillan couldn't care less about that; in fact, I wouldn't be surprised if he recalled a number himself and virtually cut off diplomatic relations with Russia, he's that angry."

Amanda laughed a fake laugh. "Well, good for him," she said. "Think of the opposite: if we allowed them to carry out these attacks and kidnaps and Mac did nothing, it would only give them the confidence to try other daft ideas. Next thing we would have is assassination of British MPs or senior military officers. Bound to start a war."

"Yes, that would light the blue touchpaper. Anyway, I'm required at the Cabinet office at nine, so I'll see you later."

The meeting was polite and run with the required diplomacy while Macmillan made sure the Russian delegates were clear about the British government's determination to deport Russian spies from the UK. Again Fitzjohn was impressed with Mac's forcefulness and fortitude. The Russian ambassador would be a fool not to make it clear to Khrushchev that the kidnap attempt was a dangerous action that would have serious repercussions and it could well have been an immediate declaration of war on the Soviet Union. But as a conciliatory gesture, Macmillan said he had authorised the release of the two bodies from Readymoney Cove for return to the Soviet Union for burial.

After the meeting, Macmillan kept Fitzjohn back for a private discussion. "Now, Henry, we are of course delighted that the kidnap attempt failed, but certain issues arise. Our secret service people have expressed concerns to me over the company you have been keeping lately. In particular one Miss Paget. It's known she is a socialite who seems to have a wealth beyond her family means."

"I think you'll find her father is very comfortably off. Tin mines and property owner."

"Not so, Henry. He has debts; his business interests are largely floundering. You will be aware that Cornish tin mines are closing as they are uneconomic, and rental incomes are flat."

Fitzjohn was taken aback. No, he wasn't aware that tin mines were struggling and had no idea what income Paget was getting from his properties. He had the sudden realisation that Vanessa wasn't the monied catch he thought she was.

Macmillan went on. "The fact is, Vanessa Paget lives on immoral earnings: she is a prostitute under the control of Stephen Walmsley. We have no proof of this, and I don't really care what the idle rich get up to, but as well as enjoying your company she has also been seen with a certain Russian cultural attaché. Did you know about this? Your relationship with her puts me in a very difficult position, you understand."

Fitzjohn said indignantly, "I only found out about this yesterday, and I don't pay for Miss Paget's company, Prime Minister. I'm not sure I do understand you."

"I think you do. If, or when, the press get hold of the fact that you are in a relationship with a woman who is also having an affair with a Russian agent, it would mean your dismissal, Henry. It's more than a coincidence that your movements are tracked by the Soviets so closely that they attempt a kidnap right under our noses. Has your little floozy been sharing secrets?"

Now Fitzjohn was offended. His feelings for Vanessa ran deep; he wasn't going to have her insulted. Certainly he was aware of the lifestyle she led and the many gifts and favours she received from admirers, but he pushed all that out of his mind. He never saw her as a prostitute, selling her services, and he wasn't going to apologise for his relationship with her. "One would hope not, Prime Minister. And as I understand it, the party in question has returned to Moscow, so we can be assured that if there was any impropriety in the past, it is all over now. I feel that Miss Paget has been a victim of an unscrupulous individual whose affairs should be looked into very carefully. She is the innocent in this business."

"Be that as it may, Henry – and I admire your loyalty – you must not continue with your connection with the lady."

"I'm not sure, sir, that I am inclined to follow your advice. After the dust has settled on the kidnap business, I am sure the press will lose interest in my personal affairs."

Macmillan banged his hand again on the table, his standard demonstration of frustration. "It's *not* advice, Henry! It's my instruction to you if you want to remain in office!"

"What are you saying, Prime Minister?"

"Can't I make it any clearer? I want you to put an end to this affair. I will not have the government at risk of scandal and ridicule over your relationship with a call girl!"

Fitzjohn picked up a pencil from the table and twiddled it thoughtfully in silence. He now saw with absolute clarity that he stood to lose his job and the prospect of becoming prime minister if he continued to see Vanessa. That was a very high price to pay. He stood up and walked to the door, knowing he had to be careful not to overreact. "Very well, Prime Minister, I will give it some thought."

FIFTY-EIGHT

October 1960

In a quiet corner of the American Bar at the Savoy, Amanda Spencer sat waiting for her old university friend, Suzie Corby, to arrive. They had agreed to meet around seven; Suzie couldn't be more precise as she was working on a photo shoot in the East End. But at half past seven she arrived, out of breath and all smiles.

"Suzie, it's so nice to see you," said Amanda, kissing her friend on both cheeks. "Let's get you a drink. You look like you've run here!"

"Well, not quite, but I have had a busy evening, rushing around behind my snapper."

"What will you have?"

"If that's a vodka martini, I'll have the same as you."

An observer might have thought that the two women were sisters. Both tall and slim, elegantly dressed in business suits, mid-fifties and exuding self-confidence. Amanda made eye contact with the waiter, who came over with his notepad.

"Who have you been chasing today?" said Amanda.

"Can't say exactly, but there's a couple of brothers, twins actually, in gangland that everyone's talking about. We got some pictures of them drinking in a pub in Bethnal Green: smart suits, Brylcreemed hair, not bad-looking boys."

"Your job is certainly full of excitement."

"That might be true, but you know what editors are like – you're only as good as your last scoop."

They laughed. "And what have you been up to lately, Amanda? Still working the political circuit? Another type of gang warfare, if you ask me!"

"Yes, I suppose you're right. I'm still working for the Conservative Party, but I've got a lead for you that you might like to follow up. High class, very much West End, not East End – involves girls, money and influence."

"Sounds interesting. Can you tell me who you have in mind?" said Suzie.

"Yes, it's Stephen Walmsley."

"The architect? What's he been up to?"

"The architectural practice is genuine – he has a lot of wealthy clients. But his real money comes from favours he does for discerning male friends: wealthy, powerful, some you could say in positions of influence. Usually involving debutantes, but also models and actresses, keen to find generous men friends and not too fussy about what they have to do with them – or for them. I believe the men pay Walmsley directly for his services, rather than passing any money to the girls. Some of them might not even realise he is controlling them."

"Is he a pimp, then, or a marriage bureau?"

"He makes introductions for money and the sex follows. I think most of the girls know the game they are in, but I have no tangible proof. I heard about his antics with debutantes a couple of years ago from a distraught mother in my constituency in Suffolk. Her daughter was a medical student in London when she got involved in Walmsley's circle. She was set up with a generous host who not only wanted sex but was violent with it. We got her out of there and she is now continuing her studies in Edinburgh."

"Nasty. Well done for helping the kid," said Suzie.

"For the police to prosecute, they need evidence. Something like photographs of him taking money from clients or passing on girls in one of the London nightclubs he frequents, or at one of his parties. Or perhaps one of his friends' parties – Lord Valley has been known to host some very glamorous gatherings down at Valley Lodge, largely in support of the Conservative Party. But Walmsley is always invited." Amanda knew her last comment would pique Suzie's interest.

"Lord Valley, goodness, that's astounding. You're painting a very sordid picture, Amanda, but why do you care what Walmsley does now? Has he offended you personally in some way?"

"Yes, but let's not go into that. All I'm asking is that you and your colleagues at the newspaper take a close look at his business and social activities. If you can get evidence of him living off immoral earnings, I'm sure the police will be interested. I want to see him in jail. The tough bit is getting the evidence. I've made enquiries myself, but investigative journalism is not my line of country."

"We have ways of getting the proof we need in stories like these."

"What do you mean?"

"Oh, come now, Amanda, you know what goes on. Maybe an undercover reporter to act as a client, or even line up a lady reporter to become one of his entourage. We might use photographs to encourage certain people to tell us a story, usually implicating one of their friends, diverting attention from themselves."

"I'm not asking you to do anything illegal."

"Don't worry, our people are skilled at staying on the right side. Anyway, it's the job of the press to expose wrongdoing, particularly where there's a scandal involved – helps to sell newspapers. And if the Establishment are tied up in it, then I like it even better."

"Do you think you can take the job on?"

"I will have to run it past the editor, but I'm sure he'll give it a go. But one more question, or the same question put another way: why do you want to see Walmsley in jail?"

"OK, but this has to be between you and me. It has to stay out of any story that gets published."

"I'll try, but you know I can't guarantee anything. Once the investigation starts, it's up to the editor what goes in and what stays out. So, if it really matters to you, don't tell me, but be prepared for it to emerge somewhere along the line."

"Alright. I have an interest that I want to protect, so perhaps I should keep it to myself for the time being."

"A wise move. Leave it to me. If you're around, perhaps we can meet this time next week? I'll buy the drinks. But do you mind if I dash just now, darling? I'm due back in Fleet Street tonight – I'm hoping we'll run a story on our luckless princess and the gallant group captain. I've got some great pictures. Can't say too much at the moment!"

"I thought that was all over, but I think I understand," said Amanda, smiling.

The two friends said their goodbyes, stood and made elaborate kisses to each other's cheeks, before Suzie departed in a hurry.

FIFTY-NINE

Adam Devon was kept busy while Hannah was in hospital. His work on assessing pilots and passing them for full maritime reconnaissance duty was stepped up by Wing Commander Valentine, who was conscious of the need to get as many pilots signed off before Devon took the three weeks of special leave he had been granted once Hannah was at home. Devon drove to St Austell hospital most evenings and made sure he had breakfast with Michael each morning. He was hugely grateful to Hannah's parents for staying in Cornwall and looking after the house and Michael.

The number of sightings of Russian submarines and surface ships had significantly reduced since the Readymoney Cove incident. Wing Commander Valentine passed on intelligence reports from the air ministry, noting the lack of any serious incursions into British waters. The reports didn't mention – but the senior officers at the ministry were aware of – the arrest of numerous people suspected of spying for the Russians. Intrusions onto military bases had all but ceased.

The Shackleton squadrons kept up their relentless long-range reconnaissance missions, extending out to mid-Atlantic, north to Iceland and west of the Iberian peninsula down to Gibraltar. Devon harboured the secret hope that they would encounter the *Leninski* again: he felt he had unfinished business there. Its men had fired upon his aircraft and while he had managed to return fire, he was disappointed at not fully disabling the submarine. More importantly, the intelligence people were convinced that it was the *Leninski* that had landed the agents at Readymoney Cove, and one of its men had shot Hannah. This made it personal, and he promised himself that if he had another opportunity to have a go at the submarine, he would make it count.

But the *Leninski* would never be seen again in the seas around the UK. The Soviet leadership had reassigned the boat to exploratory tasks more suited to its ability as a nuclear-powered submarine to stay submerged almost indefinitely: across the Atlantic, close to the coast of America and even under the Arctic ice cap as far as the North Pole. Captain Fyodor Yegorov was rewarded for his actions in the English Channel with promotion to rear admiral, and was assured that his submarine would be used as a strategic deterrent in future and not get involved in operational assignments.

When, after two weeks in hospital, Devon brought Hannah home, she was so happy to see a welcome party of Diane and Terry Trenwith with Alice, and Val and Drake Casey with Charles, as well as her parents. Michael was so excited to have his mother home that he burst into tears as she came in the house. But within a minute his laughter returned and the children went off together to play.

The adults stayed in the living room for tea and coffee, made by Hannah's mother. Devon said to Drake across the room, "How long do you have before you go back to London?"

"About two weeks, as long as everything continues to settle down the way it has recently."

Hannah's father, who knew Drake was involved in the American secret service, asked, "How are things viewed by the Americans? The risk of war, I mean?"

"Well, there's a high risk at the moment, but at least it has moved down from critical. It seems that your prime minister's challenge to Khrushchev has sobered him up, made him see sense, made him scale back the belligerent stance the Russians were taking. Who would have thought that Macmillan would put the frighteners on Khrushchev? But there you go, his show of strength has led to a stepping-down of Russian aggression. And as I understand it, NATO has also relaxed some of its military build-up. Amazingly, the Fitzjohn incident is turning out to be a catalyst for peace."

"That's good news, but will it last?"

"Again, it's impossible to be certain, but the strategists on our side seem to think that the Soviets are at last opening their doors to sensible discussion. All we want to know is that the Russians are not planning to sweep west, and they want to know that we're not about to invade East Germany and the other communist states. It's a stand-off, but a good one."

"Let's hope so, for all our sakes." Hannah's father strolled to the French doors and looked at the children playing in the garden.

Later in the evening, when the guests had gone and Hannah's parents had gone to bed, Hannah and Adam sat with coffee in the lounge. Hannah said, "Adam, I've just realised, where are my work packages? There must be something after two weeks away."

Devon smiled. "Well, I had a call from Yoel after the incident. As you asked, I explained that you would be out of action for a while and he ought to think of putting alternative arrangements in place. He did that straight away and will call you next week, after you've settled in back home, to discuss the future."

"Thank you, Adam. I'm not sure what I want to do. With the baby coming and Michael starting school, I'm going to struggle to make time for the job. But I don't want to let anyone down."

"You won't be. There are plenty of others who can take on your work."

"Yes, probably, but are they motivated in the way I am?"

SIXTY

Three days after her meeting with Suzie, Amanda's phone rang. It was just before 10p.m., and she could hear the typical background noise of a newspaper office: the clack of typewriters, voices calling out, phones ringing – she could barely hear her friend on the other end of the line.

"Hi, Amanda, do you have a minute? I've got some news for you about our society architect."

"Yes, sure. What have you found out?"

"Well, the good news is, the editor loves the story and has paired me up with a reporter to do the investigation. Philip Hicks – do you know him? Great guy. My photographer will work on the pictures, Walmsley with the girls, Walmsley receiving a plain brown envelope, that sort of thing."

"That's excellent. When will you start?" asked Amanda.

"Oh, we've started already. Got a very good lead. Look, must dash, can I call you again tomorrow?"

"Yes, please do."

"I've just had a thought. Could we meet for a drink, same place, same time? It's actually my evening off tomorrow so I won't have to rush off."

"Good idea. The Savoy at seven thirty?"

"Great. Thanks Amanda, see you then."

Amanda was excited to be part of a team that would bring about Walmsley's demise. Since hearing that Henry had become entangled with one of Walmsley's girls, she had developed a deep-seated hunger for revenge. She knew that Henry was just like any other single, rather foolish, fun-loving man. An easy target. She had used him herself for her own purposes – of a political nature rather than for profit. And their relationship showed that they cared for each other – he might even love her, she thought.

Suzie was on time for their second meeting and got straight to the point. "You were right: Lord Valley's parties are more than fundraising for the Conservatives. They are a way to introduce the most attractive debutantes, models and actresses to Walmsley, cleverly selecting girls whose families are less well off than they once were, or who can't offer the financial support their daughters want. Philip has found one who is willing to talk about her... social life, let's call it. He met her last night. Penny Vaughan-Hart – do you know her?"

"No, I don't think I do."

"An actress, mostly bit parts in the West End. It seems she loves being part of Walmsley's circus – even brags about her wealthy boyfriends and how she enjoys the life of a social escort, as she calls it. While she likes the life, she hates Walmsley, so when Philip offered her £100 and some very nice cocktails to talk, she opened up like a songbird. Initially she denied any sexual activities but instead talked about how 'other girls' sell their services. We know what that means. The gifts, holidays, use of expense accounts has attracted and retained girls, but she added that Walmsley is not the charming, unassuming architect he seems to be.

Instead he's a tough, violent, controlling man – and difficult to get away from if you want out."

"That's essentially what I heard," said Amanda.

"Look, Philip wants to see Walmsley in action. He found out that he's hosting drinks at Imogen's Club on Saturday evening. I've booked a table for Philip and me, ostensibly as a couple. The photographer will be there too. But before we go ahead with that, there's something I have to ask you." Suzie looked serious, almost fearful.

"Go ahead."

"Philip's enquiries have thrown up one very sensitive matter. Penny Vaughan-Hart has a good friend in the theatre business who is also one of Walmsley's girls – possibly his favourite, according to Penny. A charmer called Vanessa Paget. It seems she has a couple of steady clients, one of which is known to you."

Amanda sat back in her chair and gazed up at the ceiling. "I think I know what you're going to say."

Suzie stayed silent.

"It's Henry Fitzjohn, isn't it?"

"Yes. Sorry to bring this up, but he is where your interest lies, if I'm not mistaken?"

"Yes, hence my desire not to have him named."

"It's too late for that, I'm afraid. Quite apart from the story I'm working on, the business of his attempted kidnap brought lots of press attention to his relationship with a certain unnamed young lady from Cornwall. There's no problem with a senior politician having a girlfriend – until the press find out she's really a call girl, managed by a well-known pimp."

Amanda winced at Suzie's words. She knew she was right, but that didn't make accepting the truth any easier. Suzie went on. "The only way Henry can avoid damaging publicity is by ditching Vanessa immediately and saying it was all a mistake: he unknowingly got tangled up with the wrong set and is helping police with their enquiries. That might help, but he'll be lucky if his career survives. In the meantime, I expect we will run the Walmsley story a week on Sunday, hopefully with some good pictures. That should lead to what you're hoping for: a police response and eventual prosecution for running a prostitution racket. I hope that Walmsley will be jailed for a good few years."

"When you go looking for revenge, first dig two graves," Amanda mumbled to herself as she realised that her desire to expose Walmsley would also damage Fitzjohn's political career, possibly fatally. She felt sick and annoyed with herself. "What have I done? What *have* I done? This wasn't supposed to happen."

"Don't beat yourself up, my dear," said Suzie, placing her hand on Amanda's. "I'm sorry to be the bearer of bad news, but such is life. Fitzjohn has brought about his own demise. If you hadn't started the story through me, then someone else would, I'm sure, have put two and two together when all the facts about the kidnap emerge."

Amanda could see that Suzie was trying to console her, and it brought tears to her eyes. "Look, thanks for putting me in the picture. You go ahead and run your story. I hope you get the credit and it helps your career at the newspaper. I think Henry's career, and probably mine, are over."

"If that happens and you fall out with the local Tories, come to me. I'm sure the paper will take you on as a reporter – we're crying out for people who know how Westminster works. And the pay will be a whole lot more."

"That's really kind. I might well take you up on that."

"Please do, I mean it, I think you will be a great political correspondent."

When Amanda got home, she reflected upon the good news about Henry. Alright, he would lose his ministerial job, but then inevitably part from the Paget girl. Amanda felt confident that she would be able to rebuild her relationship with him and give up her liaison with Sir Robert Darnell; it had no purpose anymore. Who knew? Perhaps she would settle down and marry Henry. Getting to Number 10 had been important to her for so many years, but now she admitted to herself that what she really wanted was Henry.

SIXTY-ONE

A few days after returning to work in his London office, Mea, Sian's junior, put through a call to Fitzjohn from Richard Dunn at Gatwick airport. Fitzjohn realised that he had been so tied up with his job as an MP that he had taken his eye off the running of the airline.

"This is important, Henry," Dunn said. "We need to meet. Can you come down here for a day in the near future?"

"Of course, how about the day after tomorrow? Can you tell me what it's all about?"

"Largely good news. The flights to Europe are doing well and the air taxi business is thriving. The cash is building up at the bank – we have no debts and only a few investors. The question is, what do we do next? Some great aircraft have come on the market, if you want to expand into new areas."

"Sounds great, Dickie. I'll be there around 10a.m. on Friday – would that work for you?"

"Certainly, see you then."

***

During the drive down to Gatwick, Fitzjohn was delighted that with his career as a government minister in jeopardy, at least Granta Airlines was in great shape and providing good profits. It would not be a hardship to revert to the back benches and spend more time running the airline. Holiday flights to the Continent were booming as more people sought the sun-and-sangria experience, tired of wet days on the beach in Blackpool or Bognor. Dickie Dunn was right about the availability of aircraft, he thought, he had seen brokers' sales ads in the aviation magazines.

Fitzjohn's heart swelled with pride when he parked outside the Granta offices and looked through the fence at the two Vickers Viscounts standing on the tarmac, gleaming in the sun. The nearer one had steps in place up to the door, and passengers boarding. In the terminal, Fitzjohn stood back and observed the Granta desk. Staff were busy checking tickets and labelling baggage. Two pilots and three cabin crew were waiting to go out to the second aircraft, looking very smart in their uniforms: dark-blue suits for the men and red and grey dresses for the stewardesses, matching the livery of the aircraft.

Richard Dunn came out of his office, spotted Fitzjohn and walked over. "Good morning, Henry, good to see you. Shall we go over to the café for a bacon roll and coffee?"

"Good idea, Dickie. I guess we've both made an early start today. Nice to see the check-in desk busy."

"Yes, the ten thirty flight to Malaga is full and the eleven o'clock to Nice will be about 90 per cent occupied."

"Great stuff – well done, old chap. Now tell me about the ideas you have for the business."

"Transatlantic," was all Dunn said.

Fitzjohn's eyes widened. "You mean, we start a transatlantic service? That would require a big investment into four-engined jobs and the crews to go with them."

"It would indeed, and here's the good news. Bristol has discontinued building the long-range version of the Britannia, and several good examples are on the market. If we could get a couple we could start services to New York, Boston, Washington – maybe other destinations. One I have in mind is to Bermuda: no one flies direct there, and it's a thriving business and holiday market. We would have to register an aircraft there, but that's no hardship."

"But aren't these all covered by BOAC and the Yanks?"

"Sure, they offer the service, but it's pricey. What I'm suggesting is a low-cost alternative. Most of the flights to New York are half empty. If we can charge lower fares, we will fill the aircraft and make a good profit. The margins for transatlantic flights are excellent, so even if we discount the fares we can make more per passenger mile than on European flights. And I'm also looking at the possibility of flying to Caribbean islands."

"You know, Dickie, I could see that working: low cost, high appeal. All we need are the aircraft, and good ones would be very expensive. I would need to go to the bank again, but no problem there; we have a good credit record."

"Would any of our existing investors put up more cash?"

"Maybe, but I'm not sure that's the avenue I want to go down. In fact, we only have two remaining loans, one from Miss Spencer, which is pretty low. I'd prefer to repay these from our reserves, use some of our own cash, and get the rest under leases financed by the banks." Fitzjohn didn't feel he had to go into detail about why he wanted to end Amanda's financial interest in the airline.

"We will have the usual challenge of finding good pilots and crew," said Dunn.

"Yes, but let's look at who is coming out of the RAF – transport pilots and even maritime reconnaissance chaps. They like a long flight!"

Dunn laughed. "OK, I'll see who's available. In the meantime, let's take a look at these brochures for two of the Britannias on the market at the moment. I've drawn up a business plan for us to go through, with some financial projections. We just need to get some accurate figures for leasing the two aircraft and the operating costs."

***

Returning to London in his car, Fitzjohn thought about his priorities in life. He realised that Macmillan would undoubtedly insist that he ditched Vanessa. It annoyed him. He wanted to make his own decision about her and knew he felt inclined to stay with her, even if it meant resigning – or being sacked – from his post as Minister of Defence. With the Russian climbdown reducing the risk of war instigated by them, the Cabinet would never sanction a pre-emptive strike by Britain. So his ticket to becoming prime minister had been clipped. What the hell, he thought. It's no big deal. Richard Dunn's business ideas excited him: he would love to spend more time developing the airline. That certainly paid better than an MP's salary, even a Cabinet minister's salary, although it didn't have the kudos of being prime minister.

When Fitzjohn arrived at his flat in Kensington, he picked up the post from the doormat and took the pile into the kitchen. A couple of bills, an invitation to an England football match at Wembley, and a hand-addressed, bright-pink envelope. He caught the faint aroma of perfume and opened the envelope. It contained an invitation to the dress rehearsal of *Oliver* on Saturday evening and a short letter from Vanessa asking if he would like to meet for dinner after the show. He was delighted. Musical theatre was not usually his thing, but the chance to see her again thrilled him. He would put behind him her silliness with the Russian; no lasting harm had come of it.

***

Fitzjohn found that he very much enjoyed the music, songs and drama of *Oliver*. He was mesmerised by Vanessa's singing; she genuinely was excellent. He had a good seat, only four rows back, and when she saw him she smiled and gave him the tiniest wink. After the performance, Fitzjohn realised she needed to change and get ready to go out for dinner, so he went to the stage door and told the attendant that he would wait in the theatre bar for her. He forced his way to the counter in the packed room, bought a single shot of the best malt whisky they had, then took up a position next to the door to wait for Vanessa.

"Oh, Henry, thank you so much for coming. I wasn't sure you would." She kissed him on the cheek and embraced him. She was obviously still on an emotional high after the performance, wide-eyed and with flushed cheeks.

"It was a great show and you were marvellous, my dear – such a star!"

"Thank you. I'm glad you enjoyed it."

"I certainly did. Now, let's have a glass of champagne and we can get on our way to dinner. I've booked a table at Stella's and my driver is waiting outside."

"Of course, but before we do, I want to introduce you to my father."

"What – he's here?"

"Yes, I sent him a ticket too. Here he is."

A sprightly, upright gentleman in a tweed suit, starched shirt and airborne forces tie made his way through the crowd, smiling.

"Daddy, this is Henry."

"Pleased to meet you, young man."

"And you, Sir Bartley. I hope you enjoyed the show as much as I did, especially as you have come all the way from Cornwall to see it."

"I did indeed enjoy the show. You were marvellous, Vanessa," he said, smiling at his daughter. He turned back to Fitzjohn. "But in fact, I had to come to London this week to meet with our metal broker. We've had a bit of good fortune: in our largest mine we've discovered significant deposits of copper and other metals. One is lithium – not sure of its value, but the copper alone will be a significant earner. After a tough time in the mines we have at last struck gold – not literally, of course!" Sir Bartley chuckled.

"Really? Congratulations. Two Paget successes on the same evening." Fitzjohn felt a warming glow rise in his chest.

SIXTY-TWO

Suzie Corby didn't mind admitting to herself that she revelled in the prospect of an assignment at one of London's most exclusive nightclubs. So often she and her photographer staked out a target for hours on end, waiting in a cold, uncomfortable car or on a street corner. But tonight she would enjoy herself and at the same time get a scoop on a man she didn't know personally, but she felt she knew his type: self-confident, ostentatious, wealthy, pretentious. It would be a pleasure to expose him for running a group of prostitutes.

Philip Hicks was an experienced reporter and took the lead in setting up the pretence for the evening. It would be Suzie's fiftieth birthday. She and Philip were celebrating with dinner at Imogen's, and the photographer was there to take pictures for the society magazines. She wore her cherry-red cocktail dress and had her hair up in a beehive. To make her look wealthy, she wore a pearl choker and her most valuable item of jewellery: a sapphire and diamond ring. She looked very good – and as a resident of Sloane Square, she blended in with the crowd perfectly.

As expected, Walmsley arrived with a group of male friends and half a dozen beautiful young women. Tables had been reserved for them and champagne sat in ice buckets. Suzie ignored them and ordered smoked salmon and brown bread and a bottle of Chablis. She danced with Philip, laughed and swept strands of hair off her face, posing for the photographer: doing all that would be expected of the birthday girl. She was checking to see if any of the men were paying particular attention to any one of the girls: a sure sign that there would be a liaison between them later that night.

At about half past one, when the club became quieter, Suzie and Philip took to the dance floor again. This time, the photographer was positioned to surreptitiously take pictures of Walmsley, his friends and the women – nothing sensational, just evidence of some high-profile men in a nightclub with young escorts. Probably not something they would like their wives or employers to see. Philip Hicks would find their names, their positions in society, their jobs and their addresses and pass these to Suzie. After a quiet word with one or two, they would gladly give evidence of Walmsley's organisation of the girls and how he got paid, in return for keeping their names out of the newspaper. A promise Suzie would readily give, knowing that the chances were that the editor would renege on the agreement if the story could be enriched by including high-profile businessmen, civil servants, doctors or sportsmen in compromising situations. Running a newspaper was, after all, a business.

The story was a huge success for the newspaper – and for Suzie as leading reporter. Three days after publication, when the public furore reached a crescendo, plain-clothes detectives arrived at Walmsley's flat. He kept his composure, invited them in, asked how he could help. He believed that the newspaper article was no more than speculation and cheap scandal. He was certain that the police would not be able to trace any evidence of a criminal act back to him. It all depended on his clients being sensible and not disclosing the payments they had made to him. And why would they, with their reputations to think of? But he hadn't considered what the girls might say: seeking to gain their own moment of fame, they might sell their story to the press for much more money than came their way from Walmsley. His control over the girls would be shattered; he had hurt many of them, physically and emotionally, perhaps one or two wouldn't hesitate to seek retribution.

The police had statements from three of the young women. The most detailed was a full-on exposé by Penny Vaughan-Hart, detailing her clients' names and the locations she was taken to for lavish parties, and the inevitable sex afterwards. But, she made it clear, she had never received any cash payments: she had been given holidays, many lovely gifts and clothes, but the real money had gone to Walmsley. Much of the detail in Penny's statement was kept under wraps by police; it would cause a sensation if the full truth was known. The police had gathered more than the minimum required to prove that Walmsley was living off immoral earnings and they knew the courts took a tough line on this type of crime. Walmsley was arrested.

SIXTY-THREE

Fitzjohn was not pleased to hear from Mea that he had a meeting with the prime minister at 9a.m. on Monday. He knew what the subject would be. He realised that the Special Branch agents who watched over him were not just concerned with his personal security: they reported back to the PM's office on his movements, and the company he kept. No matter what steps he took to avoid his observers, they always seemed to be around. He wondered about a couple who came into Stella's – they seemed out of place and took too much interest in him and Vanessa. Probably agents keen to eavesdrop on their conversation, but how the hell did they know he was there? Did they really shadow him everywhere?

He decided he wasn't going to be pushed around by Old Mac; he felt affronted that his private life should be of such importance to his boss. Sure, the Russians had gained some information from Vanessa, but he didn't believe that the attempted kidnap was based solely on her pillow talk with the so-called cultural attaché. But even if Macmillan was minded to fire him for his choice of girlfriend, Fitzjohn had an ace up his sleeve he wouldn't hesitate to play.

Lionel picked him up from the flat in Kensington at eight fifteen, to allow for busy traffic across London. They said little, until Fitzjohn had a thought. "Remind me, Lionel, which regiment did you serve in during the war?"

"Grenadier Guards, sir. France and Holland, then into Germany."

"Ah yes, very impressive."

"My father's and grandfather's regiment, sir. And my uncle's."

"Quite a family tradition – going back to the first lot, or even earlier by the sound of things."

"Yes, sir. Father received the Military Cross for action on the Somme."

"Really? You must be very proud." Fitzjohn smiled, while also being a touch annoyed with himself. Why had it taken so long for him to see the connection? Macmillan's regiment in the First World War had been the Grenadiers. Mac had been wounded at the Battle of the Somme but famously returned to the front when he had recovered. Fitzjohn reflected on how cleverly Lionel balanced his loyalties: between himself, Macmillan and the regiment.

***

The prime minister was already seated in the Cabinet room. "Come in, Henry, take a seat." Also seated were Colton, a woman from the Cabinet communications team, introduced as Iona, and a junior secretary, poised with a shorthand notepad and two sharp pencils.

"Thank you, sir."

"You will, of course, understand why I have called you in. The newspaper coverage of this Walmsley business is very disturbing. You have not been named yet, but it won't be long until the press hounds find out who has been having an affair with one of Walmsley's working girls, if you see what I mean."

"And I believe we should rigorously defend my position. As you know, Prime Minister, I have never paid for the pleasure of Miss Paget's company. And more to the point, I have never paid Walmsley anything, nor have I ever done him any special favour."

"But you have paid for entertainment, dinners, drinks. Colton here has looked at the matter from a reputational standpoint, not to mention a strictly legal interpretation. I'm afraid it does not stand in your favour, and it leaves me with no choice but to take the very regrettable action of dismissing you from your position as Minister of Defence. Forthwith. The Cabinet communications team have drafted an announcement. Iona, please pass a copy to Mr Fitzjohn."

Colton couldn't resist a sideways smile at Fitzjohn as Iona passed a sheet of paper across the table. Fitzjohn scanned the two short paragraphs and threw the paper over to Colton. "Bloody ridiculous! There's no way I'm going to apologise for anything I've done. I'm the victim here, remember, almost kidnapped, possibly murdered, for my position on the approach we take to the Soviet threat."

Colton sat back, feigning empathy. "Of course we understand that, Henry, but we have to think of the prime minister's position first and foremost."

"What position?" said Fitzjohn.

"We are concerned that it will become apparent in the press that your association with the young lady has been going on for some time. We need to demonstrate that as soon as the scandal became apparent the PM took decisive action and dismissed you from your position. I'm sure you see the sense in the action we are taking." Colton stared at Henry. "And the prime minister's reputation, and that of the government, will be protected."

Slowly, Fitzjohn said, "I will not be sacked, Prime Minister, but you can have my resignation if you absolutely insist."

Colton leant forward, arms on the table in front of him. "That's not good enough, I'm afraid. It must be through the prime minister's initiative that you are removed from your ministerial office: that shows strong leadership, you see. You will be allowed to square your relationship with your local party and they will either support your continuation as their MP on the back benches or have you removed. That is a concession that the PM is willing to give. Generous, in my view."

"But not in mine. None of it is." Fitzjohn turned again to Macmillan. "As I said, I am willing to resign, citing the perfectly plausible reason that my airline needs more of my attention, as a growing business. Which is true. It is also important to me that no bad publicity comes from this Walmsley business."

Colton spoke again. "I'm sorry, but that's just not relevant here. It's the PM's reputation that we—"

"*Shut up, Colton!*" Fitzjohn's invective shocked all those in the room; the secretary's hand froze in mid-air as she transcribed Fitzjohn's words. "Prime Minister, there is something else you should know, which I have been keeping under wraps. One of Walmsley's closest friends is Lord Valley – a generous contributor to the Conservative Party, of course. You will often see at his parties many attractive young ladies: no harm in that, you might say. But they are invited by Walmsley, and he controls them. Many of the male guests who get to enjoy the company of these ladies support Lord Valley's varied business interests. I believe it is important that this connection is kept confidential. After my resignation, you can have a quiet word with Lord Valley and take whatever action you see fit. You see how damaging it could be to the government if a detailed explanation of my dismissal was required?"

Fitzjohn let the PM and Colton absorb the implication of what he had said. Colton was either dumbfounded or made the wise decision not to say anything. Macmillan looked up at the ceiling, a wry smile forming on his lips. "Very well, Henry, very well. I agree to accepting your resignation. Colton, Iona, have the necessary communiqué drawn up."

Colton's face was red with anger. "But, sir, I must protest! The press will come after you if and when Mr Fitzjohn's affair becomes public."

"That's a problem we will address if it comes along. Just get the paperwork drafted. Today, please."

Fitzjohn stood to leave the room. To his surprise and delight, Macmillan also stood up and held out his hand. "Good luck, Henry. I'm sorry you will never become prime minister."

SIXTY-FOUR

February 1961

The trial of Stephen Walmsley was covered by every newspaper in the country. Readers pored over the pictures of glamourous girls in fur coats stepping out of taxis at the Old Bailey and gloated over the businessmen and socialites called to give evidence. Bookings for parties at Imogen's and the Blue Angel soared as wealthy Londoners sought to experience the high life they had read about in the papers. Walmsley's role in the relationship between his so-called friends and the women he controlled was clear; he received substantial financial and other rewards for the introductions he made and the sexual services provided. It was not only the courts that found this abhorrent, the British public felt angered at his exploitation of young, often naïve girls.

The jury deliberation took only an hour and the judge was swift with his sentencing. Walmsley would go to prison for three years. No other persons, either call girls or clients, were prosecuted due to the police's inability, or lack of inclination, to find evidence of a criminal act.

Henry Fitzjohn's time in the witness box was short and largely kept out of the spotlight – the political Establishment worked hard to look after one of their own. The court accepted that his relationship with Miss Vanessa Paget was one of friendship and no offence had been committed by either party. Nevertheless, some reporters wrote extensive accounts of Fitzjohn's luxurious, playboy lifestyle that brought him some notoriety but won veneration and admiration by the majority of readers, who liked a fun-loving rogue.

Fitzjohn's constituency party were not so accommodating. A meeting was called which Fitzjohn attended without any enthusiasm – he had started to feel he should throw in the towel and be rid of the wranglings of politics. But as he realised the association officers for Sudbury and Woodbridge wanted him out, he was offended by their prudish stance and a new energy to fight them brewed within him. He hadn't seen Amanda for a couple of months as they had distanced themselves from each other, both knowing their relationship was over. When he saw she was at the meeting his heart sank as he expected her to deride him and ensure there would be only one outcome: disgrace and dismissal from the party.

But he misinterpreted Amanda Spencer's intentions. Her influence and powers of persuasion were deep and she pressured, badgered and cajoled the committee members until sufficient numbers agreed to support Fitzjohn as their retained MP. Once that had been achieved, and the chairman of the meeting affirmed a vote of confidence, Fitzjohn's tenancy was secured, until the next election at least. At the end of the meeting, as the chairman called for any other business, Amanda tendered her resignation as the constituency campaign manager with immediate effect.

Outside in the street, before she could dash away, Fitzjohn called to her. "Amanda, just a moment. That was good of you, thank you. But why resign?"

"Don't mention it, Henry. It was fun while it lasted but now we are no longer a partnership I have a new interest to pursue."

"Oh, really, what would that be?"

"Well, if you must know, I am joining *The Times* next month as political correspondent. An old friend made an introduction to the chief editor and the proprietor and they offered me a job on the spot."

"Bloody hell! Great stuff, Amanda, congratulations." Fitzjohn took her arm and leant forward to kiss her.

But she turned away. "No, Henry, no more of that. You have a very nice young lady to think of, and if you know what's good for you, you will remain faithful and devoted to her. You never know, she might be the one for you."

"Look, old girl, perhaps we could…"

But Amanda walked away and didn't look back as she got into a waiting taxi.

SIXTY-FIVE

Six months later – August 1961

Diane Trenwith was delighted with the final arrangements. She loved to decorate, and the pink and white crêpe paper bows, table displays of fresh flowers and balloons in the village hall all looked wonderful, even though she thought so herself. Hannah's mother had helped prepare the food: a selection of sandwiches and bridge rolls, pork pies, sausages on sticks and warm mini-pasties. The tea urn was switched on and a barrel of Cornish beer had been set up by the local publican. Diane shut the door behind her and hurried over to the church, the last person to arrive.

After the christening ceremony, everyone walked from the church to the hall. The morning sunshine threw shadows from a few light clouds, but it was a classic Cornish summer's day: breezy, fresh and bright. Some very expensive cars were parked by the hall, in the churchyard and around the village. Diane was impressed by the number of people the Devons knew and the number who had made the effort to drive down to Cornwall.

Louise Kerensa Devon had been born at home on the exact day she was expected, to the delight of the community midwife. The baby had Devon's blue eyes and a little of Hannah's dark auburn hair. Devon doted on her, spending long quiet periods just looking at her, with Michael tucked under his arm.

Hannah had no ill-effects from her injuries and had a straightforward pregnancy, helped by a much-reduced workload. She had gone back on her desire to give up work completely after discussions with Yoel Arbel and now worked fewer hours. The threats to the Israeli state were as real as ever and her secret intelligence analysis work was vital, she was told. But she had been stood down from the list of active reserve forces and now had a strictly desk-based job. She hoped she would never have to fire a gun again.

Devon continued in his role of head of maritime reconnaissance pilot training, now with a steady stream of recruits as the Cold War continued. It was less stressful than in earlier years, as the Russians, and Khrushchev in particular, were much less threatening. It wasn't the most exciting flying, but it was a regular job. He stood at the far side of the village hall, chatting to some of his ex-RAF friends and colleagues: David Porter, still flying with BOAC, John Corrigan and Stephen Young from Hong Kong. Louis Valentine and Mike Bacon had come over from St Mawgan. He introduced them to Drake Casey, but they didn't enquire into the detail of what sort of work Casey was involved in. They all had an idea, given the role he had played in the assignment Devon had undertaken in Berlin some years earlier.

Back at their house when most of the guests had left, Hannah picked up an envelope that had been delivered by the postman that morning. She called out from the garden door. "Oh, Adam, come and look at this!"

"What is it, dear?"

"It's an invitation, but look who it's from."

"Goodness me, who would have thought it? Well done, Fitzjohn." The thick white card bore finely scripted words:

> *Sir Bartley Paget requests the pleasure of the company of*
> *Mr and Mrs Adam Devon*
> *at the marriage of his daughter, Vanessa Jenna Paget, to*
> *Henry Roderick Andrew Fitzjohn*
> *on Saturday 21 October 1961 at 2p.m.*
> *St Fimbarrus Church, Fowey, Cornwall*
>
> *Reception: Fowey Harbour Hotel*
> *RSVP*

"Yes, indeed," said Hannah. "And did you see the item in yesterday's *Times*? Let me see if I can find it." She went through to the kitchen and picked up the newspaper. Several pages in, she found the article she was looking for and read the headline. "Listen to this: *Granta Leads the Way*."

"May I see?" said Devon and read the article out loud. "*British enterprise in action. Granta Airlines has secured two further Britannia aircraft to bring their total fleet to seven, leading the expansion of low-cost flights to North America and the Caribbean. Henry Fitzjohn, Granta's entrepreneurial owner and Conservative Member of Parliament, said: 'We are delighted to expand our services in the lucrative long-haul markets and to continue our European operations. Our growth will continue with services to the Middle East, Canary Islands, Africa and ultimately Singapore and Hong Kong.'* Goodness, he certainly is doing well with his business – and getting married to boot."

Hannah picked up the wedding invitation and read it again. "Good for him for sticking with Vanessa," she said. "All that press coverage of the Walmsley affair must have strained their relationship. The papers said some nasty things about her, and Henry, of course, but then he usually deserves it. Let's see what else is in the post."

She left unopened the large package that had just arrived; she would start work on the contents on Monday. There were also a couple of christening cards and a letter postmarked Horsham, Surrey. "This one's addressed to you, Adam."

"Would you open it for me?"

"Goodness me! Talking of Henry's airline, it's a letter from them, signed by the man himself. Now that is interesting – he's offering you a job as a pilot!"

"That's incredible, does Henry really think I would work for him, given the way he has treated you in the past?"

"Perhaps he thinks that's all water under the bridge now. But you're right, you can't work for him, I wouldn't allow it." Hannah walked across the kitchen and wrapped her arms around Devon. "We can go to the wedding for politeness sake, and then I hope we never hear from Henry again."

"I agree, but there's something that I haven't mentioned to you. I had a brief chat with David Porter at the christening."

"Yes, I saw you with him."

"He's invited me up to the BOAC offices in London. Said he wants me to meet Bryan Trubshaw, a test pilot at Vickers. Apparently, BOAC are taking delivery of the new Vickers VC10 next year."

"Does that mean David is offering you a job?"

"Well, who knows. The purpose of meeting Trubshaw will be to understand the role of the VC10, how it will fit into the BOAC fleet, what destinations it will serve. That sort of thing. But I think Trubshaw also helps David with recruitment of pilots."

"But if you took a job with them, it would mean us moving back up to London, wouldn't it?" Hannah moved away from Devon, her brow was furrowed and she folded her arms tightly across her chest.

"Yes, I guess that's true. Would you be unhappy if we did?"

Hannah took a breath and smiled. "No, I suppose not. It's lovely living here in Cornwall but it would be far more practical if we went back to Wimbledon. Wider choice of schools and easier to see our parents. I would miss Diane and my other friends. When are you going to the BOAC offices?"

"Could be next month. I said to David I would discuss the idea with you before confirming I would attend the meeting."

Hannah then took on a thoughtful look. "Adam, you have said you have no interest in flying passenger aircraft. What's changed?"

"I guess it's the longer term job security. And the prospect of flying the latest aircraft to interesting places. David mentioned routes to the USA and Canada and even the Far East."

"Sounds great – you should at least go and talk to them."

"I will indeed, it could be a new start for us."

ACKNOWLEDGEMENTS

Again huge thanks go to my excellent editor, Jane Hammett, who once more corrected my grammar, sometimes spelling, and provided ideas and thoughts on the text that improved the flow and pace of the story.

Huge appreciation to Mike Duval who carried out readings of early drafts of the manuscript and provided invaluable comments, particularly on the draft endings, that guided me to new ideas and thoughts on concluding sequences of the story in a way that gives some closure – but also perhaps a chink of light for the next steps in the lives of Adam, Hannah and Fitzjohn.

Thanks to all the staff at the Fowey Harbour Hotel for their skilful professionalism and providing the food, coffee, drinks and beautiful views that inspired my writing and for the welcome given to Arthur, my dog, during my visits to the hotel.

As with my previous books all the characters are fictitious but have elements of real people I know: family, friends and those I have observed from a distance. All characters, as in real life, have their flaws, but they all also have the redeeming qualities that bring out the hero in all of us.

ABOUT THE AUTHOR

Born in London, but now living in Essex, Mark Butterworth worked in the City of London in financial services for nearly 40 years, including as a Lloyd's underwriter and risk management consultant. Travelling widely on holidays and business, often the two combined, Mark developed his appreciation of the Far East, Australasia, North America, the Caribbean and Europe. Mark held a Private Pilot's Licence for 15 years, including flights from Kai Tak and over the Sydney Harbour Bridge and Niagara Falls. Mark has flown a two-seater Spitfire and made more than 50 parachute jumps. Mark enjoys running, country walking, golf and salsa dancing and has two grown-up daughters and a springer spaniel called Arthur. Mark has a BA from the Open University and an MBA from City University Business School.